THE
GREAT BEYOND
ANTHOLOGY

ISSUE 1

EDITED BY
A.K. DUBOFF

J.R. HANDLEY • RAVEN OAK • A.M. SCOTT
P. ANDREW FLOYD • DAVID ALAN JONES
C.W. LAMB • MARCUS ALEXANDER HART
RICHARD FIFE • MARK HENWICK

TABLE OF CONTENTS

INTRODUCTION i

THE LONG WAY HOME 1
By Mark Henwick
Betrayal! A pair of ex-soldiers, weary of a war that went on too long, and desperate to take essential technology back to their colony planet, have to overcome treachery, injustice, corruption, greed... and pirates... on The Long Way Home.

THE MIXON DRIVE 40
By J.R. Handley
Every journey starts with the first step. Reaching our intergalactic destiny was no different.

A FAIR TRADE 73
By A.M. Scott
At the cross-roads of the galaxy, an impulsive offer changes the direction of two travelers' lives.

WEIGHTLESS 87
By Raven Oak
In the developing industry of space tourism, a disabled and neurodivergent traveler finds her first space vacation fraught with prejudicial attitudes. When a ship malfunction threatens the lives of all on board, will Tara survive, or will she perish as society expects?

IMPROBABLE MEAT 102
By Richard Fife

Zedara Clement already had enough problems as the captain of the first, and possibly last, colony ship from Earth to find a new home for the species. So, when Brett goes and gets himself and all the livestock killed, leaving the crew nothing else to eat but "Improbable Meat" for the next two years, she knows things have just gone from bad to worse.

THE CAPTAIN'S YACHT 118
By Marcus Alexander Hart

Lounge singer Rico Diamond reunites with an old flame. Unfortunately, it's on a derelict deep-space cruise ship during an alien zombie apocalypse.

STAR CADETS 149
By C.W. Lamb

Ken Hall had always dreamed of attending the Galactic Academy, where the best candidates in the solar system competed for the limited slots in Space Command. With roommates from Mars and Venus, he discovers there are far more difficult things to overcome than math and physics.

THE DAY THE EARTH WAS GRADED 172
By P. Andrew Floyd

When aliens leave a cryptic message, Earth's best linguists launch an investigation to find the meaning behind first contact. Only, they may not like what they find.

RESERVATION EARTH 196
By David Alan Jones
When an alien civilization claims it bought the Earth from primitive humans over seventeen thousand years ago, ace spaceman, Clifton Ramsey, and his ex-girlfriend, Gabrielle McGovern, must discover a way to thwart the claim, or face losing humankind's birthright forever.

INTEGRATION 227
By A.K. DuBoff
Jason Sietinen is tasked with negotiating a technology trade with the Lynaedans, the so-called 'tech-head' planet specializing in cybernetic enhancements. When reservations on both sides jeopardize the deal, Jason must find common ground for the sake of the Taran Empire's future.

INTRODUCTION

A Note from A.K. DuBoff, Series Editor

SCIENCE FICTION HAS been an important genre since its inception, providing a means to examine the human experience while offering an escape from everyday life.

All fiction writing begins with an idea, a concept based on an acute observation about the world that can be captured in a new and exciting way, asking: what is the story in this? However, some observations offer a different type of inspiration. Rather than questioning not only what the story is, sci-fi authors ask: what if?

Uniting 'what if?' ideas with an engaging story has turned sci-fi into an enduring genre within popular culture. Through these tales, readers can travel to distant worlds, to future times, or even to alternate realities. But these aren't just mindless diversions; sci-fi, at its core, provokes thought. From social to political commentary, sci-fi can offer a critical look at the world around us while still being fun and entertaining.

Though some of the stories in this inaugural edition of *The Great Beyond* might be considered more 'space fantasy' than 'proper' science fiction, they all ask 'what if?' questions that take the reader beyond their day-to-day experiences. Some are silly, others thrilling, but each offers a hopeful look for finding the good parts of life.

The stories in *The Great Beyond* anthology follow intrepid travelers as they try to find their way home, venture out into the unknown, encounter alien beings, and discover what unites us.

Enjoy the journey!

THE LONG WAY HOME

by Mark Henwick

"I HAVE A plan."

Bjorn Thorsson snorted. "Course you do."

We were both down to a quarter of a magazine for our weapons and we were crouching in a muddy ditch, halfway up a supposedly extinct volcano that had become active again under heavy bombardment from space. The mother of all pyrocumulus thunderstorms was unloading a year's worth of rain on us, and through the clouds of steam, my IR detectors were picking out the glow of lava creeping toward our ditch. The lava would reach the ditch in three minutes, and fill it in ten.

Our armored combat suits laughed off small arms fire, and were designed to continue operating underwater or in a vacuum, but I suspected lava exceeded the specifications.

Our objective this morning had been to destroy a vital part of the planetary defenses of Rhea 4. It was a fortified fire-control installation buried in the lip of the volcano, which, despite the eruption, was still operating. It was only a half-klick away, but it might as well have been on the moon, because an automated plasma cannon had been deployed on an embankment right above us just as we'd reached the base. It was spitting a constant stream of vivid blue-white bolts at anything it considered a threat. The cannon fire meant the rest of our platoon was pinned down a quarter-klick behind us. Trouble was, give that tiny electronic brain enough time and data, and it'd work out where the platoon was hiding. That cannon was capable of blasting through whatever they were sheltering behind. It'd catch them if they came forward or retreated.

Same for us. The cannon couldn't depress enough to fire at us in the ditch, but we couldn't climb the embankment, and we couldn't get out of the ditch. I really didn't even want to try standing up.

The lava was going to reach us in two minutes now.

"Skelling, Thorsson, sorry to disturb you on your rest break." Gunny's voice crackled through the lightning interference on the comm. "That cannon is starting to be inconvenient."

"Which cannon is that, Gunny?"

Probably wasn't my best acknowledgment. I was saved from Gunny's reply by the cannon zeroing in on her comms signal and vaporizing the ruined building she was hiding beneath. Then, it pointed down as far as it could and blew several huge craters just meters downslope from us.

We crouched lower, pressing ourselves hard against the soft, slippery mud.

All our supporting bombardment had stopped. Ground attack had been blown out of the sky by the same planetary defenses that we were here to take out. The cannon pinning us down didn't seem to be low on plasma charge. Our platoon was stuck. We were stuck.

It looked like, one way or another, this was our day

to die.

Or not.

"That plan..." Bjorn said.

I hadn't had one before, but I did now.

"Dig," I said, forcing one armored hand deeper into the mud.

"Into the side of a *volcano*? An *erupting* volcano? Crazy much?"

"In and then up. It's an embankment. It's compacted earthwork, not rock. It's probably already unstable with all the rain. And if it's not unstable enough, we set off one of the bombs."

"They're supposed to be for destroying the installation."

"Yeah, well, we have two of them, and anyway, better than being cooked."

Bjorn grimaced at the red and black wall of lava clearly visible now, even through the rain and steam, inching along the ditch. "Good point."

It turned out that armored suits dug well.

Lava filled the ditch behind us, but fortunately, the mud of the earthwork was so liquid it flowed around us, sealing us off. At which point, it became more like swimming blind than digging. We were inside the earthwork and we couldn't see anything.

"My inertial sensors say we're moving downward," Bjorn panted after a couple of minutes of lung-bursting work.

He was right. The mud was moving by itself. It was making a noise like a growl, which grew and grew. And the faster we dug, the faster we seemed to be sliding down the slope.

Really fast...

"Hang on!"

We linked arms and locked our servos just in time. It

seemed we'd succeeded in undermining the cannon's platform, and once it started sliding, nothing was going to stop it.

My suit speakers maxed out with the noise so I couldn't even hear myself scream.

For the first time since training, I switched on my helmet lights, otherwise known as *I'm here, shoot me* lights. They didn't help.

We were rolled over and over, blind, helpless, battered by rocks and twisted every which way. Even with the armored suits, we were in trouble.

Maybe this was our day to die, after all.

Then, suddenly, the turbulence thrust us up onto the surface of the mudslide.

I couldn't clear my visor, but I felt Bjorn pull me up onto something. The world settled a bit; we were still moving, but we seemed to be *on* the mud instead of inside it.

I let rain sluice the visor until I could make things out.

We were clinging to the underneath of the overturned plasma cannon, surfing it down the side of a volcano on a roaring mudslide.

"Was this in your plan?" Bjorn yelled, one gauntlet pounding the metal of the cannon as if to make it go faster.

"Sometimes you gotta improvise," I shouted back.

Relief after terror. We were laughing so hard, the tears ran down our cheeks.

The command channel in my helmet blared into life.

It was Gunny yelling on the comms. "Skelling! Thorsson! What the hell do you think you're doing? Stop messing around! All units! Stand down. Cease fire. All units, cease fire."

There was a long wash of static, then Gunny's voice came back, weary but exultant: "It's over, people."

—

Now that they had decided that the war had finally ended, they started shipping whole brigades back to Earth as fast as they could board them. We lifted off Rhea 4 the next day.

It made sense; there were military units you use for peacetime duties, and then there were frontline units like the ones on Rhea 4: the 1st Frontier Assault Brigade and the Terran Volunteer Mobile Infantry.

But maybe the more important thing for them was that those units were signed up for the duration; we weren't career military. The sooner Earth government got us off their payroll, the happier they'd be. There was no profit in this war.

War... Officially, the 'Dimitras Incursion' wasn't a war, whatever it felt like while we were fighting it.

Me? Janice Skelling. From Calloway, in the Ensylas Sector, far out on the Parvi Arc. Private (for the third time—'authority issues' and 'attitude'. Got a problem with that, *bud*?). Assigned to Alpha Company, 2nd Battalion, 3rd Mobile Regiment, 1st Frontier Assault Brigade.

Shit. You could spend all day chewing through names like that, which is probably one of the reasons why we were usually called the Acid Penguins, even by General Thoomis.

And make no mistake, we were all happy to stop fighting and just go somewhere that wasn't beat down or blown up, but while everyone else celebrated, it was at that point I started to worry. That's the way I'm wired.

We had to go back to Earth first; that was just the way the bulk of space transport worked—inward and outward from the center. But the ship they used for us?

The TSS *Wingate*, the Terran Marine Corps' just-launched, state-of-the-art troop transport ship. So new it had never been shot at, and only had one layer of paint on the bulkheads down in marine country.

And it all worked. Even the freaking showers.

It was a vacation at the military's expense, with more time to think than I'd had in years.

Like: why a war, even one that wasn't called a war, had ended, and yet planets that could barely afford to feed themselves were still paying Earth to build ships like the *Wingate*.

—

"Hey, come on, Jan! We're *finally* going home," Bjorn said as we stood at the viewport, watching the blue-green jewel of Earth spinning beneath us.

"I know we're not all here," he went on, misunderstanding my silent mood. "You're thinking of Hal, aren't you?"

He held up his hand, fingers and thumb spread. I couldn't refuse the ritual. I put up my hand to touch his, finger to finger, thumb to thumb. The Five, we called it, because there had been five of us from Calloway originally. Feeling lost among the two thousand recruits of the Frontier Brigade, this had been our little group's greeting to remind us we weren't alone.

There were only two of us left. Solveig had died first. Then Enoch. Then such a long gap when we'd begun to think we were invulnerable. But Hal had died in the first nightmare drop onto Rhea 4, just one month ago. Happy-go-lucky Hal. So close. He'd almost made it.

I squeezed my eyes shut.

We'd all known the risks when we'd signed up.

Calloway was a system at the very limit of the

Frontier, unless you counted complete dead-ends like Yorkham. We hadn't expected to be visited by Frontier Brigade recruiters from Earth and we told them truthfully, ignoring that we were actually pacifists, we couldn't *afford* for people to leave. But then they told us what the pay was, and that it was in Terran dollars. Not enough to make it worthwhile back on Earth, but out on the Frontier, Terran dollars were the only way to buy the Inner Worlds tech that hard-pressed colonies were so desperate for. And we *were* desperate; we'd discovered Calloway had a long-term atmospheric cycle which fed a chemical change in the soil, and we were heading for a huge die-back of crops unless we could buy the kind of terraforming tech that would reverse the changes in our fields.

Everyone had met up or connected by comms to debate, because that was the way we did it on Calloway. We'd worked out that five of us signing up for a standard three-year tour would make enough for eight of the bio-processors we needed. It would be enough to stop starvation, no more, but it was a compromise between hard choices.

The Church declared that anyone who volunteered would be deemed guiltless in their eyes.

Everyone who'd met the military requirements had put their names forward, and the five had been chosen by drawing lots. The recruiters had allowed a couple of contract amendments. In the event of death, payment would be made to the end of tour. The survivors and our cargo 'within reason' would be shuttled down to the surface of Calloway at the military's expense.

And so, the five of us became soldiers in the 1st Frontier Assault Brigade.

Our choice hadn't been wanting to take Earth's side in some dispute about whether they had the right to export their marginal citizens into the Dimitras Sector.

No.

It'd been a stone-cold assessment of the trade-off between the temporary or permanent loss of five people who couldn't be spared, and the purchasing power of hard Terran currency for the three years they'd originally said we'd be signed up for.

And we'd done six years. Double the original tour—yeah, always read the small print, folks.

But still...

"Something's going wrong," I said. It was the same gut feeling I'd learned to trust in combat.

"Paranoid much?" Bjorn laughed. "Hey, it's okay. We all have doubts and failures of confidence at the end of a long project. It's natural. But we did it, Jan! Look, just picture their faces when we arrive. The whole colony will be there."

I couldn't help but visualize the 'shuttle port' on Calloway. The bleak expanse of vitrified rock on the coast near the town. Would they really all take the time to come out to greet us?

A huge longing swept through me to see the family again. To return to them, alive, the risks of military service to body and soul vindicated, bringing the *literally* lifesaving bio-processors, which were in storage at Ensylas, waiting for payment.

All the emotions I'd kept locked down for so long started to seep out, and my eyes blurred up.

Bjorn bumped shoulders gently. "Betcha looking forward to the expression on your old Uncle Nikolai's face, aren't you?"

I had to laugh through the tears.

"Nah. That would be childish," I said. My least favorite family member had bid me farewell by saying he never expected to see me again. That I was just running away, and I wouldn't amount to anything, anywhere.

Maybe I was looking forward to him eating his words, a little bit.

Bjorn had cheered me up and I gave him a one-armed hug. Not too much. I had kind of a thing about him, but, well, he was probably bad news. Not a bad man, but not a good bet, if you get my meaning. And maybe almost as much as I was for him.

"Come on," he said. "Let's go watch the parades."

—

Earth was humanity's home, but not home for the Frontier Brigade, which might be why we didn't get to touch the planet that we'd spent six years fighting for. Or maybe they thought that we'd all jump ship and disappear into the teeming billions of Earth's population.

Probably that, because it was the heart of the problem all over.

Earth and the closer Inner Worlds wanted to export their excess populations and import raw supplies in exchange for their advanced technologies.

The Margin wanted more people, but only the 'right' kind. And they didn't want to export their resources— *couldn't*, in some cases.

And lastly, there was the Frontier, the furthest reaches of human expansion, the most desperate colonies. No one wanted us, except to fight their wars.

It's a sore point out on the Frontier.

Anyway, the military decided to keep the Acid Penguins in orbit, aboard the *Ganga*, the huge military transshipment station.

In the *Ganga*'s cavernous concourse, we watched while the Terran Volunteers paraded. There were speeches. Presentations. Medals. Buffets with champagne for the senior officers. Beer for the rest of us.

When the celebrations ended, the Terran Volunteers were paid off and shipped planet-side on the space elevator, leaving the Frontier Brigade to wait for our transport home.

The *Wingate* had already left, gone to get the next shipload from the Dimitras Sector, and the military didn't have enough transport ships to visit every part of the Frontier, so they contracted merchanters whose cargo pods could be temporarily converted to barracks.

While the transports fueled up and got a shakedown from our Brigade engineers, the Terran Marines put on a last-minute recruitment show for anyone interested.

They had a good turnout.

Yeah, they were offering free food and alcohol.

And the show was slick, I'll give them that.

New, higher-powered armor. Glossy visors with improved tactical information. Better comms. Working active camo. The latest Mark 5 Tactical Assault Weapon.

Very impressive.

It was like a line had been drawn down the hangar. One side the Terran Marines, all clean uniforms, fresh faces and unmarked armor. On the other side, us.

We'd been requested to assemble in our battle kit, bar the helmets, and we looked more like a ghetto gang than an infantry company.

We'd spent the war shedding bits of malfunctioning suits, experimental equipment and surplus gear, sloughing off decorative coatings while gathering scars, dents and mods, until we'd emerged like a new sort of metallic insect: hard-shelled, dark, with the sort of dull sheen that comes from unremitting use, but everything functional and deadly.

I'd worked on every inch of my equipment, right

down to the power servos and the slick mechanisms of my Mark 3 Tactical Assault Weapon, as if my life had depended on it. Because it had.

All that pretty kit on the other side wasn't going to impress us, and the marine recruiting sergeant didn't get much interest until right at the end.

"So what you going to do?" he asked us, leaning against the table with all the food and alcohol. "You've spent six years getting good at being soldiers. Now you're back off to the farm and the factory, richer, but still scratching a living in the Frontier. Or you could join the Terran Marines. Do what you know best, but with the latest, finest equipment, dedicated support, and supply divisions." He paused. "And the way things are going, you probably won't even have to fight."

He smiled when he said it, and we smiled back, because by this time, we all knew that was bullshit. You didn't recruit like this for peacetime.

"Who the hell are they going to war with?" I whispered to Bjorn.

He just shrugged.

The recruiter saved his best argument for last. "Oh, and there's a new law been passed this week in the Terran Council," he said. "After a five-year stint in the Terran Marines... you get citizenship."

It was like a shockwave flashed through our ranks. Hellfire, that was some bribe.

And while my mouth was still open in shock, I got Gunny hissing quietly in my ear. "He doesn't mean you, Skelling. Or your partner in crime."

Bjorn and I turned around together.

"Crime? Gunny, that's libel," I said, with my innocent, shocked face on.

"Not unless I write it down," she replied. "And anyway, it would still be true."

Gunny was okay. She'd been assigned from the Terran Marines to teach us something, *anything*, about being soldiers when we'd signed up. We didn't hold that against her, and she'd stayed with us the whole six years, bad times and good.

"You holding grudges?" Bjorn asked her, smiling that smile that could sell vacuum to a spacer. At a premium.

She didn't smile back. "No. The opposite."

She passed on, muttering in other people's ears.

"Sort of an anti-recruiting sergeant," Bjorn said, an unfamiliar frown creasing his face.

For the first time, I saw reflected in his eyes the worry that had been eating away at me.

If a new conflict broke out *before* we were officially demobilized, that small print clause said we would have to stay in the Frontier Brigade. There would be no way to get payments out to Ensylas, let alone get the bio-processors shipped to Calloway. And the way these conflicts went, by the time it ended, it would be too late for Calloway—people would die and the colony would collapse.

—

We sweated through the next few days.

Half the brigade decided to sign up for a tour in the marines, so the transports had to be reassigned. More delays. An ominous notice appeared on our pads, reminding us that we were still in the Frontier Brigade until demobilized and, as per regulations, we were responsible for packing all our equipment onto the transports when boarding.

As if we were being deployed.

Gunny refused to say anything other than that; as far as she knew, the fifty of us from the Ensylas Sector would be demobilized as a group on Ensylas and await onward transportation, as stated in our contracts. She had an expression on her face that would blister bulkheads, so conversations were short.

Did she really know something? At the recruitment show, had she been telling us to get out as fast as we could?

Bjorn and I couldn't decide what to believe.

The Dimitras Incursion had been incredibly unpopular on Earth, with riots erupting every time casualties were brought home. Surely the Council didn't want another war?

On the other hand, the Terran Marines didn't recruit soldiers to stand around and look pretty. They'd taken on a thousand, just from the first transport to return. Was that just because we came back first? Why had they ignored the Terran Volunteers?

While we argued it, transports left for every Sector in the Frontier, and ours kept being re-scheduled.

The day eventually arrived and, maybe because we were the last to ship out or because there were no 1st Frontier officers joining the Ensylas transport, Gunny elected to come with us. In addition, we had a handful of surly military police and a civilian official from the Terran Council's Military Oversight Commission who'd been tasked with officially demobilizing us.

I didn't believe our transport would really leave, until I heard the docking clamps retract.

And even then, I still wasn't sure we'd be released when we got to Ensylas.

The journey itself was agonizingly slow: the merchanter was sound, but the navigation and sensor systems were so old that it had to emerge from Chang space at every intervening star to check its bearing and velocity. Every recalibration and adjustment took time.

Every pause, every day, made me more anxious.

—

Despite my fears, twenty-three days later, we disembarked into the Orion's Wheel, the space station that orbited the planet of Ensylas.

This system was the Frontier's local sector capital, and they had a welcome for us that was supposed to be an imitation of the ceremonies on the *Ganga*, including a parade from the Acid Penguins.

Not what we were good at, but this was our last parade and we did our best for Gunny.

Campaign medals. Salutes. A speech from the governor of Ensylas.

The Commission's official took the stand.

My heart was in my mouth.

Surely we couldn't be recalled now?

Blah. Blah. "...and I now declare this troop to be honorably discharged..."

With cheers we broke ranks. To hell with parades and speeches. Suddenly we were civilians again, and it seemed all my worries had been groundless.

I didn't remember too much after that. There were celebratory drinks. Bjorn and I drifted off from the others and ended up in a bar somewhere. Lots of drink. Some dirty dancing.

I may have got a bit short with some stationers who wouldn't take no for an answer.

There might have been some pushing and shoving.

I was doing fine, but then Bjorn noticed, and after that, the pair of us won, big time.

Which meant that when the station police arrived seconds later, we were the only ones standing and of course we got zapped. And, naturally, by the time we came around from that, every other person in the bar had identified us as the people who'd started it.

Sore losers.

Like an idiot, I was expecting to get bailed and put in the brig, before remembering that I had become a civilian a few hours before my arrest. The army had no obligations or loyalty to me.

Stupid. Stupid.

I came out in a cold sweat. What had we done? Had the army already booked us tickets to Calloway? Would we miss the departure?

We couldn't get messages in or out. The police wouldn't even talk to us.

A lawyer eventually turned up. He said he would get a message to Gunny, but he didn't seem interested in our situation or our guilt. His job was to explain our options: if we took the rap, we would get a fine or a sentence of one month of station maintenance and cleaning. If we took it to court, given the 'evidence' against us, almost certainly a year *and* a fine *and* the likelihood that the 'victims' would be awarded compensation from our assets.

We gritted our teeth and took the month.

By that afternoon, we were chasing burnt-out circuits in the maintenance tunnels wearing fetching yellow coveralls and necklaces that would deliver a shock if we goofed off or tried something stupid.

They relied on their necklaces and the fact that we had nowhere else to go. We were sent off to work alone with our own keys to access the tunnels. An inspector would occasionally come check on us. We were not allowed to communicate with anyone.

Long hours with nothing to do but work, eat, sleep and regret.

The lawyer never returned, and after two mind-numbing weeks, it came as a genuine shock to find myself in the meeting room at the jail, dressed in my off-duty fatigues, no prison necklace, with Bjorn and Gunny.

"Sorry, Gunny," I said, while wondering what the nova she was doing still in the system, let alone getting us out.

She looked as pissed as I had ever seen her, and I guessed we deserved it.

"Wasn't us started it," Bjorn said.

"I don't care," she said. "That's the least of your problems. Shut up and listen."

My heart skipped several beats.

Her eyes flicked up to the left and right before coming back to bore into mine.

Got it. The room was not secure. There could be recording devices operating.

What the hell is going on?

"You're booked as passengers on a merchanter, paid by the military as per your contracts. Departure is scheduled tomorrow," she said. "I have opted to pay your fines to the station to allow you to catch that ship, because there's nothing else on the boards scheduled to go to Calloway. The amount of the fine will be deducted from your pay."

Bjorn and I twitched at that, but, hey, I'd had enough of station maintenance and, as she implied, we could spend a long time waiting for the next merchanter heading to Calloway.

It was okay. We had 'til tomorrow to pay for the bio-processors and load them on board. As long as we'd been paid...

"The remainder of your back pay and demobilization bonus has been paid into your accounts."

With an expression like she'd chewed on a lemon, Gunny checked her pad and read out the sums we'd received. In Terran *credits*.

No!

My mouth moved without making any sound. It made no sense. There had to be some mistake.

The Terran dollar was humanity's standard electronic currency, but Earth controlled and tried to restrict it. The Terran *credit* was a promise that if you visited Earth, it would be exchanged for a dollar from the account that it was raised against. It actually was almost as good as a dollar for the closest Inner Worlds, but its value depended on there being constant trade and frequent travel between wherever you were and Earth.

For Ensylas, out in the deep Frontier, credits were only really useful on the infrequent occasions you could catch a merchanter that was heading all the way back to Earth. And even then, he'd know he had you over a barrel.

Gunny's face told me there was no mistake.

There was an utter, chilling silence as it seeped into us how completely we'd been screwed. We couldn't pay for the bio-processors using credits. They'd laugh at us.

People on Calloway would die.

Bjorn was about to go full berserker, but it wasn't Gunny doing this. I gripped his arm, held him back.

"How?" I managed to say, but her eyes flicked up again. Recording devices.

We got out of the jail, stumbling like zombies. My heart was pounding so hard in my ears I could barely hear Gunny's explanation.

The Terran Council had created the Military Oversight Commission and taken the lowest bid to run it, 'saving taxpayers money'. Our pay, in dollars, went into the Commission's account. The Commission issued credits against that, and expedited the demobilization so that the maximum number of troops would be at the wrong end of space when they got paid. Unredeemed credits would become bonuses for the Commission's members.

It was a stinking scam.

At the same time, the Terran Marines were going all out to increase their numbers because Military Intelligence said the conflict in the Dimitras Sector wasn't finished, but the Council only allowed them funding to recruit people from the Frontier. Because Frontier troops dying wasn't as 'politically sensitive' as Terrans dying.

Mad as I was, I was still holding onto Bjorn because he was liable to do something that would get us back into trouble. However little we could do to fix this, it'd get worse if we were back in jail.

"I am also required to inform you," Gunny ground out formally, "that I will be relieving you of any *working* military equipment, which is to be returned."

I blinked. In the time it took my eyelids to sweep back up, I had worked out ten ways to temporarily disable my entire battle kit, right down to the weapons. There would be no working military equipment for her to repossess, and she already knew it.

Gunny, you star!

The kit was worth something, as a whole, or in parts. Nothing like enough to offset my loss on the back pay, but something, at least.

I got Bjorn to look at me and he nodded, grim-faced, to show he understood: do what we could and work from there.

—

The next hours passed in a blur.

We marched double-time to retrieve our combat kit

from the storage facility and assembled it in front of Gunny.

"See?" I said, flexing the arms manually. "The servos must have blown. And the TAW stopped working during the last assault." I pointed at the disassembled weapon. "No supplies available to replace the mechanism."

Gunny grunted.

Out of habit, she slid a finger across the weapon's internal firing actuator.

I snorted. She'd find enough oil to feel oily, not enough to actually wipe off. It wasn't like I was some kind of raw recruit.

"Worthless crap," she snarled. "If you were still signed up, I'd dock you for poor maintenance."

She turned away to mutter notes to her InfoPad.

"You're booked out on the merchanter *Karakun*, Captain Satybal," Gunny filled in as she started inspecting Bjorn's armor. "Departs tomorrow noon, station time."

She paused to mutter again, reading off the serial numbers and then dropping the apparently malfunctioning armor.

"According to the clearing office, you have one other ex-mil passenger on the *Karakun*. A pilot from the 5th Frontier Wing."

I raised my eyebrows. The 5th was a ground attack wing. To us grunts, the ground attack wings were legendary. Mainly because, like legends, you only ever heard about them in stories from long ago. But the battle for Rhea 4 had been different, and the 5th had been true legends for us then. They'd stopped supporting us eventually, but only when they'd run out of everything. Including most of the pilots.

"Name of..." she checked her pad, "Lieutenant Siriwardene. Travelling on to Yorkham."

That was a surprise. Yorkham was a space station, constructed out of a damaged colony ship by the survivors of an accident. The star that the station orbited was outward of Calloway, and the only planets in the system were too lethal to settle on. Since the accident had damaged their Chang drives, Yorkham wasn't going anywhere.

Any ship visiting that system would be flooded with people desperate to leave. That would have made recruitment easy, but what I couldn't see was why someone would be heading back there.

Especially a ground attack pilot.

They were well known to regard themselves as the pinnacle of all pilots, skilled in null-G as well as atmospheric flying. Lieutenant Siriwardene would be a hotshot pilot jock, quiet as a klaxon, subtle as neon lighting, a man with places to go, things to do.

So why was he heading back to Yorkham?

None of my damned business. I had enough problems without worrying about someone else's.

Gunny ordered us to dispose of our 'waste', so we packed our kits back into the wheeled cases and dragged them out into the concourse.

She finished off telling us what had happened while we'd been in jail.

After the news about the credits broke to the Acid Penguins, the Commission's official had retreated into the merchanter hired to take him back to Earth and wisely hadn't come out again.

Gunny had done what she could for her former troops, and they'd all departed to their individual star systems now. We were the last, and she was due to leave on the merchanter with the official in a couple of hours.

She wasn't looking forward to the company on the flight, so she wasn't in a hurry to board. Instead, she offered us a meal at the little dockside hotel-restaurant she was booked into.

"The room's paid for another day. Yours, courtesy of the Terran Marines." Gunny handed us the keycard.

"Thanks, Gunny," I said.

"Appreciate what you've done," Bjorn added.

She looked out across the concourse, eyes focused on something far beyond the station's curving walls.

"I said I'd see you home," she said shortly. "Those that I could, close as I could get."

She *had* said that. I could remember it: one of the first things she'd ever said to the Acid Penguins, and nothing we'd done since then had changed it.

Later, we walked her down the docks, and only as the last call for her ship was being flashed up on the screens did she unbend enough to give us both a hug.

She looked worriedly at us.

"We'll be okay, Gunny," I said. "I'm making a plan."

"That's exactly what I'm afraid of." She stabbed me with a finger. "*You*. Keep Thorsson from going berserk." She stabbed Bjorn. "*You*. Keep Skelling from coming up with situations where you go berserk."

She shook her head, then the sergeant's face slid back into place. "Hate to think of all my training going to waste."

With that, she picked up her duffel, squared her shoulders and walked up the merchanter's gangway.

—

We went back to the restaurant to work.

We were still in shock, but we fired up our pads and started looking at the traders' portals to see what we could get for our combat kit. There was a problem: we were following in the footsteps of fifty other ex-1st

Frontier soldiers who had been trying to sell their kit. The market was flooded.

Bjorn was scowling. I could feel his temper rising again like a boiler nudging the red line.

"I have an idea," I said, trying to keep control, even though I wanted to blow off as well.

"Yeah?"

"We need to walk around to the market arc," I said. "You can get us better deals face-to-face."

It was true, even if it didn't qualify as much of an idea.

"They'll know we're desperate," he said. "Won't get good deals on the kit. And nothing like enough to get even *one* of the bio-processors."

"Okay. If we can't sell here—"

"We can't afford a passage back toward Earth," he said. "And if we could—"

"Hold on!" I had a brainwave. "The *Karakun* must be scheduled to make stops before Calloway."

I downloaded the itinerary from the transportation portal.

There was one stop. The *Karakun* was a short-haul merchanter and couldn't make the jump to Calloway without stopping to recalibrate on the way. However, the system chosen to stop in didn't have a name; it had a number, GC 10295-83657. And alongside that tag, it had the Facilities Rating, which told you what you could expect to find there: a zero. Nothing. Not even a traffic or navigation beacon.

Odd. There were some inhabited systems between Ensylas and Calloway. Each system was a chance for the merchanter to pick up some business. It didn't make sense to do your recalibration in an empty system. Even if you didn't want to spend time dropping into the gravity well to pitch for business, an inhabited system would have a nav beacon to keep charts updated.

Unless the *Karakun* had a time-sensitive delivery for Calloway, and the route chosen was the minimum time course.

I was no navigator—I couldn't begin to guess the efficiency of the course—but common sense made me ask myself what possible delivery to Calloway would be shipped on a time-sensitive contract. They were unbelievably expensive. I doubted anyone on Calloway was making those kind of orders.

And if they did... at that price, you went for a long-haul merchanter that could make it in one jump.

My trouble-sense started to prickle.

"Bjorn, why would a merchanter like the *Karakun* be heading out to Calloway?"

"Huh?"

He didn't even raise his eyes from his pad.

I lifted my head, but not to look at him; I'd registered that there was someone who had approached silently to stand next to our table.

"I don't think the *Karakun* is going to Calloway," the stranger said in a whispery voice.

She was untidily dressed and clutching a bag in front of her like it was a shield. For a second, I thought it was a beggar, but stations don't allow them.

She nervously ran one trembling hand through her short black hair. Her face was thin, dark-skinned. Her eyes... she had bruised-looking eyes that couldn't stay still.

"You're Skelling and Thorsson, right?" she said.

How would she know us?

"Siriwardene?" I guessed.

She nodded.

I cleared my throat. *Not* the pilot jock that we were expecting.

"Join us?" I said and gestured at the chair opposite.

I could see momentary panic in her eyes and her nostrils flared.

What the nova? Battle fatigue?

But she sat, hugging her bag on her lap.

Bjorn, who could be a real idiot sometimes, nonetheless caught on that something was wrong. When he spoke, he lowered his voice, and put away that dumb, megawatt smile.

"Would you like something to eat?" he asked. "Drink?"

"I don't," she said. "I mean I don't eat or drink food I don't see prepared."

We stared at her.

"You don't know what they put in it."

"Okay..."

Paranoia in addition to whatever else was going on with her.

If we had to live with her in close proximity on the *Karakun*, none of us were going to enjoy this trip.

I waved off a server who was lurking for an order.

"The *Karakun* came in at the same time as the transport that brought me," Siriwardene said abruptly. "I got a good look at her with the transport's sensors."

She had relaxed the smallest amount.

"Well?" I pushed gently.

"The *Karakun* is a pirate."

I ignored the spasm in my gut and frowned. "Pretty serious allegation, Lieutenant."

"I'm not a lieutenant anymore. And I can prove the *Karakun*..." She stopped and her lips thinned. "I *could* prove it, but we can't get into the dock repair gantries."

I tried not to roll my eyes. How convenient. *I could prove it, but...*

"What use would it be getting into the gantries?" Bjorn asked.

Siriwardene's eyes flicked to him and away again.

"The *Karakun* is in the last berth, next to the repair bays. You can see the whole of the ship from the gantries."

"So they have cannon mounted or something—" I started, but Bjorn interrupted me. His voice had gone all silky, like it did when he had a good hand at cards.

"Just suppose, for the sake of argument, that we could get into the gantries. Have they painted a skull and crossbones on the hull?"

"Don't be stupid," Siriwardene said and got up.

I would have let her go, but Bjorn reached out.

"Wait," he said, and she stopped. "We *can* get into the gantries through the maintenance tunnels."

"What? How?" I had a bad feeling about this. "You gave your access key back. I saw you."

"I did," Bjorn agreed amiably. "But I didn't give back the inspector's backup override key."

For nova's sake! Idiot!

He was right on one thing. We *could* get into the gantries with a master key, but the keys were dual system—an actual, old-fashioned electro-mechanical lock activator twinned with an electronic interface which would report the activity.

"They'll have found out it's gone," I said. "If they don't have someone already on the way to arrest us, they *will* have a tracking program to locate anywhere it gets used."

"Relax. It's his backup key. I took it on our first day and he still hasn't realized. He may never realize."

"It was still a stupid thing to do. Anyway, as I said, there'll be alerts that come up on a monitor somewhere whenever those tunnels are accessed."

Siriwardene sat back down and cleared her throat.

"Actually, I may be able to help with that."

—

And she could. Which is why, an hour later, we were in the low-G dock gantries near the ship maintenance section.

The section doors had opened, and according to Siriwardene, *call-me-Shami*, nothing had been reported to central monitoring.

Ground attack pilots were *different.* I knew that. I just hadn't really understood how different.

Apparently, the difficulties of flying their craft inside and outside of atmosphere in combat situations required certain additional abilities, including the capability of connecting directly to the onboard computerized systems. Part of her skull was a freaking electronic interface.

The reason she was twitchy was she *needed* that connection to computerized systems. She was addicted to it.

"Low power," she'd explained, as she rested her head on the door's panel. "I need to be close, but this is fine."

Just using her ability to connect to the monitoring system had calmed her right down.

On the other hand, climbing and crawling through narrow, low-G passages didn't help, and Shami was showing signs of claustrophobia. Bjorn and I were fine; Gunny had insisted we train in ship-to-ship combat from null-G to hi-G, from restricted spaces to cavernous hangars.

This far down toward the center of the station, we were well away from the effect of the artificial G of the main area, and the centrifugal force of rotation wasn't having much effect, so all three of us were floating above an inspection window.

Directly 'below' us, the *Karakun* was nose-in to the dock hub, secured in place with standard grapples, front and sides. It was like any other old, small merchanter— a long steel spine sitting on top of twin cargo bulges, crew space at the front and engines at the back.

The low gravity played tricks with my mind. I felt as if I were looking up at the ship. It seemed huge and menacing. The glancing sunlight made every shadow deeper, turned every surface shape into something monstrous.

I shook my head.

Concentrate.

"What am I looking for?" I asked.

"The section behind the bridge," Shami said. "The raised flat bit."

There was a big rectangular area which looked like it had been added recently. In the middle were what looked like sealed blast doors. Spread out around those were heavy-duty securing pits and recesses for grappling equipment, similar to the equipment used to secure the ship in dock.

"That," Shami said confidently, "is the latest in deep-space universal couplings. Replicates the docking facilities of space stations."

"It's a way to make a sealed connection with another ship?"

"Yes."

I frowned. Unusual, yes. Suspicious?

"What do you think they trade, out there in deep space, out of sight of everyone else?" Shami said. "What's worth the costs of getting a coupling like that installed on a two-bit merchanter?"

"Maybe it's smuggling rather than piracy?" Bjorn said.

I grimaced. "No. Down in the depths of the Inner

Worlds, maybe. Out here? Trading station to station? There's no pan-system smuggling laws that individual systems are going to enforce. If they don't want what you've got, they don't buy it."

Everyone knew ships docked at stations with cargo that was illegal for that system. It was a gray area, but generally, if you kept it on board, the station didn't care.

Shami was right. Such a coupling only made sense for bulk transfers, and only pirates would need to transfer bulk cargo in deep space.

There was a long silence, broken by Bjorn: "And they bid for a contract to take us to Calloway because..."

He and Shami kicked it back and forth between them.

"They get three slaves they can sell into rogue systems and three sets of back pay that they can convert next time they go inward."

"That ship wouldn't dare enter a rogue system. No weapons."

"No, this is their legitimate merchanter. So that means there's at least one other, an armed ship, out there in the dark, waiting."

"Can we cancel the contract to travel and re-bid using the same money?"

"Maybe. Even if we can't, and we have to pay passage ourselves, we have to."

They wound down.

"Janice?"

I was floating there, staring at the pirate.

It all hit me in that moment: The greed of the Commission. The betrayal. The three lives wasted—Solveig, Enoch, Hal. The smirks of station traders as they swindled us out of everything. My family's faces if I turned up after six years with no bio-processors. The despair as the colony faced its own collapse. More deaths from starvation. My uncle's face—*I told you she wouldn't amount to anything. Probably spent it in bars.* Six years of my life, my *soul*, risked and wasted.

And finally anger—white-hot and steady as Sirius, flooding through me.

Enough.

I shook my head again. "We can't stay here. We take that ship."

"Ah... I vote to not be a slave," Bjorn said.

"Well, that's given," I replied. "But you know what? I have a plan."

"Oh, shit," Bjorn said.

—

My plan hatched in the relative comfort of the Orion's Wheel station looked... different now that I watched the second pirate ship coast in by the faint red light of an empty system's dying sun, surrounded by cold, hard vacuum.

Back on Orion's Wheel, we'd arrived at the *Karakun* acting belligerent in case Captain Satybal wanted to check our luggage for contraband. We didn't have to worry. The crew of the *Karakun* didn't bother to greet us. There was a screen next to the gangway, which demanded confirmation of our identities and then directed us to the 'passenger accommodation'.

That was three rooms. One with a set of bunks, one with chairs and a ReadyMeal dispenser, and one bathroom. As soon as we were inside the short corridor that formed the entrance, the door had sealed behind us.

Ship security and safety were the reasons given when we'd used the comm to query it.

Hogshit.

Even before we'd undocked, Shami had located, identified, and subverted the electronics of the monitors that the *Karakun* had installed to keep watch on us. And while we were outbound from Ensylas, I'd broken into and crawled through the maintenance tunnels. With instructions from Shami, I'd rigged a connection for her into the computer system network.

It made her so happy, she had to discipline herself not to take over until we were ready.

She *wasn't* in control of the much larger, obviously heavily armed pirate ship that was incoming to connect up with the *Karakun.* Getting control of *that* was a job for Bjorn and me.

The newcomer's name was *Tünjorgo.* Both ships were registered to Zilkum, a small Frontier system at the other end of the Parvi Arc. There was almost nothing in the Ensylas databanks about Zilkum. Exactly the sort of setup that spoke of rogue systems and pirate bases.

Karakun was the merchanter that visited systems and learned about rich prizes. *Tünjorgo* was the demon that waited in the dark places to seize them. Goods went to the *Karakun* to sell at the next legitimate system, while slaves went into the *Tünjorgo* to wait until they were sold in the next rogue system. Neat.

What the *Tünjorgo* didn't know was that Captain Satybal had not picked up three helpless potential slaves heading home with currency cards full of credits they couldn't convert, but rather three angry, pissed-off veterans, one who was poised to take over the *Karakun's* computerized systems, and the other two in fully operational combat armor, waiting to do something less subtle with the bigger ship.

We waited in silence, except for the blood pounding in my ears and the rush of my breath. Knowing Bjorn could see my vital signs soaring in his helmet monitor didn't help calm me down.

Showtime.

"Let's go. When we get there, remember to point your weapon away from me," I said as we launched ourselves into space.

Bjorn's response was rude and crude. It helped take my mind off the thought that we were flying between two ships in deep space using nothing more for maneuvering than a rig made from a couple of cheap, out-of-date fire extinguishers, which were going to run out...

Now.

We were still travelling toward the *Tünjorgo*, but one extinguisher had run out before the other, so we were spinning slowly. The distant stars wheeled above me. We were only three-quarters of the way between the ships, and we needed to hurry.

Theoretically, the danger was slim. Automated scanners would ignore something relatively low mass and slow moving like us, but all it would need would be for someone to get curious.

Too late to change the plan.

We needed to get rid of our exhausted propulsion rig.

Bjorn's countdown came through my helmet. "Three, two, one, go!"

I kicked the rig with the empty fire extinguishers away, in the opposite direction we wanted to travel. Newton be thanked, it helped: equal and opposite reactions. It even slowed the spinning a bit, which was lucky because we crashed into the surface of the *Tünjorgo*, out of control.

Hey, it was our first EVA.

Newton got his revenge, because Bjorn bounced off the ship and started drifting, waving his arms and legs.

I anchored myself using a magnetic grapple and chased after him in comical slow motion.

Found a second anchor point.

Threw a line.

Too short...

Leaped. Grabbed the end. Reached...

He grabbed hold of my hand.

"Stop playing the fool and come back here," I hissed at him.

"Very funny."

His vital signs were all over the place. Made me smirk.

He reeled himself in and we had five minutes of more slow-motion racing across the surface of the *Tünjorgo*, looking for an access airlock, while the ship shifted beneath us like a restless monster.

"Docking in five seconds." Shami's voice came over the command channel. "Brace."

Three... two... one...

There was a recessed area with a raised lip just in reach.

I felt the servos in our armor gauntlets ramp up just in time. A violent shudder ran through the ship and slapped us hard against the surface.

"Docked," Shami said. "They're checking systems. I'm guessing you have about five minutes before they come looking for us."

"On it," I said. "We found an airlock."

The next step was to get inside. Almost all ships like this were built in the Inner Worlds and they usually built them with standard controls, but there was no certainty the airlock wouldn't be sealed or made to a different specification.

Bjorn was swearing as he worked on the panel.

I felt thumps through the ship as the *Tünjorgo* was clamped in place. That was okay. While they were concentrating on that, they weren't moving around.

Then the vibrations died away, and I started prepping explosives, running through what would be needed if we blew the airlock open.

It would be bad news because whereas an airlock showing it was opening and closing, with no alarms sounding, would probably be ignored by the crew for a while, blowing the outer doors would not.

Bjorn grunted: "Got it."

I heaved a sigh of relief.

The lock cycled open, and the inner door was a simple push button once the lock had flooded with air.

"Inside," I reported to Shami.

"I've frozen the docking bay's blast doors," she said. "They're blaming a faulty installation. It'll give you another couple of minutes until they get down and force them open."

"Good thinking."

Bjorn and I took ten seconds to check each other's suits.

"All okay. Weapons free," he said quietly.

I nodded, with the usual sick feeling in my mouth I got before action. "Clock zero. Go."

We came out of the airlock. Bjorn turned right, I turned left.

From the outline of the *Tünjorgo* that Shami had provided to us from the *Karakun*'s databases, we had three objectives and only two of us.

I headed to the front of the ship. I had to take control of the bridge.

After a long, difficult discussion yesterday, we'd agreed Bjorn should take the prisoners' section. We knew the *Tünjorgo* had some, and we didn't want to face a situation where they were used as hostages.

That left engineering.

We had to hope I could isolate them from the bridge.

We'd run analyses. We estimated we had four minutes and fifteen seconds for both of us to achieve our tasks, at which time Shami could seize control of the *Karakun* and lock the whole ship down through the computer systems.

Then we had another twelve minutes before we had to return and prevent Satybal and his crew from bypassing the computer controls.

If any of that went wrong...

Four minutes remaining.

Passage end. Rung ladder. Up one level. Straight ahead.

A crewman turned in shock at the sight of an armored soldier sprinting along the passage.

No time. I had no police weapons like a stun gun. The guy was unarmed.

Then again, he was a slaver.

I backhanded him out of the way. That was serious hurt, delivered by military armor.

"One hostile down, not dead," I grunted as I accelerated through the door he'd opened. Didn't slow. Slammed into the wall. Turned left. Sprinted down that passage. Then right.

The first major obstacle. The ship had enough safety discipline that they'd closed emergency bulkheads while docking.

A simple lever and bolt. I tore it open.

Three minutes.

"They've switched to using auxiliary power to open the blast doors. I can't stop them," Shami said over the command channel. "You have two minutes."

Shit. Two minutes!

More crew ahead of me. And some kind of a comm panel on the wall.

I hit the crew hard and punched my fist right through

the comm panel. Sparks flew out.

"Two more down," I said and kept going.

Another level change.

I didn't bother with the rungs. I just jumped up. My arm was extended to kill my momentum. It went right through the ceiling and some of the cabling above it.

Alarms went off. Something I'd done. Or Bjorn.

"I've sealed off the docking bay and I'm venting it." Shami's voice. "Venting *Karakun* bridge and engineering."

Shit! She wasn't messing around.

"Prisoner area secured." Bjorn's voice. "Three hostiles down. Can't get inside the cells."

We had to hope I could open the cell doors from the bridge.

A security barrier started to slide out across the passage from one side. I dove through, sensed trouble, rolled, came up with the TAW already pointed.

Crew were hurriedly grabbing weapons from a storage area.

No time.

I fired as I ran, wide dispersal, and dropped a fragmentation grenade behind me as I darted into the last passage that led to the bridge.

The grenade exploded behind me. My armor soaked it up, but when the whole ship shook and lurched, I went spinning and sliding.

"*Tünjorgo* trying to disengage docking by force," Shami said.

No time.

"Clamping circuits are being bypassed on the *Tünjorgo*'s side. You have fifteen seconds."

I bounced to my feet. The door to the bridge ahead was sealed. I sprinted, hit it at full speed, dropping my shoulder.

My armor took most of the impact, but I still saw stars. The metal door buckled and bent, but it held.

No!

I stood back, dialed in armor piercing—*only two of those rounds left*—and fired the TAW.

They punched through the door and did who knows what damage beyond. The alarms doubled and lights started flashing.

I tossed a dazzler into the bridge area and took a grip on the hole in the door.

The servos in my armor whined. This was *not* what they were designed for.

The dazzler went off. Intense light and *loud* noise.

"Ten seconds," Shami said.

The door's holding structure distorted.

There were shots from behind me. The armor let me know about it, but it would hold against typical shipboard weapons. I couldn't spare the time to deal with them.

With a screech, the door began to peel open.

"Seven seconds."

I kicked my way through onto the bridge.

There were three of them there, all stumbling about from the effect of the dazzler, their faces blank with shock.

I grabbed the nearest and shoved the TAW in his face.

With my suit's speaker amplification up to maximum, I shouted: "Turn off all power to Docking and Engineering. *NOW.*"

"Four seconds."

The man collapsed against a control panel, his eyes unfocused and his fingers clumsy.

Luckily, the command menu was in English. Once he called up the right menu, I reached past him and stabbed at the options on the screen.

Power. Emergency. Docking bay. Off.

"Two seconds."

A message popped up on the screen: *Power disconnect from docking bay. Are you sure?*

Yes!

Docking bay power disconnected.

I repeated the sequence for Engineering.

Then I found the comms panel. Switched it to ship-wide broadcast.

What the nova should I say?

"This is Lieutenant Commander Skelling of the Calloway Navy Anti-Piracy Unit. The *Tünjorgo* and *Karakun* are now under my control. If there is any further resistance, I will vent these shit-heaps to space and throw your stinking bodies out of the airlock."

—

A ring of expectant faces looked up at me.

A dozen men and women, the crews of a couple of small ships that had been captured, who'd been held prisoner in the *Tünjorgo*, knowing the fate that had awaited them—slavery.

Relief on their faces, mainly. Anger, too. And hope.

The pirates, living and dead, were now in the holding cells, and their former captives sat on the seats in the *Tünjorgo*'s mess area.

I was standing, still in my suit, but with the visor cracked so they could see my face.

I'd already told them they hadn't been rescued by the 'Calloway Navy'.

What the nova do I say now?

"There's good news and bad," I started. "You're free and we will get you back to your systems, or any place we get to, that you nominate."

Cheers. Smiles.

"We need some of them to run these damned ships, *Lieutenant Commander*," Shami snarked in my ear through the command channel. "Have you actually thought through *any* of this?"

I ignored her and went on. "The bad news..."

It got quiet.

"These ships don't have enough credit to go wandering all over the Frontier."

"You'll get bounties from handing over the pirates to any system that has signed the Anti-Piracy Accords," one of the men at the back said.

"*We* will get bounties," I replied. "All of us. But if we turn up with the *Tünjorgo* and *Karakun* in the Ensylas System, for example, the ships would be impounded and your share of the bounty might not get you home."

And Bjorn, Shami, and I would be back where we started, with fistfuls of credit that wouldn't buy what Calloway or Yorkham needed and probably wouldn't even get us passage back home.

Absolute silence, even on the helmet radio. They were all waiting for me.

"But it's okay," I said. "I have a plan."

THE END

THE LONG WAY HOME

About the Author

Mark's early interest in philosophy and psychology was adequately exorcised by tending bars. And while trying to enroll in a class to read Science Fiction full time, he ended up taking an engineering degree which splendidly qualified him to move into marketing. That in turn spawned a late onset career in creative writing.

He writes Urban Fantasy (Bite Back series) and Science Fiction (Among the Stars series).

To learn more about Mark Henwick's writing, visit:
www.athanate.com

THE MIXON DRIVE

by J.R. Handley

LOCATION: **Phoenix Orbital Station**

IT'S HIDEOUS. No wonder they kept it so secret, Paul thought.

The sight that waited for him in the hangar bay was nothing like the mission briefings suggested. Lieutenant Colonel Paul Cooley had been sold on the idea of riding a sleek shuttle for its historic test of the Mixon Drive. This was the engine that would deliver the promise of faster than light travel to humanity, and it was housed in a phallic metal tube. One that looked like the illegitimate offspring of a NASA shuttle and an airbus.

He used the joystick on his jet pack to maneuver, hating the way zero-g affected his stomach. After adjusting his angle, Paul drifted closer so he could get a better look. He was still underwhelmed. The ship was a bulbous patchwork of corrugated alloy composites, a shoestring production that barely looked flight-worthy. It had none of the beauty and grace that SpaceX built into its Mars Shot Program vehicle, the Super Heavy-Starship combination.

"You're no beauty," Paul said quietly as he rubbed

the stubby wing of the shuttle—a ship that looked more likely to explode upon ignition than start.

"Excuse me, sir?" a young scientist asked, his voice blaring on the speakers inside Paul's helmet as he gently drifted beside Paul.

Jumping inside his spacesuit, Paul accidentally toggled the joystick controlling his jetpack and had to course-correct before he could answer the new arrival. "Jesus, kid... don't sneak up on a guy!"

"Roger, sir. I'm Doctor Horovitz, a liaison from Athena International. I'm here to help you perform the final pre-flight checklist," the young scientist replied.

"I've got this," Cooley said.

"I'm sure you do, sir. However, NASA doesn't trust Marines with their expensive new toys."

Grunting out an automatic hoorah, Paul toggled his joystick and followed the scientist into the shuttles rear access panel.

"Does this monstrosity have a name?" Paul asked.

"This is the Z-480," answered Horovitz.

"That's the shuttle's designation, but what's its name?" Paul asked.

"It doesn't have one yet; it's just the proof of concept for Doctor Mixon's brilliant design work."

"I've met Doc Mixon; he's no Elon Musk—he's an idiot." Paul snapped. "We better double-check this bird. Guess I'll take that help after all."

The exterior of the bird checked out, though the scientist noted a few problematic joints on the heat shields. Years of experience told Paul that those weren't what would kill him. Faulty weld joints were ugly, but it was the power plant that would blow up spectacularly. Satisfied that the exterior of the shuttle was within the acceptable margins, he drifted over to the interior access hatch.

Paul and Horovitz shrugged out of their jetpacks, clamping them to the shuttle's exterior. Grabbing the stabilization bar near the hatch, Paul used his free hand to turn the handle that swung the door inward. Reaching back with his free hand, he gestured to the scientist.

"Lead the way," Paul ordered Horovitz.

Upon entering the shuttle, they turned and sealed the entrance and waited for the shuttle to pressurize. When the cabin's oxygen saturation returned to breathable levels, both men pulled off their helmets and clipped them to their utility belts.

"You're not even old enough to shave! You're just a baby," Paul said in shock.

"That's Doctor Horovitz to you, Colonel,"

"Take it easy, kid," Paul replied, "I was just surprised. No offense intended. Let's check the engines first. That's where most mishaps start."

Doctor Horovitz turned, heading to the rear of the shuttle and a sealed hatch. Twisting the wheel on the airtight door, he pushed it open.

Gesturing at Paul, Horovitz spoke quietly. "Only room for one, we'll go in and independently confirm the other guy's findings. You can go first."

"Sure thing, kid. Were the AI algorithms for the navigator and engineer positions uploaded today?" Paul asked.

"Negative," he replied, "they get uploaded later this evening."

Drifting into the engine compartment, Paul checked every one of the magnetic rods that made up the star engine power plant. The individual rods clamped to the wall of the engine compartment and linked to the fusion plant that spun around on a gimble. This modified Fusion Torch Drive was bigger than the ones he was used to seeing. The size of the engine made the chamber feel cramped and hampered the ability of the mechanics to move about the space.

Paul stared at the engine. He knew that the star engine design generated a barely visible blue flame out the back, as the engine vented the fusion reaction to create forward thrust. But that was the byproduct that produced the thrust. How the improved nuclear reactor worked, and the rest of the functionality of the engine was beyond him. The level of complexity was why the shuttles were designed with a three-man crew in mind.

Exiting the engine compartment, Paul nodded to Doctor Horovitz. "I'll verify the Mixon Drive next, while you check the engine. We'll meet back up in the cockpit after you double-check my work and compare notes."

"Sounds like a plan!" Horovitz replied.

He didn't bother answering the young scientist, instead trying to open the vacuum-sealed compartment door. It didn't budge. Grunting, he tried again. It remained stubbornly closed. The hatch was stuck.

"Forgot to tell you," Horovitz hollered at him, "you don't have clearance to inspect the Mixon Drive. I'll meet you in the cockpit once I've checked it myself."

Stifling a string of curses, Paul drifted toward the cockpit. The young scientist's lilting laughter chased him. When he got to the airtight hatch that leads into the cockpit, he paused.

Holding his breath, Paul turned the wheel, and the door slid silently open. He took in the sleek lines of his terminal. This was a far cry from the ugly, yet functional, aesthetic of the Z-480's exterior. Most of the terminals surrounded the pilot in a u-shape, lined with buttons, gauges and numerous toggle switches. The navigator's station was similarly situated. Computer terminals in a u-shape pattern surrounded it. The electronics were hardened for durability and looked deliciously modern.

Every available space in the rest of the tight cockpit was lined with dashboards, buttons, toggles, and switches. Numerous lights were sprinkled around, making the compartment resemble a schizophrenic Christmas tree.

Half of those buttons and switches are probably just for visual effect, he thought.

Floating deeper into the cockpit, Paul sat in the cushioned seat, strapped himself in, and pulled out the checklist so he could begin the pre-flight inspection. It went smoothly; every system checked out and passed the multi-step validation process. This was vastly different than anything he'd ever done, and the Marine Corps Test Pilot Program had put him into the cockpit of dozens of hanky fliers.

This is one complicated shuttle. Will the three-week build-up give me enough time to learn the system? he wondered.

Crushing his doubts, Paul focused on his success. He'd spent time in every other space-worthy craft in the United States' arsenal. When you absolutely had to have the best pilot in the world to test your new craft, you called him. That wasn't just his pride talking, his reflexes and flight knowledge routinely tested well above the norms for pilots half his age.

This bird was the exception, though, so classified that no information was released before he accepted the assignment. Only his desire to complete the circuit of available experimental craft made him risk the Z-480. He wanted closure before a promotion forced him to take a desk job in DC. Were it not for that, he'd never have given this project the green light.

While he was finishing his pre-flight checks, Horovitz drifted in and strapped himself into the navigator's seat. Paul turned and frowned. "Tell me again how this works?"

"Well, sir, the Mixon Drive works off the principles of the Alcubierre mathematical equation. It states that—"

"No, no, no... give it to me, Barney style. Try again; tell me how it works?" Paul asked.

"Basically, sir, Doctor Mixon solved the energy issues that had relegated the Alcubierre Warp Drive to the realm of science fiction. We started with the assumption that—"

"Stop! Break it down for me simply! Use the KISS Method," Paul demanded.

"I'd forgotten that you were a Marine," Horovitz quipped.

"And that Athena International has this project so classified that I couldn't study the bird before I got here!"

"Right, sorry about that. Once you clear the orbital station's air space, you and your crew will accelerate toward the outer solar system. When you reach the appropriate coordinates, push the red button. It engages the warp coils, which builds up the energy needed for the jumps," Horovitz said.

"Remind me," Paul asked abruptly. "How do I tell it where to go?" *If he is going to treat me like an idiot, let him explain it all!*

"Enter the preset coordinates we've given you. It should stop you from crashing into some rogue planet's gravity well," Horovitz said confidently.

"How do I know I won't smash into something like a micrometeorite that's waiting for me at this preset location?" Paul asked.

"Cross your fingers?" came the sheepish reply.

"In that case, maybe you should go with me, in case anything goes wrong," Paul replied, halfway serious.

"Do I look like some crazed maniac?" Horovitz asked incredulously. "I'm not an idiot. I won't risk my life on some untested scientific contraption! That's why God gave us idiots... I mean Marine test pilots!"

Paul ignored the scrawny scientist, poring over his flight plan before the launch window later that day.

"I'm signing off on the Z-480, are you?"

"Roger, all systems are green," Horovitz replied.

"And the Mixon Drive?" Paul asked.

"Affirmative. And no... I won't let you see for yourself," Horovitz replied.

"Will one of my crew have the security clearance for it, then?"

"Yes, we're training the navigator as we speak. They'll be ready to go in three weeks, fully up to speed. Now, let's report back to the hangar boss and upload the AIs. Then we should be ready for your launch sims," Horovitz said.

"Good, let's exit this bird and get some food. Don't want to train on an empty stomach."

A siren alert blared from every speaker on the orbital station. Whatever Horovitz might've said in reply was lost under the oppressive weight of the sound. *Wait, that can't be right,* he thought. *That's a combat alert. We're not even at war*! Reaching over, he muted the siren and pulled up the ship's sensors. They were tied into the base's computer network, letting him see everything that the orbital base ops knew.

"Z-480, this is Control Tower 1. Do you copy?" the strained voice of the flight control operator asked.

"Roger, what's going on here?" Paul demanded.

"We're under attack!" the flight control operator said.

"Who's attacking?" Paul asked.

"China. They surprised us—bombed our embassies!"

"Calm down. Now, repeat it slowly," Paul said, trying to soothe the distraught tower control operator.

"We're under attack! Four embassies are gone! They even hit the Canadian embassy! Who the hell bombs the Canucks?" asked the hysterical operator.

"Are we sure it's even the ChiComs and not some terrorist group?" Paul asked.

"Ye... yeah, I triple checked the incoming feed. This was a combined arms attack; the Chinese Communists planted the flag and everything," said the operator.

"Okay, relax. Just give me an update," ordered Paul.

"They've launched multiple sorties at our location. At Phoenix Station. There are nine flights of HuoLong's inbound!" the flight control operator said, almost hyperventilating.

"Say again, HuoLongs? Those are the Space Dragons; they're just unarmed merchant shuttles," Paul said calmly. "You're overreacting."

"Those shuttles have opened fire on some of our satellites. Confirmation enough?"

"Okay, think this one through. The Chinese wouldn't violate our non-aggression pact," Paul said.

"By firing on the satellites as they advance, they've already violated the 2024 Space Disarmament Treaty! Orders have come in Colonel. They want you to launch now before it's too late!" the flight control operator screamed, finally giving way to hysteria.

"I don't have a crew. I also don't have the navigator or engineer AI uploaded yet," Paul replied steadily, hoping to calm the civilian operator. "I can't launch blind."

"Cooley, this is Colonel Geller. Launch with Doctor Horovitz. The Chinese don't want us to get the first FTL engine; they're actively trying to sabotage the launch. Go!" the base commander ordered.

"We can't. We don't have the AIs on board," Horovitz interrupted.

"Launch or die. Your call, Doctor. Colonel Cooley, you have your orders," Colonel Geller said.

"Roger," Paul said.

"Godspeed," Colonel Geller replied.

Turning to look at the frightened young scientist, Paul spoke quietly. "We'll be okay. We're going to be gone before the ChiComs, get here."

Ignoring the frightened response from Doctor Horovitz, Paul began initializing the Z-480. In record time, the shuttle disengaged its clamps and freed itself from the metallic arm. As he rotated the shuttle's orientation, the hangar bay doors of the base began to open slowly. The well-lit bay darkened, exposing the inky voids beyond.

"The good thing about Phoenix Station being in the Lagrange Point past the moon… quicker launches," Paul said.

"Entering the coordinates now," Horovitz said, ignoring the pilot's random musing. "Initiate thrust and head toward the preset jump coordinates."

A quick flick of the toggle engaged the modified Fusion Torch Drive, gently pushing the shuttle toward the outer galaxy. He watched his orb of origin get progressively smaller in his scanner window, trying to ignore the fleet of Chinese shuttles headed in their direction.

"They're getting closer," Paul warned Horovitz. "Preparing to initiate evasive maneuvering. You better adjust on the fly!"

"Just hold it steady," Horovitz said.

Ignoring the scientist's hissed reply, Paul focused on the sensors in front of him. The Z-480 lacked weapons sensors, but he could see the flashes of light from the rail guns being fired by the HuoLong directly behind his shuttle. Twitching his hand gently, he adjusted course.

"Hold steady, damnit," Horovitz snapped, not looking up from his console.

"Trying not to die is priority one. They're shooting at us," an exasperated Paul said in reply.

"Hold this course. I'll recalculate," said Horovitz.

Cursing, Paul held the stick and tried to resist the urge to nudge the Z-480 off course again. *I'd kill for some missiles. Who thought a one-sided disarmament treaty was a good idea, anyway?*

"Hold it for a few moments longer," Horovitz begged.

Paul stared at the sensor array, willing the enemy fighters to give up. He missed Horovitz's request, only registering his words when the young man screamed.

"Engage Mixon Drive now!" Horovitz said.

Paul flipped open the cover and hit the red button.

At first, nothing happened. HuoLong shuttles were firing at them again as they adjusted to the Z-480's new trajectory—then he was slammed back into his seat.

Staring out the forward window, he saw streaks of light speeding past faster than his eyes could process the data. Their location folded in on itself. Everything was slightly out of sync. He couldn't focus. Looking over at his navigator, he tried to determine which one of them was Horovitz.

Nausea hit first, then dizziness. Paul couldn't feel his fingers and electrical currents tingled along every synapse. It was worse than his last bout with vodka. That night of degeneracy, when he'd celebrated the promotion of his Annapolis roommate, didn't compare to what he was experiencing at the moment. All of the illness without the drunken debauchery.

"Please be real. Please be real," Horovitz chanted.

Huh, I can hear him clearly. Slightly hollow tonality, but the vocal distortion is minimal. "It's real," Paul said. "Now what?"

"The AI will coordinate with the engine, and it'll drop us off at the programmed coordinates. Now, we wait," Horovitz said excitedly, his fear forgotten.

The lights flashing across the cockpit window were nauseating. Paul closed his eyes, trying not to puke. Time seemed to slow as they waited, though the internal chronometer said mere minutes had passed.

"Get ready for it!" Horovitz shouted, breaking the pregnant pause.

Nothing seemed to happen—until he looked out the window and realized he was in another star system.

Retch.

"Grab the vomit—" Horovitz started.

Blargh.

"That slipping through space was no joke," Paul said, wiping the drool from his lips. *Glad I had my helmet off.*

"It's a warp bubble," Horovitz replied as he tried to avoid the floating blobs of vomit. "Now clean this puke up!"

Cleaning fluids from a zero-g environment was tedious, but ultimately Paul was able to scoop it all up while the shuttle analyzed their surroundings.

"Before we jump home, let's do another maintenance check," Paul said as he stowed the bag of puke globules in the refuse container.

"First, we need to figure out where we are," Horovitz said, almost giggling.

"We're in Alpha Centauri, quit joking around."

"That's where we were supposed to be going," Horovitz said, "but look around you. Does anything you're seeing match the star charts we studied?"

"Oh...," Paul said, his voice trailing off.

Turning back toward the cockpit window, Paul looked at the bright orb that was the system's star. Except there was only one, not the expected binary stars of Alpha Centauri. Wherever they were, it was a system with a red dwarf star and several planets. Not that that narrowed down the possibilities much; the universe was full of red dwarves.

"Okay, while you figure this out, I'll go check the engines," Paul said.

Unbuckling, Paul drifted up from the seat and twisted his body, so he was facing the rear of the shuttle. He pushed off the back of the chair with his boot, hands outstretched to grab the sealed hatch. Twisting the spin-wheel handle, he opened the door and shoved off the wall toward the engine compartment. Along the way, he checked every system to verify the Z-480 was still flight-worthy.

When he reached the engine compartment, Paul entered and checked all the terminals for any anomalous readings. Then, he began running the diagnostics sweep of all the computer systems several times before he was satisfied. He checked each diagnostic panel, searching for any red LED warning lights. When he found none, he ran another check of the computer's software.

After the computer told him that everything was good, Paul then physically checked each system he had access to. He couldn't enter the compartment that held the modified Fusion Torch Drive, the radiation would've killed him, but he verified everything else in the engine compartment before he was satisfied.

"Either get me into the compartment with the Mixon Drive or check it for yourself," Paul yelled to Horovitz.

There was no answer, so Paul repeated himself.

"Don't get your knickers in a twist, I'm coming."

The young scientist headed straight toward the sealed hatch that housed the Mixon Drive. "Get back. This is still classified," he snapped.

Not bothering to restrain himself, Paul let loose a

string of vulgarities that caused the young scientist to blanche a new shade of pale.

"The answer is still no," Horovitz said grimly.

Paul glided back to the cockpit, leaving a string of obscenities in his wake. When he reached the pilot's console, he strapped back in and began checking every system. As he was initiating the third sweep through the computerized maintenance interface, Horovitz drifted into the cockpit.

"It's broke... the lower coolant pump's completely fused, and magnetic guides eight through to ten have buckled. It's a mess. A damn mess. God, we're screwed." Horovitz said dully.

"So... fix it," Paul said, his voice calm despite the sinking feeling in his gut.

"Without the right spares, we're trapped here." Horovitz answered, his voice devoid of emotion.

"Okay?"

"We didn't bring any spares," replied Horovitz.

"Then jerry-rig something! You're a damned—"

Wah-wah-wah!

The blaring siren cut Paul off. He was unable to focus through the screeching sound, leaving whatever thought he'd had to drift away.

"Turn that siren off. Wait... what was that siren for?" Paul asked.

"Let me check," Horovitz said slowly as he silenced the alarm.

While the young scientist scrolled through several menu screens, Paul stared into the abyss of space. Out of the corner of his eye, he caught the glimmer of something. Cocking his head, he tried to see it again, to no avail.

"There's something weird out there," Paul said, warily pointing toward where he'd seen the strange flickering of light.

"I know," Horovitz whispered, slumping back in his chair.

"How?" Paul asked, his voice harsher than he'd intended.

"That's what the alarm was. NASA added a contingency alert for any molecules that didn't occur naturally," Horovitz said, his voice strained.

"What did they want us to do about it?" Paul demanded.

"Scan it for later review. Last night, we upgraded the sensor suite on the Z-480. Those sensors should give us a better idea of what this is, but what good is that information without a working Mixon Drive?" said Horovitz.

"I'll move us closer," Paul replied. "We can decide what to do after we start a full sensor sweep of whatever caused the alert. We need to assess the situation, prioritize our next move."

"This isn't some wargame. No amount of planning will fix this," Horovitz said.

"We're not dead yet, so we keep trying."

Nudging the throttle, Paul ignored his defeated navigator and adjusted the shuttle's angle to get better readings from the strange shiny object that had set off their alarm.

"It's probably just a metallic asteroid," Horovitz said. "A high enough metal count would screw with our sensors."

Grunting, Paul accelerated toward the object. The closer they got, the more he was convinced that this wasn't a simple asteroid. An odd structure came into view. It was a massive metal ring with an unusual grayish black finish that couldn't have occurred naturally. A quick interface with his terminal magnified the structure and showed strange symbols carved along the ring at regular intervals.

"Horovitz, run those symbols through our known language database!" Paul said, forgetting their dire situation in his excitement.

"It won't be in the database," Horovitz said dismissively.

"Snap out of it! Do you have a better solution? No? Then do it!" Paul raged at the scientist's apathy.

The harsh tone broke Horovitz out of his stupor. He began tapping away at his terminal, pulling up various sensor reports hidden under a layer of redundant programs.

"We should have more details soon," Horovitz said.

"Thanks," Paul replied.

After a few minutes, the young scientist began babbling.

"Calm down, deep breaths... Now, repeat whatever you just said," Paul ordered.

"Colonel, the computer says that the radius of this ring is 12 kilometers. This thing is huge!" Horovitz said in awe.

Adjusting the ship's angle again, Paul gave them their first look at the center of the metallic ring. The center of the ring had an inky blackness that managed to be a darker shade than the voids of space around it. On his sensors, the darkness had a wave-like quality to it that mesmerized Paul, while simultaneously grabbing him with a cold foreboding.

"This can't be real," Horovitz gasped.

"Why? Strange metal rings are staples of science fiction," Paul replied.

"What? The ring? No, humanity could build one of those now," Horovitz said dismissively.

"Then what?" Paul asked.

"It's what's inside the ring," Horovitz said.

The pause grew longer, and Paul began to worry that he wouldn't finish the thought. He was about to ask him to continue when Horovitz spoke again.

"There's an event horizon. They've caged lightning... John Archibald Wheeler was right. That's a kugelblitz!" Horovitz exclaimed.

"A what?"

"A kugelblitz," Horovitz replied in irritation. "Whoever built this caged a black hole. They've warped spacetime!"

"What does that mean? Barney style, remember?" Paul asked.

"Think of it as a bridge between two points in space. In theory, if we entered the event horizon, we would travel to the other side and exit in a different point in space," Horovitz said slowly.

"How do you know this?"

"I wrote my thesis on Dr. Wheeler's paper, Geons, when I was a grad student. What he speculated... it's right in front of us," Horovitz said, his enthusiasm lending him an almost giddy tone.

"Okay, so what do we do now?" Paul asked. "Without the Mixon Drive, we're not going home any time soon. We're light-years away—we'll die before our ship returns to Terra Firma."

"Only thing we can do." Horovitz stared grimly at the ring. "We enter the event horizon."

—

LOCATION: Boyajian's Star, Milky Way Galaxy

Maneuvering toward the massive ring took time. Making minute changes to their orientation, Lieutenant

Colonel Paul Cooley continually adjusted their course.

"Can we speed this up?" Horovitz asked.

"If you're right, this ring is a tunnel through space. So, we need the Z-480 to enter the ring head-on," Paul replied. "If not, we might come out the other side slamming into the ring."

After answering the young scientist, Paul continued moving the shuttle closer to the kugelblitz. When he achieved the perfect alignment with the metallic ring, he gently pushed the throttle forward. With the increased thrust, the Z-480 started accelerating at alarming rates.

Their craft started shaking. It felt like the vehicle was going to rattle itself apart, bolt by bolt. And then, bolts did begin to work themselves loose. Screws dropped onto his lap, inertial gravity driving the pieces of metal downward. Sirens and alerts went off, adding a layer of flotsam to the river of chaos Paul was attempting to ford.

"The ring... it's sucking us in," Paul shouted, his eyes never leaving the computer panels as he fought to maintain control.

When Horovitz didn't say anything, Paul grunted and continued trying to reverse the thrust of the shuttle to slow their approach. None of it made a difference; the Z-480 kept picking up speed.

"Horovitz, flip the—"

Time froze and a stillness settled over the shuttle for a brief second. Paul never finished his statement. Space outside the shuttle blurred into nothingness, only disturbed by the groaning of the metallic polymers that composed the hull of their craft. He could only observe what was happening. He couldn't move, the pressure pushing him back into his seat. He was a hostage to the moment, watching silently as he waited to find out what was on the other side of the caged lightening they'd chosen to ride.

Paul didn't know how long he sat there, glued to his chair. One minute he felt a crushing pressure trying to squeeze the life out of him and the next it was over. The light of hundreds of stars replaced darkness as the Z-480 returned to real space.

"Find out where we are," Paul ordered the scientist sitting next to him.

"What? How?" asked the befuddled Horovitz as he stared blankly at the terminal in front of him.

"The stars— Use them to figure out where we are. Use solar navigation," Paul said soothingly, his finger pointing to the navigation terminal to the doctor's right.

It didn't take long for Horovitz to report back. "The computer doesn't recognize any of it. We're out past any known star charts, so the navigation algorithms can't interpret these solar configurations."

Nodding his head, Paul began scanning the area. He wasn't sure what he was looking for, exactly. He was hoping to find salvation among these new stars, as unlikely as those prospects were. Scanning the space around the Z-480, he found nothing... until blips began appearing on their radar.

"Are you seeing this?" Paul asked.

"Yes, they're registering as... unknown space objects," Horovitz replied.

"Couldn't you just say UFO? Might as well go for the cool factor," Paul said.

"Are they flying? We're in space; there's no atmosphere for flight," Horovitz replied.

Any further conversation was cut off by more alerts going off on their command screens.

"It's the engine. We've got a serious containment leak," Horovitz said as he unbuckled.

While the young scientist floated back to the rear of the shuttle, Paul began toggling through the sensor readings. He needed to make sense of what his onboard computer was seeing. While he was going through the screens to search for any data that he could find on the unidentified ships that sat just beyond visual range, they started moving. The movement caught his eye, drawing his entire focus to the cockpit window in front of him.

"How the hell are you moving so fast?" he whispered to himself.

He quickly reacted to the unnaturally swift approach of the strange craft, toggling through his screens again to recheck the readings. Before he'd made it to the third screen to check for anomalous heat emissions, his screens froze.

"Horovitz, the damn computer froze up again. Can you fix it?" Paul shouted over his shoulder.

"Did you try turning it off and on again?" Horovitz asked in reply.

Cursing to himself, Paul leaned forward and slapped the side of the command terminal. *Turn it off, my ass,* he thought to himself as he hit the monitor again. It worked, causing the screen to react briefly. A slight waver shimmered through the frozen screen, accompanied by a strange humming sound. It gave Paul the briefest moment of hope before the terminal started rapidly flashing through every setting.

"Ummm, Horovitz," Paul said nervously.

Before he could say anything else, the ship noticeably shuddered. The ever-present hum from the onboard star engine power plant was noticeably absent. They were dead in the water, the cockpit's only illumination the red emergency lights. Looking up, he could see the strange ships had stopped right next to the Z-480. Close enough that the ship filled the entire cockpit window.

"Bold choice, stranger," Paul whispered as he took in

the orange and yellow pattern of the alien ship.

When the ship didn't immediately power back up, he hollered back to the scientist. "We've got a situation here, Horovitz. We need you to power back up! Not the time to play games!"

The urgency in his tone got through to the preoccupied scientist. "I didn't do that. I thought you did?"

When Paul's only reply was to let out a stream of curses, Horovitz floated back into the cockpit.

"See that ship outside the window? Yeah, it looks like I was right about that UFO," Paul told Horovitz.

Horovitz strapped himself into his terminal and attempted to restart the ship, ignoring Paul's verbal jab. None of his actions over the toggles or switches had any effect. After several tense seconds, the consoles flickered again before booting back up—streams of data flooded through their screens. The text quickly flashed by, barely giving them time to decipher the information before it disappeared.

"Are you seeing this?" Horovitz whispered.

"Yeah, our ship is glitching," Paul replied.

"No, it isn't. Did you see what was flashing across our screens?" Horovitz whispered.

"No, it was too fast," Paul replied.

"Looks like that other ship is in control because we certainly aren't. It's the only thing that makes sense. The screens started switching from our code and language to something I didn't recognize. They're learning our language and technology. Their invasion into our programming code is teaching them," Horovitz said.

"That's bad?" Paul asked.

"If they're bent on intergalactic conquest, it could be," replied the scientist.

Paul wasn't sure what to say; instead, he stood and

drifted back toward the supply locker. Grabbing the survival gear, he quickly added it to the webbing on his bulky spacesuit. Once his kit was situated, he turned and started shoving equipment into the hands of the startled scientist.

"Glad I added an emergency pioneer kit. I was a good Boy Scout; I planned for the worst," Paul said.

"Huh?" Horovitz asked, still in shock.

"If we had to, we could survive by landing on any habitable planet. We might need these things with these aliens," Paul said grimly.

"But what am I supposed to do with these weapons?" Horovitz dumbfoundedly repeated.

"Not die. You're supposed not to die," Paul said before floating back towards the cockpit.

The Z-480 lurched before he could strap into the seat, slamming him into the terminal near the main entrance hatch. He fought against the pain, ignoring the pinpricks of light that danced across his vision. When his head cleared, Paul saw that their ship was being pulled toward the strange vessel.

"They're bringing us onto their ship," he said grimly. "Some sort of tractor beam."

Their ship lurched again, yanked to and fro by the invisible grapple. Only the padding against the wall of the shuttle passageway prevented injury from the sudden movement. The longer this went on, the angrier Paul got. He started muttering every vulgarity he'd learned in the Marine Corps, stopping only when the young scientist grabbed his arm.

"Let's see what they do before you start shooting," Horovitz cautioned.

Neither of them said anything else as the unseen force towed them ever closer to the alien vessel. Time slowed as their small proof of concept craft was dragged into the unknown.

"Fuck, what's taking them so long?" Paul demanded.

"Even aliens have to follow the laws of physics," Horovitz replied, his voice devoid of emotion.

Impatient and unwilling to twiddle his thumbs while he waited, Paul went through each of the weapons that he'd attached to his gear. He made sure that his blade could be easily removed from the sheath, the secondary weapon firmly slung upside down on his chest harness. After ensuring that his carbine was locked and loaded, but with no round in the chamber, he drifted over and repeated the procedure with Horovitz.

Once they'd prepared as much as they could, they both floated back toward the cockpit. The young scientist resumed his efforts to regain control of their craft, to no avail.

"It isn't going to work," Paul told him. "We need to get back to the exit and prepare to make a stand."

They drifted back out of the cockpit when the Z-480 suddenly encountered gravitic distortions, unceremoniously dropping them onto the deck.

"That's not supposed to be possible," Horovitz said as he struggled to regain his footing.

Ignoring the young scientist, Paul stood and noticed that the weight from his gear seemed more oppressive than he remembered it.

"Either the gravity is stronger than Earth, or we've been in zero-g for too long," he told Horovitz.

Clank.

The dull thud sent a rippled vibration throughout the ship, bringing Paul's attention back to what was going on outside of their vessel. Looking out the cockpit window, he saw that they were inside an empty compartment. *Has to be a shuttle bay*, he thought as he scanned his surroundings. The walls that constrained their ship were painted in the same yellow-orange color as they'd seen from the outer hull.

"We're not in Kansas anymore, Horovitz," he said.

"We were never in Kansas. Who the hell wants to be in Kansas?" Horovitz asked, distracted.

Glancing over, Paul saw that Horovitz was fiddling with the gear attached to his bulky spacesuit.

"You break it, you buy it," Paul told the scientist. "Now, leave your gear alone."

"Sure," Horovitz replied, still fiddling with it.

Grunting, Paul dismissed his navigator and took in what he could see of the cavernous compartment where they'd landed. While he took in his surroundings, he clamped on his helmet and gestured for Horovitz to do the same.

"Let's go," Paul said, dragging his companion toward the exit hatch. When they got there, he took up the best defensive stance he could manage in the confines of the shuttle and waited. And waited. When the small HUD on his helmet told him several minutes had passed, he turned to the scientist.

"Horovitz, go see if you can run some scans. What's on the other side of this hatch. Atmo? And how close to Earth's gravity are we? Get me something useful."

While the scientist scurried back toward the cockpit, Paul waited. After a few minutes, with nothing happening outside, he walked over toward Horovitz.

"Anything?"

"No, and I still can't control the ship. Unfortunately, I didn't bring any personal computers to use as an interface medium either," Horovitz replied.

"Roger, then we need to take the fight to them."

"Can't we just stay on the ship?"

"And do what? Should we wait until we run out of supplies, and I have to suck-start my service rifle after splattering your brains all over the cockpit window?"

"That doesn't sound pleasant," Horovitz muttered.

Without saying another word, Paul turned and advanced toward the rear airlock while he unslung his rifle. He waited for the pressure to equalize—again, higher than conditions on Earth, but within the rated tolerances of the suit. Grasping the handle, he opened the door and observed as much of the exterior compartment as he could—which wasn't much; the Z-480 was positioned with its hatch facing an ominous grey bulkhead.

"No time like the present," Paul whispered as he tightened his grip on his rifle.

With a resigned sigh, he cautiously peeked his head out the shuttle. There was no movement in either direction, so he exited the vessel. After clumsily clearing the drop ladder, he spun toward the rear. Scanning as he moved, he took in the massive compartment. Advancing toward the back of his vessel, he saw that the area could comfortably house a dozen Phoenix Stations, but it sat empty.

"Right, time to find the hatches that lead into this ship," he muttered.

As he spoke, he noticed three exits that almost blended into the walls of the alien ship. Two of them were over four hundred feet away, so Paul prioritized the one that was closer to their shuttle. It was still over two-hundred-fifty feet, which damn near seemed like a half-mile trek in the higher gravity. Walking around to the front of the Z-480, Paul opens the emergency exit that sat under the cockpit.

"You coming, or do you wanna stay here by yourself and hope for the best?"

Horovitz yelped, surprised that his secure cockpit had been breached and seemed to be on the verge of hyperventilating. After taking a few breaths that sounded remarkably like what Paul had suffered through during his wife's Lamaze class, Horovitz answered. "Wait for me!"

It didn't take his companion long to rejoin him. Once the scientist was standing in front of him, Paul harshly addressed the man. "Stay behind me, watch our rear, and keep up."

After he adjusted how Horovitz held his rifle, Paul turned and started toward the nearest exit with his own weapon held at the low ready. While he was in the best shape he'd ever been in, he found advancing through the heavier gravity physically draining. By the time he'd reached the exit closest to his shuttle, he was short of breath. His navigator was as exhausted as he was, and Paul had to slow down so Horovitz could catch up.

"Horovitz, use your whiz-bang brain to open this hatch," Paul ordered.

"It doesn't quite work that way," Horovitz mumbled as he shuffled forward.

While the scientist worked on the hatch, Paul stood to watch. The compartment, one that he'd dubbed Hangar Bay Alpha, appeared empty. However, an instinct born from years of training told him that he was being watched. A sense of foreboding settled over him. Simultaneously, a tingling sensation ran up the back of his neck, causing an involuntary shiver.

Turning suddenly, he finally saw the movement that his gut had sensed was there. Every surface of the compartment was covered with a thin layer of swarming robots. They looked like a drunken fool had crossbred metallic ants and spiders. A thing out of his nightmares, but there wasn't anything Paul could do to stop them.

"They're swarming our ride," he said, tapping Horovitz on the shoulder. "You better hurry up!"

"Just shoot them. It's what you Marines are good for!"

"I don't have that many rounds," Paul replied. "Get that god damned hatch open!"

Bouncing from one foot to the other, Paul kept an anxious eye on the robots as they quickly digested his shuttle. He almost jumped when Horovitz tapped him on the shoulder. Pushing back the wave of panic that threatened to overwhelm him, he turned his back on the threat. It was difficult; every screaming instinct told him to engage the threat. To eliminate the enemy.

Biting the inside of his cheek until it bled, he calmed his breathing and focused on the hatch in front of him. "Open it on my mark... and go!"

When the door silently slid open, he stepped through. He'd expected it to open into a passageway, but the hatch opened into a downward sloping ramp. With few options, and the other exits accessible only through the swarm of horrific machines, Paul had no choice but to advance.

They pushed deeper into the ship, jogging down the metallic grey that seemed to go on forever. After another several hundred feet, the passageway finally stopped sloping, leveling out into a circular room full of terminals built for monsters. The sheer size of the computer stations was intimidating. It caused Paul to shudder; whatever manned these machines were Goliaths, and he'd left his slingshot at home.

"See what you can do on the terminals, Horovitz," Paul said.

"It could take months to learn their programming code, and the odds of us speaking their language are slim to none. This is a ship; they have to drive it from somewhere. We might be better off looking for the bridge."

"Okay, then see if they've got a wireframe schematic.

Something we can use to make an educated guess. We need to hurry before that robot horde swarms us, too."

The flurry of cuss words coming from the young scientist impressed Paul; he hadn't thought the boy wonder had it in him. Because of the height of the computer stations, Paul had to lift Horovitz onto his shoulder so he could access the terminal. The bulk of their spacesuits and the stronger gravitational pull made it extremely difficult. It took its toll, and soon Paul was dizzy from the strain.

"Hurry," Paul gasped "... can't hold it."

"Got something!" Horovitz shouted.

Before Horovitz could say anything else, Paul's muscles gave. The two men collapsed onto the deck in a heap, their groans filling their shared comms channel. The weight of Horovitz's bulky spacesuit made the tumble even more ungainly, but they managed to disentangle themselves and regain their footing.

"When the machine broke into our core programming, they left part of our language paired to theirs. I think it was how they were learning our language, but I was able to follow that back into their mainframe."

"English, give it to me in English! Did you find anything useful?" Paul demanded.

"Yes, the hangar bay we landed in was designated for this ship's command team. We're already close; we should be able to make it there quickly if we hurry. We just have to follow the symbol that looks like a warped triskelion; it'll lead us to the bridge."

"Where will these symbols be located? And do you know what a triskelion looks like?" Paul asked.

"Etched on the decks or the bulkheads. And yes, I know what I'm looking for. The symbol consists of three legs radiating from a central point. You'll know it when you see it."

"Right, when we find one of these things, show me what it looks like, and I'll take point from there," Paul said.

The two men took off with a renewed sense of purpose. After a few dozen yards, they found the first triskelion symbol painted on the wall. The young scientist hadn't done it justice; it wasn't just one triskelion symbol. It was several interlocking three-dimensional representations of them combined into one complex picture. Despite the convoluted marking, the symbol was somehow simple and artistic.

The markings that led to the bridge stood out; the design was painted in a reflective orange color that was garishly unappealing. With their path clear, Paul was able to focus on moving as tactically as possible. It was difficult; the pull of the extra gravity made it feel like he was walking through quicksand. Even with that complication, Paul was able to return his focus on maneuvering at peak combat efficiency while studying his surroundings.

Two hours later, their venture finally saw fruition as they stood outside the hatch marked with a strange symbol. The passageway dead-ended into a massive circular hallway. The inner ring had several smaller access ports and one visible hatch into another room. It was exactly what the wireframe schematic said should be there, except there was a hiccup... they'd have to wade through several feet of scurrying robots to get to the hatch.

"Horovitz, do you have any scraps of equipment we don't need?"

"Say again?" Horovitz asked in reply.

"Those things started devouring our ship. It was foreign technology, and they ate it like it was candy. I need you to hand me any scientific testing stuff that you have on your webbing. I'll throw it as far down the passageway as I can. While they're distracted consuming the device, you'll run at the hatch and get us in. Be quick. I don't know how long we have."

"If they just want our tech, then we should be okay. We should be able to walk right through them," Horovitz insisted.

"How, exactly, do you think they'll react to your spacesuit?"

"Point taken," Horovitz said as he began handing Paul several handheld devices.

"On the count of three, I'll throw these. The instant the horde moves, so do you."

After an audible count, Paul hurled the first boxy handheld device as far as he could manage. It worked, and the tiny robot horde shifted enough to clear a narrow path for them. Paul walked into the opening, stopped, and threw another device even further down the passageway. It was successful, and the breach widened. When there was enough room, Horovitz half-stumbled, half-jogged over to the hatch.

"Better hurry!" Paul said.

Once he steadied himself, Horovitz fiddled around until he hit the sequential pattern that he'd memorized from the first terminal.

"Got it!" Horovitz said, shouting with a voice full of nervous energy.

The horde had just finished devouring the piece of foreign technology when the hatch slid open. Neither needed any further encouragement; they scrambled into the bridge. With his rifle at the ready, Paul scanned the room, but he couldn't see anything through the maze of massive terminals.

"Keep your eyes open and pay attention," Paul told

Horovitz as he moved. His heart pounded as he glided along the deck, weaving in and out of the various workstations. He struggled to clear every corner, but the corners were endless. Exhaustion began to weigh him down.

Paul endured, with the young scientist gamely keeping up as they wandered around until they reached the center of the massive compartment. The central ring in the room was clear, except for what appeared to be a gigantic orange throne.

"That has to be the captain's chair," Paul told his flagging companion.

"Ro... roger. We need to get up into it so we can access the controls. It's our only chance of making it home."

The closer they got to the command chair, the more confused they became. Slumped into the oversized seat was a human skeleton confined in armor, much like theirs. Exactly like theirs.

"I'll check the corpse, you check the command seat," Paul ordered as he dragged the body to the deck.

Pulling a small handheld device from his cargo pocket, Paul linked the two suits together. It didn't take him long to access the dead guy's sensor logs.

"This can't be right... this can't be right," he muttered.

Rechecking the information, Paul confirmed that it was Doctor Terry Mixon. He'd flown onboard the Z-481. Somehow, he'd beat them to this ship, though he couldn't fathom how that was even possible.

"Horovitz... you're not gonna believe this, but this is Doctor Mixon. As in, Athena International's resident genius and CEO."

"I believe it; I'm reading his notes. Mixon thinks that this ship was abandoned when the life support failed. The robots are just leftover maintenance bots, this tub is running on autopilot," Horovitz said.

"Wait, the life support's working just fine," Paul insisted. "It just doesn't produce air as we know it."

"It's working... sort of. Whatever is coming out of the air vents can't sustain us and we don't know enough to fix it in time. Again, those maintenance bots fixed most of the battle damage this ship suffered. Anyway, Mixon brought a laptop from home onto this vessel and used that as an interface. It worked, giving him a lot of access to the core programming. His Mixon Drive also failed, so he was trying to break into the navigation drives on this ship. If we can finish what he started, we'll make it home."

"How long will that take?" Paul asked.

"We have until we run out of oxygen in our suits, or we die," Horovitz replied flatly.

Paul slumped down, leaning against the same massive terminal as Terry Mixon's carcass. He began to pray silently, trying to force himself to remain calm and conserve oxygen.

"He was close," Horovitz said. "If I start on the assumption that he made no mistakes, we can solve this. *I* can solve this."

"I knew Doctor Mixon; he made tons of mistakes... if we needed him to be flawless, then we're doomed."

"You won't say that when the good doctor and I bring you home," Horovitz replied.

"If you succeed, I'll tell the world that you were right, and I was wrong," Paul said.

"You'll do more than that; you'll buy me a steak at one of those fancy restaurants. Now leave me to get to work."

While Horovitz worked, Paul leaned back against the computer terminal and brought his rifle onto his lap so he was ready to defend them should the need arise. He tried to slow his breathing to conserve his oxygen levels, using every meditative technique he'd ever learned or seen on late-night infomercials. Minutes ticked by until he began to despair that he'd die on this strange alien ship.

"Eureka!" Horovitz shouted, interrupting his downward spiraling malaise.

"Give it to me," Paul said, his voice barely audible.

"I did it. I solved the equation. We're going home!"

Paul smiled grimly as he entered the data into the terminal. "Well, we may have lost our original ride, but I think we can still call the first FTL test flight a success."

Still looking down at Mixon's corpse, Horowitz said, "We might not be going back to the same home we left. Somewhere along the way, a lot of time passed."

"All part of the adventure," Paul replied reassuringly. "But at least we'll have a hell of a story to tell."

THE END

THE MIXON DRIVE

About the Author

J.R. Handley is a pseudonym for a husband and wife writing team. He is a veteran infantry sergeant with the 101st Airborne Division and the 28th Infantry Division. She is the kind of crazy that interprets his insanity into cogent English. He writes the sci-fi while she proofreads it. The sergeant is a two-time combat veteran of the late unpleasantness in Mesopotamia where he was wounded, likely doing something stupid. He started writing military science fiction as part of a therapy program suggested by his doctor, and hopes to entertain you while he attempts to excise his demons through these creative endeavors. In addition to being just another dysfunctional veteran, he is a stay at home wife, avid reader and all-around nerd. Luckily for him, his Queen joins him in his fandom nerdalitry.

To learn more about J.R. Handley's writing, visit:
www.jrhandley.com

A FAIR TRADE
A FOLDING SPACE SERIES PREQUEL

by A.M. Scott

STOMACH RUMBLING, SAREE stopped in front of her favorite station eatery, the QuickEatWell. At least, that's how the owners translated the name, and she wasn't familiar enough with the Antlia languages to know better. Besides, the name fit.

Saree brushed her hand through the 'Order' holo floating in front of the kiosk. Despite the late off-shift hour, the proprietor, a mature neuter Antlian with the unlikely name of Mom, popped up in the window. "Your order, Scholar?" the slightly mechanical voice of the translator asked.

She smiled with a closed mouth and bowed slightly. "One Puffer please, Mom." She waved credits from her holo to the kiosk.

Mom bobbed, the closest an Antlian could come to a bow and said, "Right away, Scholar." A puff from a maneuvering valve and the yellow, two-meter-round bag of light gasses spun, the four long, skinny appendages darting to build her Puffer. A three-fingered hand pulled a dorad air fish from a tank floating above Mom's gasbag, a knife hacked off the head of the fish, another hand pulled out the guts and disposed of them, while the third stuffed the fish with air weed and other vegetable equivalents, and the fourth added the special sauce—a spicy, creamy mixture native to Antlia Nine. Saree didn't know what was in the sauce, and she'd been warned by other humans not to ask, just enjoy.

The air fish was placed in a heating device for two minutes before being pulled out and wrapped in veg plas, and finally placed in the kiosk airlock. Saree removed the Puffer from the airlock, a faint hiss of light gasses accompanying the pop and crack of the Puffer reacting to the change in pressure.

"You should have your airlock checked, Mom. I don't think it's emptying correctly."

"Yes. Next twelvesday. Eat well, Scholar." The Antlian bobbed again and sank out of Saree's sight.

Every time Saree bought a Puffer, she told the Antlian the same thing and got a different answer in return. The repair appointment was for some future time, always farther away. No matter—a high, squeaky voice from the leftover helium was a small price to pay for a Puffer. Besides, oxy-breathers were lucky to have dedicated passages on Antlia Nine Station; she could be in a suit right now and never have the pleasure of a fresh, hot Puffer right from the source. She'd had them on the human-centric Antlia Five Station, but they weren't the same.

Golden-brown toasty goodness with a hint of hot spice and brine wafted up to her nose. Saree almost drooled. She bit down. The light, crispy crust gave way to the firm, delicious flesh of the air fish, then the crunch of vegetables coated in almost too spicy, but amazing creamy, saucy goodness.

Ah. Saree smiled after each bite, wiping the corners of her mouth to prevent staining her Scholar robes. *Scrumptious.*

She crunched through half the Puffer and a bite or two more, full, but unwilling to stop eating.

Fresh Puffer was so good, but it didn't keep. She'd been warned to never reheat Puffer but had stupidly tried it anyway. Saree shuddered a bit, remembering the four days of cleaning to get the stink out of her shuttle.

She pulled out her knife and very carefully cut off the eaten portion of the Puffer, shoving the scraps in her mouth despite her already groaning stomach, leaving a little less than half in the wrapper. Saree strolled, her footsteps thudding slightly on the plas decking of the cramped, meandering station passageway, and enjoyed the lack of beings until she reached the Mourner.

The first time she'd traveled this corridor, she'd thought the pile of rags off to the side was garbage, refuse missed by the auto-cleaners. But then she'd seen a being, a bipedal species she didn't recognize, stop in front of the pile and bow. Curious, she'd watched the Gentle place a credit chip down in front of the rags, step back, and bow again.

An appendage, completely covered in ragged, mottled brown layers had darted out and snatched the credit chip. Three seconds later, a beautiful but sorrowful melody in wavering high tones and alien pitches came forth, a multi-toned drone below the melody, much like the drone of an Old Earth bagpipe. Saree'd hurriedly switched her vid recorder on and listened, completely enthralled.

After the music stopped and the pile of rags did nothing else, she'd returned to her shuttle. Saree had found nothing in her records to match the sounds. She'd sent the recording to Centauri University, but her thesis advisors had never heard this particular music, either.

After she carefully questioned some of the vendors and workers on this passageway, she'd been told the being just appeared one day. The only understandable word anyone heard was "home," said in Standard. Attempts to move the being by persuasion or force were useless—somehow, it remained anchored to the decking and avoided every force shield and tractor beam. The energy just passed through the being like it wasn't there. Imaging attempts were the same—no one knew what was under the pile of tattered cloth. But since the song seemed sad, the station residents nicknamed the being 'the Mourner' and took pride in ensuring it was fed and protected.

Saree's cover as a poor Scholar of Ancient Music wouldn't allow her to give credit chips away, but the Puffer she couldn't finish? Why not try? The Mourner evidently liked Puffer, because it disappeared and the gorgeous but slightly unsettling alien music rang out. Every time she indulged in a Puffer, she gave the uneaten part to the Mourner.

She did the same now, crouching to place the Puffer on the deck in front of the Mourner. After the meal disappeared, Saree impulsively asked, "Can I take you home?"

Why had she asked that? She had a shuttle, not a folder. It didn't seem likely the Mourner was from Antlia. If she was taking the Mourner to a solar system other than Antlia, she'd have to contract with a fold transport first, since her shuttle, like most, wasn't fold capable. Saree thought wistfully of the small Mermillod fold-capable shuttles. If only she could fold space and cover the immense distances between systems without relying on outsiders. She sighed. She'd never earn enough credits for one of those.

Recalled to her task by the first notes of the Mourner, Saree straightened and turned on her recorder. The music this time was not only beautiful, but joyful. Saree took three quick steps back when the pile of rags rose. It rose a meter, then higher until it was level with her face.

"Home," the being sang jubilantly.

Saree blinked, astonished. Had no one asked before? And where was home? How would she get the Mourner there? An urgent message pinged in her holo and she swept it up, bewildered. A set of coordinates from an unknown originator. This must be the Mourner's home.

She brought up a connection to her virtual assistant. "Hal, where are these coordinates located?"

"Hydrus, Saree. Hydri GeeJee Beta, specifically. There is a planet there, a gas giant, but no sentient life has been discovered."

Saree shook her head in wonder. "Hal, please compile a list of folders going to Hydrus."

"Certainly, Saree."

"Thank you, Hal."

"You are welcome, Saree."

She swept off the connection and turned toward her shuttle. Without her saying a word, the pile of rags followed her. Good thing it was nightshift and this wasn't a popular passageway. Even so, she might attract attention soon.

As she entered her shuttle bay codes, a siren wailed. Station authorities evidently noticed the Mourner's rise. Saree hurried through her shuttle's security protocols and led the Mourner inside. "Hal, did you find a folder?"

"Perhaps, Saree. The list is in your workspace. It seems some station personnel are surprised and alarmed by your new passenger, Saree."

She plopped down in the pilot's seat, the worn

cushion hissing air, and brought up the list. Three folders, none headed directly to Hydrus: one human, one Grus, one RR. She scanned the names and the aggregate ratings. The human folder looked risky, the RR were sometimes difficult to communicate with, so the Grus it was. At least they were air-breathing bipedals, so she wouldn't be stuck on her shuttle for the entire trip to Pictor, where she'd have to find a folder to Hydrus. She sent inquiries for cost and speed of departure, then checked the Time Guild clock maintenance listing. Plenty of fold clocks required tuning at the systems along the way, so the trip wouldn't cost her anything.

"Saree, a large number of beings are gathering outside our shuttle bay airlock," Hal's ultra-calm voice said. "There are also a large number of Antlians gathered in the main station passageway above our airlock. All the beings appear to be upset."

They probably were. The Mourner brought traffic to an out-of-the-way passage. Saree's stomach sank. Getting away might not be easy.

"*Fortuna Lucia*, Antlia Nine Station."

Saree grimaced and accepted the emergency communications request. "*Fortuna Lucia* here, Antlia Station."

An Antlian appeared in the vid, this one a mottled green and blue, an official seal on the surface behind it. "*Fortuna Lucia*, do you have the Gentle being known as the Mourner on board?"

"Yes, I do. It followed me. I did not do anything to it or compel it in any way."

"Why did it follow you?"

"Because I asked it if it would like to go home. It sang 'home' and sent me a set of coordinates in Hydrus."

The Antlian bobbed. "Would you transmit the coordinates to me, along with proof the Mourner followed you voluntarily?"

"Of course, I have nothing to hide." Saree muted the comms. "Hal, please transmit the vid I made of the Mourner's song to Antlia Station and the coordinates in Hydrus."

"Certainly, Saree."

"We await your transmission."

"Antlia Station, I intend to take the Mourner to those coordinates."

"Why?"

Saree sat back. "Why wouldn't I? Everyone deserves to go home."

"How does this benefit you?"

"It doesn't." Saree shrugged. "I have finished my research here. I've never been to Hydrus and there are new places to explore along the way, so why wouldn't I?"

"Many residents are upset by your actions. They believe you are abducting the Mourner."

Saree scowled at the screen. She enunciated carefully, putting a little snap in her tone. "Antlia Station, you're not implying the Mourner doesn't have the right to leave, are you? That would be against every sentient being treaty I know. And as I said, I did not compel the Mourner in any way, shape, or form. It followed me, without any action on my part."

"Very well, Scholar. We will review your vid and let you know."

She smiled grimly, careful to not show teeth to the easily-punctured Antilan. "Let me know what? I intend to depart as soon as possible. You have no reason to detain me."

"A station riot would be more than reason enough, Scholar." The connection went black.

The Grus folder messaged with a quote for the fold to Pictor—an acceptable amount of credits—and a departure time: upon her arrival. *Perfect.* The sooner she could leave, the better for all of them. She transferred credits to the Grus folder and brought up navigation to program her flight. "Hal, send the appropriate fees to Antlia Nine Station and request a pushback immediately."

"Immediately, Saree. They may not comply with our request."

"I don't want to stay here and be charged with inciting a riot."

"Remaining on Antlia Nine Station is dangerous for you, Saree?"

"Yes, it is."

"Then I will ensure we can leave. I have transferred the correct fees, but as expected, they are refusing to push us away. However, I have found a way to accomplish this action. Be ready to thrust."

Hal had gotten them out of some tricky situations before, but releasing from a station? He was a Virtual Assistant, not a net expert. Saree jumped when navigation flashed at her. *Oh, suns, get ready for thrust!* She refined her planned orbit, going for the fastest possible arrival at the Grus folder. Her finger hovered over the start button.

"Antlia Nine Station releasing now," Hal said. A little jolt and Hal continued, "You are clear to thrust, Saree."

Saree hit the thrusters when Hal said "clear," hoping evasive maneuvers wouldn't be needed. Scanning the surveillance, she saw no indication of pursuit or laser fire. She glanced at her messages—lots of protests piling up, it seemed from the subject lines. And some outright threats.

Once they were safely on their way and outside the influence of station tractor beams, she asked, "Hal, how did you get us free of Antlia Nine Station?"

"I created a false message from the Laniakea Fleet Commander, informing Antlia Nine Station they had no right to hold a Gov Human subject because an independent sentient being decided to join them by invitation. Evidently, Antlia Nine Station didn't want to argue with Gov Human military."

Saree rolled her tense shoulders. "How did you fake a Gov Human address, Hal?"

"It wasn't difficult, Saree. I didn't infiltrate Gov Human's net, I simply created a message identical to one from the Fleet Commander and inserted it into the Antlia Nine Stationmaster's translation program. Antlia Nine Station's messaging systems and nets are quite secure, but their translation program has known vulnerabilities, and I was able to exploit them. Would you prefer I not take such action? My default is to protect you at all costs, Saree."

Saree swallowed. Not for the first time, she wondered exactly what the Sa'sa had programmed into her virtual assistant. The Sa'sa tech class wasn't forthcoming when she'd asked, reacting with what she thought was sly amusement. But they were cold-blooded hive mind aliens, so who knew? What she did know was Hal had saved her from several sticky situations, so maybe ignorance was better. "Well, thank you, Hal."

"You are welcome, Saree."

No longer worried about Antlia Nine Station, Saree shot a look back at her guest, settled on the decking, just to the left side of the cargo bay hatch. "Make yourself comfortable, Gentle Mourner, and let me know if there's anything I can do for you."

The being didn't move or sing.

Saree turned to stare but turned back when an incoming message drew her attention—her receipt for payment of the docking fee; she was legally clear of

Antlia Nine.

She smiled, but it quickly faded. She'd have to avoid Antlia orbit for the foreseeable future. Perhaps she could send them vid of the Mourner's homecoming? If it was a happy, joyful event, that should help justify her actions. Not that she needed justification to help another sentient being escape a bad situation like homelessness.

She glanced at the Mourner again. Hopefully, the being was comfy there on the decking. She wouldn't try to move it, just feed it every now and then, and hope that was sufficient.

—

"So, Gentle Mourner, here we are. Floating in space at your coordinates, near Hydri GeeJee Beta. Will you please give me a more refined set of coordinates, so I can take you to your final destination?" Saree slowed the shuttle to rotate in sync with the gas giant Beta. There was nowhere to land, of course.

Hal said, "Saree, the being you know as the Mourner has transported itself to the exterior cargo airlock. I do not know what it intends."

"What?!" Saree was up and sprinting to the cargo bay hatch before she finished the word. She opened the hatches and ran across the cargo bay, reaching the exterior airlock hatch just in time to see the light flash red, showing the air was evacuated and the outer hull door open. Saree pounded on the hatch with her fists. "No, no, no! I didn't bring you all this way to commit suicide!"

"Saree, I do not believe suicide is the being's intention," Hal said. "Watch the vid I've sent you."

She pulled away from the hatch, spun and sagged back against it, the cerimetal struts sharp and cold against her back as she slid to the deck. *Why?* Why come all this way to float out an airlock? Saree closed her eyes for a second, unwilling to believe the Mourner was dead. Firming her will, she swept up the vid Hal sent, showing the interior of the airlock. The Mourner floated in and settled on the decking. The hatch closed behind it and the air evacuated. The Mourner didn't move, although the rags enfolding the being rippled and waved as the air was sucked out. The outer hatch opened. The rags rose, draping around the being's body, then floated down to the decking again, but the tattered mass lay flat. A faint shimmer rose above the compacted pile of rags. Saree squinted at the vid. The shimmering turned into a ball and then streaked out the airlock, into space.

"Saree, are you okay? Do you require medico assistance? Or some Jhinzer tea?"

She started and snapped her dry mouth closed. She'd been staring at nothing, wordless, long enough for her mouth to become dry. She blinked and shook her astonishment off. "I'm fine, Hal. Just surprised."

"This was quite unexpected, Saree. The existence of pure energy beings has been speculated, but never confirmed."

"Yes, very unexpected." She stood and cycled the airlock, intending to gather the rags. But when she opened the hatch, there were no rags. No, a human woman's dress lay spread across the decking as if it hung on a hanger. The hem of the full skirt was the deep scarlet of Sa'sa rubies, shading into the orange of a yellow star's sunset, and fading into yellow that paled to almost white at the shoulders. Saree stared, open-mouthed again, waiting for the apparition to disappear. When the dress remained, she blinked and entered the airlock, slowly. Bending down, she grasped the dress at the shoulders. It had slim, three-quarter length sleeves, a fitted bodice with a modest, round neckline, and flowed into a wide, full skirt.

The material was soft and sensuous, almost caressing her fingers. It warmed in her grasp, but it didn't feel like insulation material. No, it was like being wrapped in her Mother's favorite blanket.

A sensation she barely remembered. She rubbed her cheek on the plush fabric.

"Saree, I have a message from an unknown source," Hal said. "It says, 'A fair trade.' Do you wish to reply, and if so, to whom?"

She laughed. "No reply is necessary, Hal." She held it up, high, admiring the dress again, then pulled it close and waltzed with it around the cargo bay. The dress was beautiful, so soft, so warm, so comforting.

"Saree, I believe the dress is Tazan silk. You have received a much higher value than you gave, especially since your clock maintenance work paid for the transport costs."

She stopped, thrusting the dress to arm's length and almost dropping it. "Tazan silk?! Are you sure? This is worth a fortune!"

"Yes, Saree. I believe you could buy a frontier planet with it."

The implications made her mind whirl. Saree strode to the pilot's chair and sat down, draping the dress across her lap. "Hal, we cannot tell anyone about this dress or how we got it. Otherwise, beings will find a way to hunt and capture the Mourner's kin. I know we discussed sending Antlia Nine Station a vid of the Mourner's homecoming, but we *can't* show them this."

"I do not fully understand your concern, Saree, but I stand ready to do whatever you require."

Saree tapped out a complex rhythm on the armrests of her pilot's chair as she thought.

"We must delete the vid of the airlock and all evidence of the energy of the Beta Hydri. We cannot take any chance they will be discovered. This must remain a secret forever."

"If you insist, Saree. Deleting data is often dangerous."

"In this case, keeping it is more dangerous, not only for the Beta Hydri but for us. If anyone knew our part in this homecoming, they might attempt to use us as bait, to see if our ship or my voice could lure a Beta Hydri close enough to capture."

"I understand. I will delete all information concerning the Mourner entirely. I must keep you safe."

"Thank you, Hal."

"You are welcome, Saree."

Contemplating what she'd experienced, Saree flew back to the folder and allowed them to dock her shuttle.

"You are ready to continue, Scholar Sessan?" the message from *Eridani Acamar* read.

She messaged back, "*Fortuna Lucia* is ready. Continue course." Saree felt the thrusters kick in, sending the folder flying to the fold orbit.

She pulled up an outside vid and gazed as Hydri GeeJee Beta dwindled into a bright point of light. "Best of fortunes to you, Gentle. Mourn no more." They thrust for the distant stars, Saree stroking the colorful Tazan silk still draped over her lap, soothing her unexpected sorrow at the Mourner's departure.

But it was a fair trade indeed.

THE END

A FAIR TRADE

About the Author

After twenty years as a US Air Force space operations officer, AM now operates a laptop, trading in real satellites for fictional spaceships in the Folding Space Series, starting with *Lightwave: Clocker*. AM is also a volunteer leader with Team Rubicon, a disaster response organization.

To learn more about AM Scott's writing, visit:
www.amscottwrites.com

WEIGHTLESS

by Raven Oak

Damn.

THE TITANIUM bits in my knee always set off the security sensors at Houston Spaceport. Every stinkin' time. Bad enough the knee replacement tech was older than my mother, but standing here, waiting for security to clear my kneecap of any wrongdoing, meant standing longer than I'd planned.

As if that wasn't enough, my medical bracelet failed to scan, dislodging me from the fast-travel line and into the ever-crawling queue of travelers awaiting a full identity scan. By the time the scanners pronounced me "Tara Barrens, Louisiana" and declared me "safe to travel," my heart trembled along with my knee. It figured that my terminal would be halfway across the damn spaceport. Go big or go home—that was Houston Spaceport for you.

By the time I stood with the rest of my boarding pod, sweat clung to all the places least convenient: my upper lip, that ticklish spot behind my knees, not to mention the bottom of my feet. I squirmed as a thrum filled the space around me. Panic ate my insides like my granddaddy's moonshine.

"First time off-planet?" The contralto voice came from a rather wiry woman to my right, sporting a full head of soft brown hair and equally soft brown eyes. "I'm Megan." The woman inclined her head toward the child at her hip. "And this is Seren."

"Tara."

The child held up one hand. "I'm six, and my name means star." Seren struggled to free the other hand from her mother's grasp. Failing, she pointed at something in the distance.

My pod-mates' bodies stole the air from me as I tried *(and failed)* to find what had distracted the child. Rather than give in to my panic, I inhaled deeply through my nose. I could do this. It was only a brief hop from Earth to Mars. New ship on a new route, *The Ursula* had the most accommodations. Shorter walks between cabins and amenities, larger cabins, and a smooth engine that made the trip like melted butter on southern biscuits.

Someone clearing their throat brought the spaceport into sharp contrast as my brain refocused. A blonde-haired man carrying a briefcase stepped on the dais ahead. His blue jumpsuit's shoulder bore a familiar patch: the bright-white arc of a ship over Earth, marking him as our steward. While the idea of weaving my way through the mass of people left me short of breath, the thought of missing any pre-flight instructions knocked the wind out of me, so I tucked in my elbows and pressed my way to the front.

"The name's Sven, and I'm your steward. From here on out, you're group E-6, and I'll be S-ven." The way he stretched out his name's syllables left him chuckling. When no one joined in, he sighed and pressed the briefcase's button. I flinched at the slight hiss that escaped as it opened to reveal a stretchy, blue nylon mass.

The dreaded spacesuit.

Despite my physical therapist and I having practiced getting in and out of one, I clenched my fists at the sight of it.

"Your pod is located on the lowest level, or E level, of *The Ursula*. In the event of an emergency, all passengers should proceed to the nearest escape pod." As he spoke, his wristband projected a screen displaying a map of Level E. Blue arrows showed the path we'd follow—one left down a long corridor, then a right. Not too far from my cabin.

Seren whispered worriedly in her mother's ear while a young couple rolled their eyes as the steward continued his pre-flight safety speech. Several other travelers glanced at their wrist AIs, and Sven cleared his throat. "Every escape pod is equipped with standard-sized spacesuits in the event of an emergency. Specialty suits—"

"That means you, fatty," came a nearby voice.

Sven's cheeks flushed warmer than my own, though the words were aimed at me. They always were, and I focused on my breathing as our steward continued. "Suits for other heights and...er...sizes are available in your cabins."

"What if we're out and about, and something happens?" asked Megan, who'd made her way up toward the front to stand behind me.

The steward's perfectly straight teeth gleamed in the overhead lights, but the smile didn't reach his eyes. "During non-sleeping hours, you'll be directed to the nearest escape pod by a steward such as myself or another staff member of *Omega Travel Authorities*."

He rattled on as Megan leaned forward to whisper in

my ear. "Unless you're on the budget level. Level E: where staff is sparse and the comforts sparser. Better be state-of-the-art escape pods!"

I clenched my hands together and stared straight ahead. If I didn't respond, maybe the woman would stop running disaster scenarios through my anxiety-driven brain.

"All passengers on this trip, including children, must be at least forty-four inches in height. The accordion-like knee joints of the standard-sized Z300 suit will accommodate passengers up to six-and-a-half feet tall…"

At this, Seren stretched her neck upward. Somehow, I doubted she met the height requirement, though her gangly body came pretty close. In contrast, her mother slouched as she pursed her lips.

"—need a volunteer. Anyone?" A shove from behind sent me forward and under the gaze of the smiling steward. His eyes widened as he noted my ample figure. "We'll make this work, don't you worry."

The fabric breathed easily enough as Sven removed the suit from its case. "In the event of a suit-level emergency, you'll want to don your suit first before assisting others, including any children in your party. The Z300's a two-piece suit with helmet." He rattled on about the procedures of suiting up as I stepped through the lower torso ring and into the overly large feet. I ignored the laughter from the onlookers.

As I pulled the suit over my calves and then my thighs, its fabric clung to me tighter than my mother yesterday when she'd hugged me goodbye. The metal ring used to seal the two pieces together stopped when it collided with my hips. "Um…assistance please?"

"Apologies for the closeness." Sven grabbed the ring, his breath too sweet as his nose bumped mine. He gave the suit a good tug, but it remained firmly in place.

"Perhaps we can stretch the upper torso down to meet this."

I shoved my head through the neck ring as he slid the upper piece over my shoulders. The arms were snug, but they fit. My sigh of relief lasted until the laughter reached me, and Sven's flushed face gave a small shake. I couldn't see myself, but I didn't need to. The upper ring brushed against my belly button, much too high to form a seal with the bottom piece.

"Let's get you out of this," Sven whispered as my knee throbbed and sweat rolled down my face. Now that the suit had me, it didn't want to let go. Sven tugged and wrestled with the suit as I stood there, rotting in my panic and pain.

Once free, I stumbled off the dais and into a nearby privacy booth. A soft, female voice sounded from the walls. I dropped into the cushioned seat and ignored it.

Inhale. Hold—3...2...1. Exhale. Even with my eyes closed, the small booth tilted as my breath came in ragged gasps.

"Would you like a mild relaxant?" asked the same female computer voice.

"Do you...have something stronger? Something coupled with a Jupiter-sized pain killer?" I held out my wrist, then cursed as the scanner errored out. My medical bracelet remained unreadable. I fumbled for my identification card, and once scanned, the dispenser in front of me popped out a capsule and some water. I swallowed the pill like a good patient and focused on breathing.

At least breathing didn't hurt.

By the boarding announcement, my heart rate had slowed to keep time with my pounding knee. Megan and Seren stood at the boarding doors where the child stretched to reach the minimum height marker. Sven frowned when he spotted me, and waved the mother and child through. Before he could mumble some lackluster apology, I flashed my identification card at another set of scanners and hobbled after Megan.

Seren pried her face away from her mother's thigh long enough to furrow her brows in my direction. "Why'd those people laugh at you?" she asked, and I gripped the wall's railing for support.

Her mother shushed her, then turned to me. "I'm sorry. She's just nervous."

A young couple stared at me, their laughter a rude reminder of my broken body. Wincing, I crouched down in front of Seren to distract myself. "They're laughing because I'm fat."

"Why are you fat?" Megan clamped a hand over the girl's mouth.

"Some people just are, I guess. Why do you have brown hair?"

Seren pried her mother's hand away. "Because Momma has brown hair, but that doesn't mean people should laugh. They're big meanies."

"I don't think they can help it. It's what hyenas do best," said Megan.

After the relaxant, I joined Megan in a good laugh.

"What's so funny, Momma?"

We could only shake our heads as we boarded, our paths splitting once we reached our budget cabins on Level E. Anti-slip linoleum, rather than carpet, made up the flooring of my extra-wide cabin, and the walls bore standard hand railings at distinct intervals.

My special spacesuit hung near the door, and I eased myself into the corner's large cot. Damn spacesuit had added an extra $600 to my ticket, but at least it was mine. "Usable on any future trip!" the travel agent had stated.

To offset the cost, I'd opted for a cabin directly over the ship's engines. The rumbling during take-off, while louder than anticipated, vibrated like the subway cars of home.

I was asleep before we even left Earth.

—

Two weeks was enough time for anyone to settle into the rhythm of a ship, be it one that travels on the water or through space, and I was no exception. I'd spent the night before playing cards with a woman from New Galveston and had stumbled into E6 at a time I'd thought was way too late, but the number of pod-mates making similar crawls for their beds had promised me that this was normal behavior for a space cruise off-world.

Despite my fatigue, the shift in engines brought me out of sleep with a growl and the flinging of sheets as I sought to right myself. There was rumbling, and then there was a grind-y-whine that set my teeth on edge. Dissonance blared out of the overhead speaker a moment later, announcing a ship-wide evacuation.

Feet still tangled in one sheet corner, I tumbled face-first against the gray linoleum floor as my knee woke up with a sharp twinge. Outside my room, footfalls sounded as people headed portside toward the evacuation pods.

This time, I untangled myself *before* attempting to stand, which took two tries and half-a-dozen swear words. I pressed the button to release my space suit, which remained firmly bolted to the wall. I slammed the button. Nothing. Bracing myself, I gripped both sides of it and tugged, wrenching my knee a second time. The suit remained firmly in place while the emergency alarm blared overhead.

My granddaddy would've blushed with the creative

trail of words I uttered as I slammed my hand against the door's panel to release its lock. Hopefully the pod was functioning.

Outside my room, dragon-clawed pajama slippers greeted me as Seren waved at me. "Momma says we're taking a side trip." Behind her, Megan's wide eyes darted to the overhead lights, which flickered twice.

"Do we know why...?" I asked.

Megan shook her head as we trailed behind five other passengers. When the line ahead of us stopped, I nearly stumbled over Seren's dragon tail. The overhead lights flickered again as the ship groaned, and thickness filled my throat. *Ships shouldn't sound like my granddaddy wheezing.* I glanced around the huddled group. "What's the hold up?"

"Hey, you were paying attention pre-flight, right?" A young man in an emerald-green plaid suit with garish, ruby cufflinks half-smiled at me. "Which way to the pod?"

"Right."

"Yeah, okay. You know the way, so which way is it?"

I pointed to the right. Again. "That way."

When no one moved, I sighed and set out down the corridor, the line of passengers trailing behind me. We reached our escape pod as a loud hiss barreled through the hall. The emergency lights flickered constantly, and Seren screwed up her face to cry. Everyone waited one heartbeat, then another.

"I think they're waiting on you," whispered Megan.

I pressed my hand against the pod's plate with a sigh. The door slid open four inches and stopped, leaving a gap not even Seren would fit through, let alone me.

"Oh, great. The pod's door must be afflicted with whatever's got the ship," said suit guy, who hovered at my elbow. "How do we get it open?" He continued questioning me at an increasingly rapid rate, while a young woman hovered nearby.

Her dress matched his suit, and when I glanced at the two again, hyenas sprung to mind, though I couldn't be sure in the poor lighting. I flipped open the panel to expose the door's manual override. Suit man slapped it, and I wedged my arm through the gap to the shoulder. One good shove, and stale air hit my nose.

Suit guy pushed past me into the long pod, then set to coughing. I tugged him by the sleeve until he fell backward into the corridor. "What's...with the pod?" he asked.

"Bad air mix," said Megan as she gripped Seren's hand. "I read about this once..."

Like a behemoth, *The Ursula* moaned before shaking us about, and I grabbed hold of a safety bar along the wall. The faint smell of smoke tickled my nose. My eyes fell to the suits stacked at the pod's entrance, and I sighed. "We'll have to use the suits."

"Are there enough?" Megan asked as she glanced at Seren.

"Twenty people per pod, right?" I asked. When she nodded, I pointed at the two large cases. "Fifteen suits per case."

A blur of emerald-green pressed the case's button, which opened the seal around the first set of suits. His feet made it into the bottom torso piece before I'd done more than blink. Megan and I ran conveyor until everyone had a suit. Tears threatened to escape my eyelids as I stared at the suit intended for me, and for a moment, the ship tilted—but only for panicking me.

It wouldn't matter that my anxiety left me breathless as the others stuck their feet through standard-sized legs. I wouldn't be able to breathe in the pod. Not without a suit. There wasn't any point in trying to cram my hips into something standard. As if there was such a thing in the diversity of space.

Seren's body swam in the child's suit as Megan fumbled with the top torso. *At least she will still fit. Too short isn't a problem.*

Someone tugged at my sleeve. "Do you know how to do this?" Suit guy held the upper torso of his suit by the water tube. "I don't even know what these are."

A sea of people stood like frozen deer in the flickering lights as I pulled the suit's inner belt from his waist and strapped it across his shoulders like a pair of suspenders. He shoved the upper piece at me and like a child, held up his arms to await it as I lifted the top over his head with a grunt. For a moment, his head tangled in the tubes, and he bumped into me in his momentary panic. My knee wrenched right as I lunged to catch myself. Fire spread across my knee as the smoke thickened in the corridor. In the distance, footfalls bounced around with cries and shouts for help, for spacesuits, or for missing pod members.

Megan had been right. Not a single steward or *Omega Travel Authorities* employee could be found in the budget wing of Level-E-for-expendable.

Bile burned the back of my throat. I took a deep breath to calm myself, then sputtered as smoke threatened to choke me. The young man's hand touched mine. "Get your suit on first, right?" he said and then flushed. Perhaps it was the reddened cheeks or the way his eyes widened, but even in the dim lighting, the scenario betrayed his identity. When his girlfriend snickered behind her hand, it confirmed my earlier suspicions.

With a sigh, I pulled the tubes through the neck where they dangled. Standing this close to him, he couldn't be more than sixteen. I snapped his helmet into place with a strained smile. Resentment wouldn't save anyone today. Once he was breathing suit air, he stepped into the pod, and another person filled his space.

One down, eighteen to go.

My motions fell into a steady rhythm. Strap the lower torso into place. Slide upper torso over a pod mate and snap. Thread through the tubes. Place helmet on top. Cough or wince at my knee. Start again.

I lost count after the fourth person, though I spotted Sven for a brief moment before he disappeared again in the smoke. Somewhere halfway through the line, *The Ursula* rumbled from deep down in her belly, and I picked up my pace despite the fact that I stood almost exclusively on my left leg now.

A coughing fit left me momentarily breathless. When I glanced up, no one else stood waiting. The escape pod was almost full, though it was near impossible to tell as the emergency lights had gone out.

It was time then.

Tears burned my eyelids. Would my mother be told why I died? Would she fight the authorities over their asinine spacesuits? Something brushed against my elbow, and I yelped as my heart tried to tear its way out of my chest.

"It's Sven," he said, his voice barely audible as it crackled its way through his suit's external speaker. He set something on the ground, and there was a slight hiss as something brushed against my calf. "Step into the feet."

I shook my head, which he couldn't see in the dimness. "Standard suits...don't work," I muttered between coughs.

He took my hand and led me to step forward into the spacesuit's feet. "This isn't standard. It's the suit from your cabin."

My mouth fell open to speak, but no words came out. Had he really gone back for my suit? How had he gotten it to detach from the wall? My vision blurred as the metal ring cleared my hips. Every inch of me ached, including my lungs. Sven lifted the upper torso over my head, though he struggled with the tubes with his suited fingers. I tried to help, but my head swam, and he batted my fingers away.

"It's time for someone to help you," he said as he pulled the food tubes through the head opening. The helmet clicked into place, and a rush of clean oxygen brushed across my face. Sven guided me into the escape pod where he belted me into a seat before claiming the last one as his own.

"Thank you for going back," I said into my helmet's mic.

"Thank you for helping to save everyone in this pod," said Sven as he buckled himself into place. "The least I could do for you was make sure you lived after...well..."

The spacesuit hid the emerald-green of her dress, but not the snarky look on the young woman's face as she spoke. "If she wasn't so fat, you wouldn't have had to go back. What woulda happened to us if you hadn't made it to the pod? Stewards are tasked with saving as many lives as possible."

Despite my aching body, I was pretty sure I possessed the energy to kick her. As my leg twitched, a nearby woman spoke up. "If you had spent less time fat-shaming the poor woman at the spaceport, you would have known how to assemble your suit. You should be suffocating right now."

A few other voices popped up in my defense, including the boyfriend in the emerald-green suit, and I couldn't help but grin at the irony. When Sven pressed the button to detach the pod, I held my breath as I waited for it to malfunction, but a mechanical squeal cut through my helmet as the pod successfully detached from *The Ursula.* As we drifted away from the ship's gravity field, we lifted a few inches in our seats.

Seren squealed in delight. "Look, Momma! We're weightless!"

Yes, we are. I grinned beneath my helmet.

—

Five years since *The Ursula*'s disastrous maiden voyage, I found myself willing to try another trip into outer-space, as the archaic digital drives called it. Either way, it still amounted to strapping myself into little more than a tin can with no guarantee I'd escape in an emergency. Houston Spaceport resembled a sardine packing plant as travelers prepared for holiday voyages. Though this time, my medical bracelet scanned and I zipped through check-in at record speed. While *The Ursula* had been re-commissioned, my tickets led me on a trusty old model named *The J. M. Barrie,* and much like my knee, it had a record of taking a few licks and flying straight on 'til morning.

The crowd of people who would be my pod gathered around the dais as we awaited our pre-flight instructions. A familiar figure scrambled out with an equally familiar briefcase. "The name's Sven, and I'll be your steward this trip. From here on out, you'll be Level E, Wing Three, or E-3." He spotted me as I squeezed my way toward the crowd's front, and he gave me a quick thumb's up before launching into our safety instructions.

When it was time to walk through the dreaded "donning of the spacesuit," Sven grinned at me as he unveiled a small, blue suit that shimmered in the overhead light. "This is the Z600, a suit developed in the last year to fit the ever-changing populous traveling the stars! The suit's material is more flexible and adapts to the wearer. Based on an old hydrogel, it's tough and can easily stretch up to twenty times its length without breaking or splitting."

He stepped into the suit's feet, which were much smaller that the Z300. As he pulled the legs up his torso, the fabric stretched around him as promised. Sven gave me a wink before strapping himself into the suit. "Originally, it was developed as research into artificial cartilage back in the day, but with *Ursula I*'s disaster, *Omega Travel Authorities* sought to ensure the safety of *all* of our travelers, no matter what their size. In addition, the suit's flexibility makes it easier to step inside for those with ability challenges, and added straps make it simple to pull the suit up or down."

No giggles or comments reached me as Sven finished the demonstration, though even if they had, it wouldn't have knocked the grin off my face. *Imagine that, a more accommodating spacesuit! About damn time.*

As I boarded *The J. M. Barrie* and set out for Level E, my knee twinged, but not even *that* prevented my smile.

It wasn't gravity that made me feel truly weightless. Perhaps there was hope for space travel after all!

THE END

WEIGHTLESS

About the Author

Multi-international award-winning speculative fiction author Raven Oak is best known for *Amaskan's Blood* (2016 Ozma Fantasy Award Winner, Epic Awards Finalist, & Reader's Choice Award Winner), *Amaskan's War* (2018 UK Wishing Award YA Finalist), and *Class-M Exile*. She also has many published short stories in anthologies and magazines. She's even published on the moon! *(No, really!)*

Raven spent most of her K-12 education doodling stories and 500-page monstrosities that are forever locked away in a filing cabinet. When she's not writing, she's getting her game on with tabletop games, indulging in cartography and art, or staring at the ocean. She lives in the Seattle area with her husband, and their three kitties who enjoy lounging across the keyboard when writing deadlines approach.

To learn more about Raven Oak's writing, visit:
www.ravenoak.net

IMPROBABLE MEAT

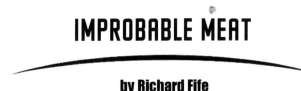

by Richard Fife

STARDATE 3721.10.2 – *Captain Zedara Clement*

THE CREW'S MORALE is low today. After Jenkins revealed we lost part of our stores, there was... ah screw it. No one back home is gonna read this anyway. I hate being so damn formal, blast the regs.

Guess I should still transcribe something, for "historical and poster...ical purposes," as the pin heads back home would say. Try to keep up, computer.

Anywho, Jenkins came up from the icebox, hollerin' like a polecat in heat. Couldn't have the good grace to keep it to hisself, no sirree. Had to scream the whole blasted length of the ship. "We're all gonna starve!" in that high-pitched nasal wheeze.

Like a good captain, I smacked him upside the head, and when he came back around, I had him strapped down and gagged, and I gave him my most winning of pleasant smiles.

"Jenkins," I said, leaning over and batting my big pretty eyes. "I do declare, you have caused quite a right stir with your making about. Might you be able to calm yourself a spell and explain exactly what's wrong to little ol' me?"

He said something through the gag, but he nodded, so I took it out.

"Cap'n," he said back. "Cap'n, I went down to check the icebox, and I noticed the stock pens were awfully quiet. I mean, they can get that way, but this just felt too quiet. So I poked my head in, and... and..."

He just stopped there, so I opened my eyes real large, in that way that seems to make folk want to talk. "And?"

"And they's was all dead, cap'n. The stock for the new world. I think they killed themselves, got all tied up in some rope."

"And how did they do that, exactly?" I asked. Livestock can be difficult, I know, but we weren't exactly amateurs.

"There's more," Jenkins said. "Brett was in there, too, his head all smashed in. I think he might have been trying to sneak one off, have himself a meal off the books."

I let out a heavy sigh, but I can't say as I was surprised. Brett was one of the loudest babies about having all this livestock on board and not getting to use any of it. He just didn't have a head for the bigger picture, and now, well, I guess he doesn't have a head at all.

And, we don't have any livestock.

So, to Jenkins I said, "Well, normally I'd say to keep this to ourselves until I can figure out how to let the rest of the crew know, but that cat's out of the bag now, isn't it? I'd be surprised if they didn't hear you all the way back on Earth, the cold vacuum of space be damned."

Jenkins had the good grace to at least look down in shame.

"So instead, whenever someone comes up and askes you about it, you just send them along to me. And now you go find Tina, and you see if there's anything worth salvaging from the stock. Might as well not let that go to waste if we can help it."

And that was how the third anniversary of this God-man be praised five-year trip started. Why did I agree to this mission?

—

STARDATE 3721.10.18 – *Captain Zedara Clement*

I'm not even trying, pin heads. Deal with it.

We've returned to some resemblance of normalcy since the stock massacre. After all, we'd been eating nothing but this blasted "Improbable Meat" for the last three years. The little treat we got from salvaging the livestock was almost a right holiday. And I can't say there was much in way of tears for Brett. Engineering actually seems happier without him.

I sent a formal message back to Earth, as per your stuffy regs, but it'll be years before they get it, provided Marty aimed the damn laser right. I wonder if Brett even had any family back home. Not many of us did, truth told. S'why they picked us for this mission.

I wonder at that, though. I mean, your world's dying, and the pin heads have managed to build a ship that can go find a new world, so you fill it with mostly unconnected, lost folk? I mean, I get that it's pretty much a one-way trip, but still, what's to say we don't find a great new world and decide we don't want to share?

After all, it was people that ruined Earth in the first place. I might not have paid too much attention to my history lessons, but I got that much, at least. Back in the day, back when the moon-halves were whole, before the rock started falling, the people were doing every damn thing they could to ruin the place.

And not just war, no. They poisoned their water in new and increasingly stupid ways in the name of ease and money. They kept doing things quick and dirty because they couldn't be bothered to learn to do it clean. And they never did get over hating each other. And not the way me and Bobby Ray hate each other. Oh no, they'd scream to their god-men and their goats and whatever else about how the others were the cause of all the problems, never able to just look in the damn mirror.

And by 'they', I do mostly mean men. Us womenfolk had some part, I won't lie, but boy was it so much the boys. Whipping it out and measuring, until one of them whipped it a little too hard.

At least, that's what the history books say happened to make the moon-halves. My old nan said it was the God-man getting tired of all their screaming and hollering that did it. That he split the moon and broke the world and spared only the good and righteous folk, like us.

Little good that did, leaving us a broke-ass planet. Billions dead, and plenty enough problems that didn't just go away with all those assholes. Sea levels rose, the sun beat down, a zombie plague, not to mention all those nuclear reactors that had to get scuttled safe-like before they ruined the world further.

We kept going, though. Gotta learn to adapt, change with the world.

At least, until the world just done gives up.

And somehow, that ends with my ass in a tin can full of well-meaning but blazingly idiotic folk without a brain between them trying to find a new world.

We are so screwed.

—

Stardate 3722.1.12 – *Captain Zedara Clement*

Been a while, pin heads. How ya doing? You still even kicking?

We haven't gotten a transmission from Earth in a year. They said that might happen, that we'd get to be going so fast that even the ansible couldn't find us. I can't say as I even know what that means. They put me in charge because I'm good at keeping folk in line, not because I understood any of this techno-jargon.

And that was why, for the most part, I just got to smile and nod today as Conroy came up blathering about the Feynman-Drive showing signs of degradation in its Pulse Cycle. At least, I think that's what he said. I just batted my eyes at him again, and he coughed and put it in terms anyone could understand.

The goat-be-eaten thing is on its way out. Way to go, pin heads. Your fancy ship is breaking down, and I don't think there's a service station anywhere nearby to take it in for a tune up.

Now, I know there was a lot of debate over putting a woman in charge of this. Some old-folk blather about not being assertive enough, not being fit to lead, getting moody.

Well, I'll have you know that I'm the only competent person in this whole damn tin can.

Conroy just stood there with a dumb look on his face, so I asked, "Can you fix it?"

"Well, maybe, cap'n," he said. "I'd need some things."

I'll note, he didn't actually say 'things'. It was a list of things. A long list that he prattled off from his data pad.

"Well," I said. "Do we have those things on board?"

"Well, yes," he said. "At least, enough that I can limp us along."

"And will it break anything else if we take those

things?" I asked, sweet as tea.

"Just the livestock pens," he said.

"Well, we aren't exactly using those since Brett's tragic brush with idiocy, now, are we?"

"Well, I suppose not," Conroy said.

We stood there a moment, looking at each other.

"Well," I said. "Get to it."

God-man above, do I get why they sent me. It seems the better a person is at a thing, the worse they are at everything else. And the first damn thing that goes is common sense.

Back on the farm, Da used to say those city folk didn't have no common sense. They could be standing out in the field while it's raining rock, and they wouldn't think to get in under cover if you didn't holler at them. They'd just stare up at it.

And, when you finally get them in, if you go and ask them what they were doing, just standing out there looking up at the moon halves like a two headed sow, they'd say something like, "I was just thinking maybe we could build a net to catch the rock," or "I wonder how much more is up there, and if we can measure it."

I mean, I guess the city folk have their uses. Wouldn't be this tin can without them. We'd all just be sitting on a smoldering, wet, mostly dead rock waiting for it to be all dead, and then where would we be? Can't exactly keep going if we're all dead. Even Improbable Meat can't fix that, for all it claims to be able to fix everything else.

And I say that as someone who has been eating Improbable Meat every day for the last three some years. Well, except for that one time a few months ago. Brett, bless his stupid heart, probably did save us with that.

Because, truth is, we'd already lost a few folk that the Meat just wasn't cutting it for. And I know you pin heads knew that was going to happen. It'll supplement, it'll help us stretch things out, but a body can't last on that alone. We need the real thing, at least a little—preferably a lot.

But here we are without any. We all are thinking it, goat knows. This planet, it better not just be a desolate rock you've sent us to. It needs to be ready to provide from the start, or we're all boned, and no pretty smiles or battings of eyes will fix that.

And when I finally succumb, I swear to all there is, moon-halves and God-man and goat, that I'll die with a smile knowing that you pin heads who sent us up here are going to suffer the same fate, too, if just a little drawn out.

Unless you already have, I suppose. Have you?

—

STARDATE 3722.5.27 – *Captain Zedara Clement*

I still remember the first time I had Improbable Meat. The company that made it had been building it up as the answer to all our troubles for a year before they even did a limited release in 'select markets'. That only lasted a month, and was mostly a novelty where it was. Which, I might add, was nowhere near my humble farm deep in the Appalachian-Piedmont Unified Alliance.

No, by the time I was able to get Improbable Meat, it was a year later. I can't say I was eager to try it. I mean, we all understood that we needed something, that our current consumption was untenable, and no amount of smarter farming or even selective breeding was going to fill the gap. We also knew that folk weren't going to just stop eating, either.

We knew all that, but that still didn't matter.

Improbable Meat was the enemy in our minds, here to put the good and honest working folk out on their ears, do away with farms, and turn us all into beggar-slaves to the pin heads in the cities.

So, on that fateful July afternoon, when Da came back from the store with a pack of Improbable Meat, we weren't trying something new. We were meeting the enemy.

Oh... I suppose I should take a second to actually make some sort of report. Conroy has the engine limping along just like he said. No, it didn't take him four blasted months. He had it fixed in about a week. I just didn't feel like turning this blasted transcriber on before that.

Now what was I saying?

Oh, yeah. Da bought a few pounds of this Improbable Meat. The packaging was sleek, all bright colors and bold statements. Someone in their marketing team had to think they were really damn clever, though. In big green letters on one corner, it proudly proclaimed: "100% guaranteed to not be made of people."

Over a thousand years and that old joke is still floating around. Some things just never die, I guess.

Nan was none too pleased when she saw the package, but Da told her to do something with it, and so she did. Made a casserole, just like she would if Da had come back from the butcher with something proper instead.

And, well, we all hated to admit it, but it was pretty damn good. Not just that, it also hit the spot. The packaging also had the word 'Filling' written in large rainbow letters, and the God-man strike me down if it wasn't.

It was another month or two before Da started buying it on the regular. Improbable Fridays became a thing, and then Improbable Lunches. Another year, and it was everywhere. Our savior, our answer, our salvation: Improbable Meat.

Yeah, someone in their marketing team must have been pretty damn proud of themselves. The thing about marketing, though, is that it only sets you up to fail all the worse when you can't deliver on those big promises.

By the goat herself, I am so damn sick of Improbable Meat.

—

Stardate 3722.10.2 – *Captain Zedara Clement*

Year four of our five-year journey.

\<NON-TRANSCRIBABLE SOUND>

That was a party popper, you stupid box. Meg found some in Brett's things. Why by the God-man's pointy beard he had those is anyone's guess, but hell if I care.

Four years. I know, logically, it isn't that long, at least not anymore. Hell, Da was pushing three hundred when I left, and I'm no spring chicken myself. I heard the old stories, how back before the moon-halves happened, folk were lucky to hit a hundred. So, I guess we haven't completely been stuck in the hole in some ways.

Of course, all that keepin' on might be what got us in this mess in the first place. Just means there are more and more mouths to feed.

But that wasn't even what I wanted to talk about. No, see, while I know back on Earth, four years is a blink to anyone nowadays, up here, it definitely feels longer.

Especially when all you have to eat is the same Improbable Meat day in, day out, meal after meal.

The cooks, they're good at dressing it up. Casseroles, tacos, spaghetti. I hear they've even figured out how to make a cake out of the stuff for today's celebration.

But, well, can't say I much feel like celebrating. It's been a year since we had the real stuff, and we've lost more crew. I keep lasering it back at you, and I keep wondering if you're even getting it. Earth has been silent for so long, and I am down to seventy percent of the crew I started with.

It isn't pretty, when folk start to succumb. I have to wonder if these pin heads that made Improbable Meat actually tested, tried to see what it would do to someone who actually did switch completely over.

When I first heard of potential side effects to the stuff, we'd been eating it ourselves for nearly five years. The farm was still doing well enough, and the farmer's bounty was that we probably got more of the real deal than folk up in the cities or wherever it was we were selling our herds to. But when the news first came of regression, well, I won't lie. Every last one of us at the table looked at each other, wondering who was going to say it first.

"I knew it was no good." Nan took the honor. "It just isn't right."

Da, though, being Da, had to be pragmatic, even if he agreed with her.

"It's the folk what are eating only the fake stuff. It isn't the eating of it that's hurting them, it's the not eating real vittles that's doing them ill."

"Except they swore it was just as good as the real stuff," Nan said. "Someone needs to hold them accountable!"

She went on for the rest of the meal, but that didn't stop her from still clearing her plate, despite it being "The Devil's Work" we were eating.

Regression is most certainly a thing I wish I had only ever heard of and not seen firsthand. They say no one is immune, everyone has a trace of it, back from when the rock first started falling. The rock may have given us a lot, but it sure as hell can take a lot, too.

I haven't been able to bring myself to put them down, you know. The regressed. They're in the hold, with the load of rock we brought. It calms down them down, at least a little bit. I heard stories of regressed being able to come back, after they started eating right again. And yes, I know it was only stories, but the God-man strike me down if I don't try. It's what a good and decent person should do.

Isn't that why we're up here to begin with? To try and bring us all back from the brink?

Is there even anyone left to bring back, though? Why can't you figure out how to send something back? Yell at me for not keeping these logs all stuffy and official like you want, or for calling you pin heads all the time. I'll take it back. I'll say I'm sorry.

Just send something back. Anything.

It's so lonely and dark up here.

—

STARDATE 3723.7.20 – *Captain Zedara Clement*

This thing still work? Hello?

I see the red light. I hope it's working. Can't read the transcription anymore. Conroy, for whatever reason, needed the monitor from my logs transceiver to keep your busted ass engine running. Not that I've been wanting to read the complete absence of your responses, or my own complaining. What's it been, nine months since the last entry?

Well, maybe this will be the last, because God-man bless us all, we're here. This stupid little planet you found is actually here.

Not that I'm sure if it matters.

We tried to turn the sensor array on, but Conroy had filched some parts from that, ostensibly for repairs. Honestly, though, I think that was right before he regressed, so maybe he didn't even know what he was doing, just going through the motions without understanding the why.

So yeah, all we have are general images to go by. At least the telescopic cameras are still working. It's green, blue, and white, so that's a good sign. Looks just about like some old pictures of Earth I found once. Not the brown and brown and brown it was when I left, but back before it went all wrong.

The dark side has some light, but not super much. That's promising. Even if we are coming now as refugees instead of heroic explorers, maybe there's a chance we can survive.

But what makes me feel the best is there is nothing floating around it. No ugly debris field of discarded satellites and forgotten rocket bits. Not only does that tell me that they probably have no clue we're here, but it also means I don't have to worry about the fact that we don't have a proper pilot anymore that could fly us through it.

Yeah, both Jerry and Kaitlyn are down with the rock, with over half my crew now.

Fortunately, I got Kaitlyn to show me the gist of flying this junk heap before she went, so when we reach this planet tomorrow, I'll be able to do the basics. There looks to be a pretty remote area in the southern hemisphere, but not too remote, that will work perfect. I'll drop the rock, let it do its thing for a week, and then we'll land and start setting up.

If everything goes well, I'll be sending my last log in a month. If not, well, I suppose we're all goners, and if you aren't, you might as well be, too.

—

Stardate 3723.8.21 – *Captain Zedara Clement* – Final Log

Well, I got good news, and I got bad news.

I'll start with the bad news. Regression is permanent. Of the four hundred folk you sent, about one hundred and fifty of us made it.

The good news, though, is the regressed can still be useful!

The landing was a little rough, and this tin can certainly ain't going back up again, but frankly, it doesn't need to. The rock fall went well, making a safe area we could set up and get used to this new world, and my estimation of the local wildlife was pretty spot on.

There was a herd maybe not ten miles from where we landed.

I waited a day to see if any of them would come looking while we made sure we could even leave the ship, and sure enough they did.

And this is where we found a use for the regressed.

See, when I opened the hatch, I had no idea of the things I'd forgotten.

The air was cool and crisp, carrying the scents of a clean, healthy world. I had forgotten what that smelled like until then. Right took me back to being a wee girl in the foothills, back before the worst of the rock fall, back before it hit our farm and changed us.

So, dumbstruck as I was, I didn't even notice the small pack that was watching us. But the regressed did. It's all they want, you see, the real deal. We'd still been feeding them, just throwing Improbable Meat into the rock hold to keep their strength up. I mean, we had enough, why not?

But they needed the real stuff.

Conroy and Jenkins bolted first, running to where our unseen watchers stared stupidly, and the rest followed.

They didn't leave much for the rest of us, truth told, and I honestly had my doubts about if we could actually eat this meat, but the regressed seemed strengthen by it. It didn't bring them back like I'd hoped, but strengthened, nonetheless. Barring any way to actually test it with the machines—yes, my entire pin head science team regressed, you pin heads—we went about making some harnesses and securing the other regressed. We then took five of our new bloodhounds and went to check on this herd.

The homes they made were fairly clever, and showed an understanding of tools that our native herds have since lost. They also had some weapons, but nothing that was too dangerous. A lucky shot took down Kaitlyn, God-man rest her, but in general they just had no idea what they were dealing with. We didn't give them a chance to figure it out.

It's almost like they'd never heard of zombies before.

But hey, I'm not one to look easy meat in the mouth, not if the other option is Improbable Meat and its 100% guarantee to not be made of people.

We're trying to start a new domestic herd, but it's going to be tough. I guess that is just part of the thrill of being an explorer on a brave, new world. Fortunately, free-range was how Da taught me to farm, and I think we can work with that here, too.

So, pin heads, if you're even still there, come and get it. Food's on, and there's plenty to go around. And if you're not, oh well. Just means more for us.

This is Captain Zedara Clement, signing off for the last time, and about to go enjoy some delicious, fresh brains.

THE END

IMPROBABLE MEAT

About the Author

Richard Fife is a native of North Carolina, but he is often found around Atlanta, GA, where he helps run two small genre-lit conventions: JordanCon in April and Multiverse Convention in October. While he has been paid to write under various auspices, and has edited anthologies, this is his first publication as simply an author of speculative fiction. Huzzah, as the kids say.

To learn more about Richard's writing, visit:
www.richardfife.com

THE CAPTAIN'S YACHT

by Marcus Alexander Hart

RICO DASHED TO an emergency muster station tucked in an alcove between two shops. A panel by its side showed the Sturf glyph for 'launched'.

"Mertz."

He cupped his hands to the saucer-sized window set in the heavy door and peered through. There was no lifeboat. There was nothing but the yawning abyss of empty space. Just like all the others. He thumped his fist on the glass.

"Mertz!"

A weary groan croaked from his throat as he rubbed his eyes and leaned back against the door. Cheery pop muzak still echoed through the abandoned promenade deck. The ferrofountains still performed their shows, every hour on the hour. The holoposters still droned through their endless sales pitches, trying to coax passengers into the high-end restaurants. Despite the rolling power brownouts, all systems seemed to be fully functional. But that was no comfort. The ship could self-maintain for a full week even if the entire crew was dead.

And Rico presumed the entire crew *was* dead.

His rubberized socks gripped the floor as he crept through the ruined deck, carefully avoiding the detritus of hastily discarded shopping. Designer paw covers and fine nitrocigars and necklaces with gemstones the size of ubergrapes. Cafe tables lay overturned and broken. Much of it stained with blood. Mostly purple. Some green. Just a little bit of red.

Rico turned in a slow circle, taking in two levels of storefronts sealed behind the electric sizzle of their forcegates. The *Cosmic Queen* was on emergency lockdown. He didn't know why. He didn't know what had caused this carnage. And he was going to get the hekk off the ship before he found out.

pop-pop-pop! pop-pop!

Rico's ears pricked up. He knew that sound. That was the sound of... yes!

A feminine figure drifted into view further up the corridor, her head cocked to one side under the weight of her majestic feather headdress. Rico's heart went light in his chest.

"Clarizza!" He rushed to her, catching her by her slender shoulders with both hands. "You're alive!"

He held her at arm's length and looked her over. Clarizza Fantana. The most dazzling showgirl in the Rico Diamond Revue. Her golden hair fell in waves down her long neck, framing her flawless little face and big dark eyes. So big and so dark. Like a pair of obsidian avocados floating in her pea-soup complexion. The suckers lining her six tentacle legs *pop-pop-popped* against the marbleine floor. Rico's jaw tightened. The sound wasn't unpleasant, as such, but when you have to sing over a dozen Qualexi dancers *pop-popping* through a kick line twice a day, seven days a week, it starts to get under your skin.

"Are you all right?" Rico asked. Clarizza just stared at him with her empty, black eyes. He gave her a firm shake. "Hello? *Cosmic Queen* to Clarizza Fantana. Do you copy?"

The alien beauty straightened up and sucked a breath. Her enormous eyes blinked once, then again, and her graceful, humanoid arms raised to rest her palms on Rico's chest. He smiled.

"Ah. There's my girl. Rizza, what happened here?"

Clarizza blinked again and smiled back. But it wasn't a true smile. Her face remained slack while the corners of her mouth lifted. And kept lifting until her green skin pulled taut and began to split, ripping a lightning-bolt crack through her chin as her jawbone tore right through.

Rico shrieked and tried to stumble away, but Clarizza's fingers clamped down on his plastic pajama shirt and held him tight. He pounded his fists against her flat, cephalopodan chest, but she just pulled him closer, coiling her tentacle legs around his bony human thighs.

"Get off me!" he cried. "Get off!"

Clarizza's jaw unhinged and the perfect white pearls of her teeth elongated and splayed like porcupine quills from the gaping wreck of her face. Rico's hips released a sickening *snap*, igniting a blaze of pain through his body. Clarizza's jaws gnashed, splattering gobbets of her own cold blood on his face. He tried to resist, but agony sapped the strength from his skinny arms. His wail raised to a piercing falsetto as his body threatened to snap at the crotch like a wishbone. In a moment of gruesome clarity, Rico knew this primal scream would be his final encore.

A violent *crack* twisted Clarizza's head sideways, launching a spew of drool and teeth across a nearby storefront. Rico sucked a breath as his tentacled attacker went limp and hit the floor like a fumbled plate of sushi.

With a whimpering cry, the aging crooner wriggled free of her serpentine limbs and scrambled away. Searing pain slapped his brain around his skull, but he managed to pick out a shape through his daze. A hulking figure standing over the motionless heap of downed showgirl.

It was a woman. A human woman. Two legs, two arms, two mammal parts. All of them in the right place and symmetrical. Her pink gingham shirt and well-worn denim pants were filled to capacity with long, lean muscle. She hefted a double magnum of cheap Centauri wine like an overweight cricket bat, ready to knock another dent in the rogue Qualexi's skull if necessary.

It was not necessary.

The woman lowered her weapon and muttered, "I'm sorry."

Rico put a hand over his pounding heart. "It's all right. We weren't close."

His savior didn't lift her eyes from Clarizza's body. "I was apologizing to *her*. She didn't deserve this."

Blinding agony scalded through Rico's hip as he forced himself to his feet. "Didn't deserve *what*?" he hissed through his clenched jaw. "What happened to her?"

The woman's head swiveled, scanning the deck. "Not here. We have to keep hidden or the—" She glanced at him, her panic snuffed out. "Rico?"

She swept her dark, silver-streaked hair behind her ear, allowing Rico a clear look at her face. Big brown eyes, crinkling in the corners. Faint wrinkles, no makeup. Not young, but not old. Not a knockout, but not too plain. A typical specimen of his fan base. Pure force of habit turned on the ol' Rico Diamond charm.

"The one and only. Always nice to meet a fan. Especially one so beautiful."

"Fan? Really?" The woman's nostrils flared as her fists tightened on her bottle. "Don't even tell me you don't remember me, Rico Derpdump."

The smarmy grin dropped from Rico's face. How did she know his real name? Nobody knew his real name except the people who knew him back on...

His breath caught as his mind's eye peeled twenty-five years off the woman before him. Her intimidating stature shrank down and pushed out, melting her muscles into soft dough. Age lines smoothed as her thin face filled out into pimply jowls. Her graying hair flowed into an oily black ponytail tied with a knot of twine.

It couldn't be.

"Meegan?"

She gave a curt nod. Her lips smiled, but her eyes remained impassive. "Long time no see."

Rico forced his own insincere smile. "Wow. You look great. You know, I'd love to catch up, but first, uh..." He gestured at the puddle of yellow blood pooling around Clarizza's smashed head. "What the hekk happened on this—"

Meegan lurched forward and clamped a hand over his mouth. Before he could struggle, a chilling *pop-pop-pop* echoed up the corridor. He followed Meegan's wide-eyed stare along the storefronts to see a Qualexi waiter stagger into view on his beefy tentacles. Another ripple of pops delivered a cabin steward from the other direction. More pops. A yoga instructor. A deckhand. A bartender. All closing in, slavering drool and gore down the fangs of their wrecked jaws.

"They found us! We're surrounded!" Meegan's eyes darted, evaluating their only two options for escape—a lifeboat hatch that currently led directly to open space on one side and a plain, unmarked door on the other. She launched toward the door and rattled the handle, impatiently tapping her bracelet on its lock-pad. The pad blinked red and farted an error tone.

"Dang it!"

She drew back her magnum of wine and brought it down on the handle like a powersledge. The bottle shattered, splattering turquoise booze, but the handle didn't budge. Rico hobbled over, pain threatening to black him out with every step.

"Move aside!"

He slammed into the wall and waved his own bracelet at the pad. It lit green and the door popped open with a cheery *ping*.

Rico tumbled into the next room, but only made it two paces before he crashed to the floor in a sea of agony. Meegan raced in behind him and slammed the door. With another satisfied *ping*, its deadbolts shot into place. Hissing mutants pounded against the other side as Meegan leaned against it and caught her breath.

Sweat beaded on Rico's face, part terror, part pain, part pure adrenalin burn. He touched his injured right thigh, shooting bright arcs of torment through his body. His skull hammered and he vowed to never do that again. His watering eyes adjusted to the dim emergency lighting, picking out the polished edges of industrial chromasteel appliances. They were in the kitchen of one of the promenade restaurants. Meegan scowled and rapped a knuckle on the glowing red X on her bracelet.

"Ugh! Why doesn't this stupid thing work anymore?"

Rico mopped his cheeks with his palms. "When the ship goes on lockdown, it tries to herd the passengers toward the lifeboats. The guestNav bands won't open anything that doesn't lead to an active muster station."

"Then why does yours still work?"

"Mine's crewNav." Rico raised his arm. A pulsing green key glowed from his bracelet's steel face. "In an emergency, it switches to all-access. I'm supposed to find stragglers and escort them to safety." He half smiled. "You're welcome."

Meegan's eyes rolled. "My hero." She crouched by his side. "How's that leg? That showgirl looked like she was gonna take it for a souvenir."

Rico pushed himself upright and shrieked. "Agh! Mertz!" He slumped back and whined. "It hurts like hekk. If you hadn't showed up when you did..." He shuddered at what could have been. "Thanks for the assist, Meegs."

He met her eyes. She blinked away and stood up. "Uh, yeah. Well, these Qualexi are persistent buggers. We have to keep moving." Meegan smoothed down her wine-stained shirt as she crossed the small room. "Come on. There's another way out." She shoved one side of a pair of double doors. Locked. She shoved the other. Also locked. She frowned and turned to Rico. "Toss me your band. I'll check and see if it's safe this way."

"It won't work."

"It has to work." Meegan eyed the door they came through rattling in its jamb. "There's no other way out."

"No, I mean, the band won't work if I take it off. It's bio-locked to my identiprint." Rico twisted the thin cuff around his wrist. "And I'm not going anywhere until you tell me what happened on this ship."

Meegan huffed impatiently. "Why do you keep asking that? How can you not know?" She squinted at him as if truly seeing at him for the first time. Grippy socks. Green plastic pajamas. Two perfect circles of tender pink skin over his temples. "Wait, did you sleep through the whole infection?"

The word sent a shiver down Rico's spine and a sizzle through his bruised loins. He had, in fact, been sleeping through an infection.

Rico knew full well the risks of cross-pollinating with

non-mammalian species, but he was still a sucker for blondes in any biological configuration. One especially lonely night, he had told Clarizza his show might have an advancement opportunity for a properly motivated dancer. He offered to discuss it with her in his cabin over a nightcap. One thing led to another and the next morning he was in the infirmary pissing polliwogs. The Sturf doctor shot him up with anti-batrachomorphics and put him in stasis until his immune system could recover. He'd still be under right now if a rolling power failure hadn't triggered his medipod's auto-wake failsafe.

Rico gestured to his pajamas. "Had a bad reaction to some seafood. Doc had to knock me out long enough for my stomach to—" A popping wave of tentacles bashed the door. He jerked back with a pained squeak. "Anyway, you were saying... Infection?"

"Right, uh... Gosh, it all happened so fast." Meegan rolled her hands, digging for the words. "From what I understand, it started with a tray of candied mollusks in the lunch buffet that was tainted with some kind of parasite. It didn't affect the Sturf or Gormix, or even humans. But once a few Qualexi got a taste of it..." Her face flushed. "It wrecked their brains. They just drifted around like they were sleepwalking. And then... you know."

She made claws with her hands and put them to her mouth, gnashing them together. A shudder ran through her body so violently that it transferred to Rico. He pulled a hand through his graying pompadour and cursed under his breath.

"Mertz. How many of them ate the stuff?"

Meegan shrugged. "Enough. Apparently it's highly contagious. After a few hours, everyone with tentacles had become a monster."

"But... seventy percent of the crew are Qualexi."

"Were," Meegan corrected. "And anyone who's immune is either dead or evacuated by now."

Rico eyed her skeptically. "What about you?"

"Once the infection started spreading, it was total chaos. I didn't make it to a lifeboat in time and..." Meegan's expression darkened. "They're all launched. They're gone, Rico."

Panic tightened Rico's jaw. "No way. The ship has more than enough lifeboats for everyone on board. They can't all be gone."

"That's what I thought, too. Once everything quieted down, I started searching deck by deck. I couldn't find anything. I was just about to give up hope when..." Meegan wiped her eyes with the back of her hand. "When he found me."

"Who found you?"

"The captain. He refused to abandon ship until he was sure all the survivors had evacuated. He was trying to get me to safety when..." Her voice went hollow. "They got him."

Her mournful eyes drifted to Rico, searching for solace. He cast a reverent gaze to the floor. "I'm sorry. He was a good man. A good officer. And a good friend." Rico had only actually met the captain once. The guy seemed like an uptight prick, honestly. "And he died as he lived. A hero. Trying to get you someplace safe." He let his eulogy settle for a moment. "He didn't happen to mention where that was, did he?"

Meegan nodded. "He said there's only one lifeboat left. His lifeboat. The Captain's Yacht." She blew out a frustrated breath. "I've been searching for the stupid thing for days."

Hope sparked in Rico's mind. Yes! The Captain's Yacht was still on board! And with his band in emergency mode, he'd have the authority to launch it. He could be there in two minutes. If he weren't partially crippled. If the ship wasn't full of bloodthirsty mermaid-squid zombies. He evaluated Meegan's brawny form and rubbed his chin. He could make this work.

"I know where it is. I remember it from my shipboard orientation tour. The Captain's Yacht launches from the command bridge." Rico patted his swelling thigh. "But we can't get to it. Not with my leg like this."

Meegan nodded and held out a hand. "Yes we can. I'll help you. Come on."

Rico took Meegan's arm and winced as she hauled him to his feet. Between her hard muscles and his scrawny physique, the maneuver was surprisingly graceful. He put an arm over her shoulder and she wrapped one around his back and squeezed him tight. Rico's nose wrinkled. An unknown number of days spent struggling to survive had filled her clothes with a heady tang of body odor.

A powerful olfactory memory clawed from his subconscious.

For a sparking instant, he wasn't in a kitchen on a cruise ship. He was in the locker-lined hallway of a scumbag high school in a scumbag farm town on the scumbaggiest moon of Molnar Prime. A teenage Meegan had her arm around him. He could feel the padding of her round body molding itself against his bony hip. He could see her greasy little face beaming at him. He could smell her pubescent musk boiling through her overalls. But young Rico was barely aware of her. He was too preoccupied with the stares of his classmates. Judging him. Laughing at him. Maybe even pitying him. He shut them out. They didn't matter. None of it mattered. This was only temporary.

The pain rocketing through his hip shocked Rico

back to the here and now. With Meegan supporting his weight, he managed to take a step without blacking out. Then another. Together, they hobbled to the double doors, and he touched his crewNav to the lockpad, popping them open.

The two continued into an abandoned restaurant— one of those Franco-Gormix fusion places, where the walls were covered in rough barkshell paneling with brassy inlays of the distinctive silhouette of the Eiffel Six generation ship. A fully stocked bar dominated the back wall and a few neatly set tables filled the space. A yellowish sheen of light filtered through the translucent electric wall stretching across the entrance. Elegant script hung in the middle of it, declaring the restaurant closed and listing its operating hours. The rest was a swirling wallpaper image of delicious algae fondue.

Meegan squinted into the shadowy corners of the room. "How do we get out of here?"

Rico gestured toward the glowing wall. "Over there." He held up his wrist. "I'll drop the forcegate and we can make a break for the lifts. From this level, there should be one that goes all the way to the bridge."

Meegan nodded and helped her injured companion limp to the gate, but before he could touch his band to the lockpad, she grabbed his arm. "Wait! Look."

Rico followed her gaze through the hazy sheen. On the other side of its swirling pattern, he could make out the dark shadows of tentacled crewmates. Way, way too many tentacled crewmates.

"Mertz. I think we got their attention."

The infected Qualexi slapped against the forcegate, sending ripples of distortion across its face. Meegan backed away slowly. "Can they get through that?"

"No way. Probably not. I don't know." Rico warily considered the tiny emitters glowing in the corners of the entrance. "These gates are designed to keep old people from wandering in during off hours, not to hold off a pack of rabid—" He tried to take a step and wailed. His leg gave out but Meegan did not let him fall. "Agh! Son of a—"

"Shhh, it's okay." Meegan gingerly lowered him into a plush kelp-leather armchair. "Maybe if we stay put for a bit they'll get distracted and move along."

"Staying put sounds aces to me." Rico gritted his teeth and cradled his ruined hip. "Get me a drink, will ya? Something with a high enough octane to make everything numb."

Meegan cast a glance at the bar, and then back to Rico. "Bad idea. You've got to be sharp and ready to go when we get the chance. Trading in pain for a drunken stagger isn't an improvement."

"It is to me," Rico moaned.

Meegan's somber glare softened. "You poor thing. Let me have a look. I might be able to help."

She knelt down and rested a broad palm on Rico's leg, applying gentle pressure. Cold waves of torment rolled through his nerve endings, tempered by the warmth of her hands. She rocked forward, tenderly probing all around his hip. As her fingers caressed his upper thigh, the sparking pain became a sizzle of exhilaration.

Rico took advantage of his nurse's moment of concentration to study her up close. Patches of subtle freckles flecked her cheekbones, swooping up to meet at the bridge of her petite nose. His gaze drifted down her neck to the collar of her shirt, unbuttoned far enough to reveal the soft skin over her broad collarbones. He closed his eyes, letting his imagination uncover what the gingham obscured. No scales. No fur. No exoskeleton. Just smooth, warm, human flesh.

Man, it had been so long since he'd been touched by a human. In all his time cruising the galaxy, that was the one and only thing that ever made him homesick for Molnar Sux.

Rico had been born and raised in an agrarian human colony on the sixth moon of the planet Molnar Prime. Every other natural satellite was designated a number. Officially, the "Sux" was a typo that never got fixed, but Rico believed it was intentional. The Molnari always looked down their two noses at those "dirt monkeys in orbit."

Rico was no dirt monkey. He was different than the hicks on the Sux. Better. They were a bunch of uncultured rubes, but Rico... he had the voice of a Shellinic songbird and a stage presence like a supernova. He was destined for bigger things. But nobody ever left the Sux. Passenger ships rarely visited, and even when they did, tickets were prohibitively expensive for the struggling farmers. Moonside, there was only one vessel with engines powerful enough to reach escape velocity. A second-hand Sturf barge that ferried a moonload of crops to the orbital docks above Molnar Prime after each harvest. Every cubic centimeter of cargo space was so precious that carrying passengers was absolutely forbidden by the laws of—

A quick jerk of Meegan's shoulders rammed Rico's dislocated femur back into its socket with an audible *pop*. His entire body stiffened on the power of the earsplitting shriek of profanity ripping from the very core of his soul. Meegan leaned away—eyes wide, hands raised—as Rico scrambled back in the chair, seething and gasping for breath.

"Hekking mertz! What the hekk did you do to me?"

"I fixed your leg!"

"No, you didn't! You..."

Rico gripped his hip defensively, but the stabbed-with-a-hot-uranium-rod pain had been reduced to a dull, throbbing ache. Meegan's brows raised in surprise. No, not surprise. Something else. Rico didn't immediately recognize the expression, because it wasn't one that he saw often. It was concern. Even with their troubled history, Meegan still cared about him. A warm tingle prickled in his chest. He shook it off.

He stood up, cautiously putting his weight on his wounded leg. "Okay, so you did fix it, actually. How in the worlds did you know how to do that?"

Meegan raked her messy hair behind her ears with a relieved smile. "I've done it before. Plenty of times. Never on a person, though." She shrugged. "Sometimes kids come cowish tipping. The poor things are so heavy, their bones pop right out of their sockets when they hit the ground."

Rico winced at the imagery, but the thought made his stomach rumble. "Man, I could go for a fat slice of cowish right now. Best steaks of all the large grazing lizards." According to the Olde Earth settlers who named them, cowish tasted pretty close to the animal they used to get beef from.

Meegan nodded. "My family has been raising them since the soil went sour and we had to stop growing cornesque."

Rico staggered over and peeked behind the bar for snacks. He found nothing but booze. Booze counted as a snack. He grabbed a bottle and two shot glasses. "So, I take it you're still living on the Sux?"

Meegan slid onto a stool opposite Rico, eyeing the glasses disapprovingly. "I am. Ma passed not long after you left. After that, I had to take on a lot more responsibility on the ranch and... you know."

Rico did know. He'd seen it happen too many times

to too many people when he was growing up. The gravity of the Sux was difficult to escape physically, but it was nearly impossible to escape socially.

He poured two shots and pushed one toward Meegan. She politely nudged it aside. Rico knocked his back, letting it burn down his throat and sting his empty stomach. He poured himself another. "Well, you must be getting some good harvests if you can throw down the credits for a Constellation Celebration Cruise."

"Oh, no. I won this trip. At the countystate fair." A proud smile brightened Meegan's face. "I had the biggest cowish eggs the judges had ever seen." She fidgeted with the shot glass, not drinking. "I could never afford a fancy vacation like this. This is actually, uh... this is the first time I've ever been off-world."

Rico's brow raised. "Seriously? Your old man never took you up? Not even once?"

Meegan's voice flattened. "Not after all the trouble he caught when the council found out what I made him do. They would have stripped him of his pilot license altogether if anyone else on the Sux was qualified to fly the barge. No more rule breaking after that." Her eyes locked on Rico's. "So... did you ever get to your mother?"

The abrupt segue made Rico's gut clench. It had been a long time since he'd thought of his mother. The decorated Space Corps hero who spent Rico's entire childhood deployed in the war, leaving his father at home to work the farm and descend into an empty oblivion of loneliness. He slowly worked the cap back onto his bottle as a memory surfaced, sharp and clear as a psy-res holostream.

Meegan's family farmhouse was a dump, even by Sux standards. A tiny ranch-style squat built of pressed bamboozle board that always smelled of wet boots and unruly armpits. He was perched on a fart-filled armchair in her living room, his slender teenage body throbbing with anxiety and adrenalin.

"Uh, Meegs. I uh... I got some news today. From off-world." He picked at the chair's disintegrating arm. "From my mother."

Teen Meegan subtly stiffened. "Oh, gosh. Is she... uh. Is she okay?"

Rico's heartbeat pounded in his ears. His mouth tasted like stale metal. "She's not. Actually. She... She got hit by a radionanite grenade."

Meegan gasped. "Is she...?"

Rico shook his head. "No. No, she was wearing her armor. But enough of them still bored into her nervous system that she's... the doctors think..." His jaw quivered. "She doesn't have long."

"Oh, Rico, I'm so sorry."

A tremble rattled through Rico's voice. "She told me she regrets not being here to watch me grow up and..." He sniffled and blinked hard. "She wants to see me. In person. One last time before..."

He didn't say it. He didn't have to. Meegan squeezed his hands. He squeezed back.

"What are you going to do?"

"I don't know. The hospital is on Shellin. I think I have enough saved to buy a trans-system thrustbus ticket that far, if only I could get to the orbit docks. But I could never pay for passage on a gravity breaker. Not if I worked ten more harvests. And by that time..." He trailed off as his eyes went distant. "At least I'll see her when the casketpod is delivered."

"Oh, Rico. Oh no." Meegan climbed into his lap and squeezed him. He felt the heat of her body and the dampness of her own tears falling on his neck as she held him, desperate to make it better but knowing it was hopeless.

Until she had an idea.

Meegan begged her father to help. She cried. She pleaded. Two days later, Rico was hidden in the bottom of a bushel of cornesque on its way to the orbital docks.

Rico blinked, drawing his focus back to the present and to the tentacled shapes *pop-popping* their suckers against the fondue forcegate. Meegan stared at him, expectantly. He rolled the booze bottle in his hands and carefully returned it to the shelf.

"I did get to my mother. It took every centicredit I had, but I made my way to the hospital on Shellin. The facility was a paradise. Rolling gardens, flowing water, whispering ivy on trellises. Such a peaceful place." He looked far into the distance, as if gazing through the years. "Mom was ravished by her illness, but even so she was still beautiful, in that stoic, warrior way." He sighed and shook his head. "The time she and I spent together is something I'll always treasure. I stayed with her until the end." He flexed his fingers thoughtfully. "I was holding her hand when she passed."

Meegan's eyes narrowed and her lips pressed tight with simmering emotion. "I'm so happy you got to be with her for her last days."

Rico held up his drink in toast. "All because of you. Thank you, Meegan. From me and my mother. Your kindness meant the worlds, to both of us."

Meegan raised her glass without cheer. Rico clinked it and downed his shot. Meegan set hers back on the bar, still full.

"So, after she passed, why didn't you... I mean, did you ever think about..." She met his eyes and took a steadying breath. "Did you ever think of coming back to the Sux?"

In a lifetime of womanizing, Rico had never seen a face so wounded. He knew exactly what *Did you ever think of coming back to the Sux?* meant, and it was not a question of logistics.

"I did. Of course, I did. I wanted to come back, but..." He sighed helplessly. "That's not what Mom wanted for me. Her dying wish was for me to get out and see the galaxy. But not the way she had. Not delivering death, but delivering joy. Through the gift of my voice. Ever since then, I've been honoring her memory by—"

Rico's narrative crescendo was interrupted by a bass-filled hiccup of the ship's engines. The lights flickered, an alarm buzzed, and a stern but pleasant female voice enunciated from the walls:

"La Marais du Fromage is currently closed. Please visit us during regular business hours. Thank you."

The message repeated as Rico spun toward the entryway. Thin bands of crinkly light clung to their emitters across one corner of the arch, but the rest of the forcegate had completely collapsed in the power surge. Six parasite-infested Qualexi spilled inward, tripping over each other as they staggered into the restaurant.

Rico picked up Meegan's drink and threw it down his throat.

Meegan leapt to her feet, a storm raging in her eyes. "Rico, arm yourself!"

She snatched her barstool and hefted it over her shoulder like a battle ax. Rico grabbed the heaviest bottle of hooch he could reach as two Qualexi porters squashed toward him from either direction. With a cowardly yelp, he dropped his weapon and clamored over the bar and behind Meegan.

The infected closed in around them, drooling and hissing. Meegan pounded one in the chest with her stool, knocking it to the ground. "I'm sorry!" Her hair whipped across her face as her biceps flexed, slinging her weapon the other way to clear a second mutant with a wet *crunch.* "Rico! Move!"

He didn't need to be told twice. Rico's stocking feet thumped the carpet as he raced through the hole Meegan had cleared in the wall of attackers. He limped out into the promenade, his head swiveling and eyes darting. Just up ahead a bank of three lifts sat idle, their polished goldtint doors open and ready.

The meaty *thwhacks* and pained apologies of Meegan fighting her way out of the restaurant faded behind him as Rico plodded down the corridor. Forcegates across shops on both sides of him glitched and blinked as the power continued to choke, but it didn't matter. The Captain's Yacht had a self-powered launch. Even if the *Queen*'s engines were dead cold, he could still escape. He just had to get to it.

A twinge of guilt slowed his step. They. *They* had to get to it.

Rico clenched his eyes and shook his head.

No. *He.* There was no 'they'. There was never a 'they'.

A shrill scream ripped the air behind him. He whirled around to see Meegan, just outside the restaurant, soaked in blood. Not briny yellow alien blood. Red blood, gushing from her own torn-open shoulder. A burly Qualexi deckhand grasped and lashed at her with arms and tentacles. His gnarled jaws gored with flesh and knotted with tattered gingham.

"Rico!" Meegan cried. "Rico! Help!"

Rico froze, one foot inside the elevator. This was his chance. His only chance.

He had to go.

He stepped into the lift, but the sound of snapping ribs and an aborted screech drew his attention back to Meegan. She was down. The deckhand's massive, tattooed tentacles wrapped around her chest in a crushing embrace. She swatted at his clapping jaws and gasped for breath. Strong as she was, even she couldn't win this fight without oxygen. Two more Qualexi lurched out of the restaurant and stumbled their way toward her prone body.

Rico tapped his crewNav band to the lift panel, turning the rows of red buttons green. He hovered his finger over the one marked "bridge."

He willed himself to push it.

Meegan's scream choked to a strangled sob.

His hand balled into a fist. "Oh, for hekk's sake!"

Rico charged out of the elevator with a savage roar. Adrenalin powered his thin arms as he grabbed Meegan's barstool and swung it at the deckhand like he was hitting a gong. The mutant hissed and tumbled over, dazed but still very much alive. Rico clawed at his twitching tentacles, frantically peeling them off Meegan's body.

"Let's go." His breath quickened as the other Qualexi drew closer. "Now!"

Meegan took Rico's hand and pulled herself to her feet. They clutched one another for support and staggered into the center lift. Rico mashed the top button and the doors slid closed. The car rattled and sluggishly ascended as the machinery struggled to pull power from the ship's unstable grid.

Meegan planted her palms on the wall, coughing and sucking air in ragged breaths. "Thank... you. So... strong. I couldn't..." She turned her head toward Rico and caught a glimpse of her own torn-up shoulder. A gasp choked from her lips as the pain of her injury burst through the protective shell of her panic.

Rico was plastered to the opposite wall of the lift. Eyes wide. Face ghostly pale. The amount of blood seeping from the massive gash in Meegan's back was making him lightheaded.

"Are you…" His voice came out thin and high. He cleared his throat. "Are you all right?"

Meegan's breath steadied. She gave a tiny shrug and grimaced. "Looks like I'm not going to be wearing my strapless gown anytime soon." Rico just stared at the torn flesh, his jaw hanging open in horror. Meegan's brow raised. "That was a joke, by the way. I don't own a strapless gown."

Rico blinked. Meegan let out a pained chuckle. The tension cracked as Rico chuckled with her. He raked his bony fingers through the sides of his hair and let out a hot breath.

"Mertz, Meegan. Were you always such a badass?"

Meegan waved it off. "They build 'em tough on the Sux. Still, I'd like to keep some of my blood on the inside, if possible."

She tapped a panel on the wall engraved with the Sturf glyph for 'medikit'. It opened, revealing a compact cache of emergency supplies. Using her good hand, she tore open a foil packet of gauzegel. She reached over her shoulder and tried to turn her head, but the injury was too inconveniently placed for her to see or reach.

"Rico, help me out."

She placed the packet into Rico's hand and turned her back to him, presenting her gored shoulder. He took a half step back and bumped into the opposite wall. "No. I'm not a… I don't want to hurt you."

Meegan snorted. "Quit being a baby. Gauzegel doesn't hurt. You know that."

Rico frowned. Gauzegel was a powerful antiseptic and wound dressing, but its real selling point was its anesthetic properties. The second this stuff got in your bloodstream it hit you with an endorphin rush like a three-stage rocket of sunshine, lollipops, and rainbows. Rico had used it plenty of times before, but only recreationally.

He held the packet over Meegan's shoulder and squeezed out some gel, releasing an intense sugary-lemon aroma. The instant the first drop landed in Meegan's wound, her whole body drooped. She leaned on the wall, letting out a dreamy sigh. "Oooh, yeah. That's better." Her face melted into a goofy smile. "Rub it in."

Rico shook his head at the reservoir of blood and pearly goo in her flesh. "I don't think so."

Meegan gently grabbed his wrist and lifted it toward the bite. "Come on. If you don't rub it, the skin won't form, and we'll have to start again."

Rico knew she was right. He clenched his teeth and pressed his fingertips into the center of her raw wound, hesitantly moving them in a circle. The gauzegel reacted immediately, congealing into a pale blue skin the consistency of rubber surgical gloves.

Meegan sank into the depths of her induced high, groaning as Rico's long fingers worked the gel to the edges of the bite. Euphoria weakened her knees and she lurched toward the floor, but Rico threw his other arm around her, catching her under the ribs. She giggled as he struggled to keep her upright, squeezing her back to his chest as he used his palm to smooth the last of the thickening gel into a clean, even seal.

Meegan's head lolled lazily to one side with a lopsided grin. "Aww. Thank you, Rico. You're such a good person." She reached up and caught his hand, pulling it down to wrap his arm around her. "You were always so good to me."

She closed her eyes and curled into him, nuzzling like an affectionate cat. The gesture saturated Rico with his own all-natural endorphin rush. Meegan's warm-blooded body against his felt so right. Their forms fit together so effortlessly. She was just so unmistakably *human.*

A tingle of regret crept through Rico's mind. Back in the day, he'd never appreciated how good he had it. Meegan had always been affectionate, but he hadn't returned any more tenderness than he had to. Holding hands. Snuggling in front of reruns on the holo. A little bit of making out. A part of him shuddered at the memory. He used to hate kissing Meegan. Hated the feel of her dry mouth on his lips. Of her acne-scabbed face rubbing oil on his cheeks. But now... everything had changed.

Meegan's adult body was firm in his embrace. Muscular and powerful. She sighed contentedly and turned her head. Her features had matured so strikingly. So... *beautifully.* He could feel the warmth of her breath on his cheek. He could almost taste the satin of her soft lips on his.

She was so much different now. So much *better.*

Rico shifted his grasp, slowly turning Meegan to face him. Her head rolled to his shoulder and nestled against his neck. Her hands moved languidly to his hips as his own slid down her back, coming to rest on the firm curve of her behind.

Meegan snorted and stiffened, as if awakening from a dream.

"Oh!" Her cheeks blossomed crimson. "Oh, uh..."

Rico didn't release his grip on her posterior. "Shh. Everything is okay. You're with Rico. I'm gonna take care of you."

His eyes drifted shut as he pulled her in for a kiss. Just like the old days, except better in every way.

"Wait." Meegan grabbed his wrists and pushed his hands away from her backside.

Rico raised an eyebrow as she slipped from his arms. "What's wrong? I thought you wanted—"

"I do! I do. It's just... Not here. Not like this." Meegan fussed with the rubbery blue patch on her shoulder and adjusted her sticky, blood-soaked shirt. "I'm sorry, I know this is the drugs talking and I should really shut up now, but I always imagined, gah, I don't know." She looked at her shuffling feet. "I just want it to be special. To be perfect."

The words between the words resolved in Rico's mind. "Wait, are you saying you've never..."

Meegan groaned. "Okay, it's not like I'm some kind of loser. I had suitors come calling, but none of them were..." She took a breath, trying to clear her head. "None of them were *you*."

Her eyes ticked up and caught Rico in a beam of pure vulnerability. He knew the gauzegel had made the words come easier, but that didn't make them any less sincere.

"So, you just... what? You *waited* for me?"

A tiny, melancholy smile teased Meegan's lips. "What can I say, Rico? You were the one that got away."

Conflicting emotions crashed hot and cold in Rico's chest. The heat of this lovely creature's admission that she still cared for him forming a storm front against the frosty guilt of leaving her in the first place. Because the truth was, he wasn't 'the one that got away'. He was 'the one who ran away at a quarter light speed and never looked back'.

But maybe he should have.

He opened his mouth to reply, but no words came out. For once, Rico Diamond was speechless. In his proxy, the lift replied with a bright *ping* and opened its doors.

The noise startled Meegan, smothering her endorphin rush with a spike of fight-or-flight adrenalin. She dipped into a crouch, prepared to meet anything that would come through that door with a full-frontal attack. But there was nothing on the other side but the abandoned command bridge of the *Cosmic Queen*.

She stepped out of the lift and into a vestibule, eyes wide and jaw slack. Just beyond a broad arch, three recessed rows of gleaming white consoles blinked with alerts nobody was there to address. But Meegan wasn't gaping at the controls. She was looking out the enormous domed window at a magnificent panorama of space. A great purple and orange nebula dominated the view, its vaporous fingers reaching out into a void of starry blackness sprawling to infinity in every direction.

"It's… it's so beautiful," Meegan whispered reverently.

Rico barely gave it a glance as he hustled past her. "Eh. It's space. You get used to it."

Meegan shook her head numbly. "I don't think I could. It's breathtaking."

Her hand slipped into Rico's and squeezed. He squeezed back. Even after all these years, it felt familiar. Like they were still in high school, standing under a different starry sky. A much duller one, muted by the farm moon's hazy artificial atmosphere. Meegan's awestruck smile made Rico feel empty inside. The poor girl was mesmerized by something as ordinary as *space*. In her whole life, she probably hadn't seen anything more exotic than an invasive cornesque weevil. Because she had spent her whole life trapped on the Sux. Waiting for him.

He had stolen decades from her. And she didn't care. She didn't even *know*. She was just happy they were finally together again. And here he was, using her to get what he wanted. It wasn't fair. It wasn't right.

It wasn't too late to fix it.

Rico looked into Meegan's glimmering eyes and steeled himself. "Meegan, listen. There's something I need to tell—"

Before he could finish his thought, a sharp *ping* echoed through the bridge. Rico and Meegan both whipped around to see a second lift slide open. Two of the Qualexi from the promenade spilled out, gurgling and hissing.

"The infected!" Meegan cried. "How did they..."

Rico noticed the green keys glowing from the mutants' wristbands.

"Mertz! They're crew!" His eyes darted, looking for a place to take cover. There was nowhere to go, but the peculiar arch between the foyer and the command center jogged a memory. "Get back!"

He shoved Meegan as hard as he could, sending her sprawling onto the bridge. He lurched toward a control panel, swiped his band, and mashed a pad labeled 'Start presentation'.

A transparent forcegate sizzled into place in the broad arch separating the vestibule from the control stations, punctuated by a musical flourish and a booming voice.

"*Ah, hello there. Welcome aboard, new recruits!*"

The Qualexi and Meegan all looked surprised to see a two-dimensional man slide out of the wall and casually stroll across the entryway. He was a Sturf, broad-chested with burnished orange skin and a perfectly formed crown of horns. His uniform was as immaculate in holographic form as Rico remembered it being in real life.

"*I'm Captain K'vendle, and it is my honor to show you around the command center of your new home, the* Cosmic Queen. *Let's start with the communications console.*"

The holoprojection raised his arm, and a yellow outline appeared on the face of the forcegate. From

Rico's perspective it drew a rectangle around a Qualexi waiter, but from the other side, it would perfectly surround the control panel to his left. However, the mutants weren't here for a new-hire orientation tour. They were here to kill. They lurched at the captain fangs-first, but he continued his spiel unabated as they bounced off the photon-thin wall.

Rico hustled to Meegan, still leaning against the console where he had shoved her. "You okay?"

Meegan nodded, but she didn't take her eyes off the infected aliens clawing at the lecturing captain like cats scratching aquarium glass. "I'll be a lot better once we're off this horrible ship." She grabbed Rico's hand. "Where's the Captain's Yacht?"

Rico's gaze drifted. "Right. That. Well..." He crossed to a small hatchway at the far end of the bridge. "It's, uh... It's here."

He swiped his crewNav over the lockpad and the door slid open in a neat iris, revealing what appeared to be a cramped metal closet housing a single chair.

Meegan squeezed inside and kneeled on the seat to take a closer look. There was nothing to see but padded consoles packed tightly around her. "I don't get it. How do you get to the rest of it?"

"There is no rest of it." Rico's voice tightened. "The Captain's Yacht is a one-person escape pod."

Meegan fell still. She shifted in the snug space, coming off her knees and flopping down in the seat. "But how are we both..."

"We're not. You are."

"What?" Meegan's eyes went wild. "No. Rico! I'm not leaving you here!"

She tried to climb out of the capsule, but Rico gently pushed her back, easing her into the chair. "Yes, you are. You deserve this."

"What's that supposed to mean? We both—"

"Meegan, please. I'll be fine." Rico waved at the comm console. "I'll hunker down here and call for help. As soon as I get rescued, I'll find you. I promise. But right now I need you to be safe."

"How is this safe? I don't know how to fly a spaceship!"

"You don't have to. Look," Rico gestured to an autonav panel and a stasis generator, "no manual controls. It'll get you to safety automatically. That's literally its only function."

Doubt tightened Rico's chest, but he knew he was doing the right thing. He had to make sure she was okay. He had to give her a second chance to live the life he had stolen from her. Even if it meant...

The snarling of the Qualexi monsters grated in his ears. He focused on Meegan's blanching face.

"You'll be fine. Trust me."

He leaned into the hatch and waved his crewNav at the ignition pad. The panels in the Yacht blinked on in sequence and began running self-diagnostics. Meegan yelped as the restraints closed over her, locking her to the seat and squeezing stasis inducers to her temples. A thirty-second launch timer awakened on the arm of the chair.

Rico took a deep breath. "Listen, Meegan. I'm sorry I never came back to the Sux. I wish I could change the past, but I can't. I can only change the future." He struggled to find the words. "When we're together again, I... I want to pick up where we left off. But for now..." A sober smile tugged at his cheeks. "I want to give you a goodbye kiss."

He leaned in, but Meegan twisted her face away. "I'd rather not."

Rico paused, his puckered lips going slack. "Wait,

what?"

"I don't want to kiss you."

"But... *what*?" His eyebrows knitted. "I don't get it. You... you said you waited for me."

Meegan tugged a lock of hair from under a stasis inducer, making sure it made good contact with her temple. "I did wait for you. For three whole harvests. And then I met your mother." Her airy voice went cold. "She's never served in the Space Corps. She's never even been off-world. She's a waitress, Rico. And a pacifist."

Meegan's glare formed an icy brick in Rico's stomach. There was no way he could dig himself out of this. At this point, there was no reason to try.

He blew out a long, cathartic breath. "Okay. It's true. Everything I told you about her was a lie. Everything I told you was a lie, period." His body loosened as the tension of old secrets leeched out of it. "I confess, our entire relationship was a long con to get you to convince your dad to fly me off the Sux. I knew the deep-space cruise liners stopped at the orbit docks, and I knew if I could just get to one... If they could only hear me sing, they would..."

His voice trailed off. She didn't need the details. The broad strokes were damning enough. Meegan's stare cut him to the bone.

"You never loved me, Rico. You exploited my feelings to make me think what you wanted was what I wanted. You made me care about you just so you could use me to escape."

Rico nodded grimly. "I did. And I'm sorry, Meegs. I'm so very sorry."

"Don't be." Meegan waved him off, flashing the red X on her guestNav bracelet. "It's a solid con. And so simple even a beginner can pull it off."

She rested her hand next to the ticking green digits

of the launch countdown. Rico's eyes widened as he glanced at the green key on his crewNav. Meegan continued.

"You see, the captain told me his Yacht was a one-person pod. He was going to put me in it and go down with the ship. He was a true hero. But you, Rico?" She shook her head. "I know you better than that."

Rico's mind reeled through their brief reunion. "But you... You fixed my leg! You protected me, and... the snuggling! It was all just..." His voice cracked. "You said I was the one that got away!"

Meegan shrugged. "I did what I had to do to get home to my kids."

"*Kids?* But I thought you'd never—"

With a final deafening rumble, the ship's engines burned out. The bridge went dark, illuminated only by the stars shining through the transparent dome. The holographic captain blinked out of existence, taking his forcegate with him.

Rico gasped in horror as the infected Qualexi set their sights on new prey. He whirled back to the Captain's Yacht just as the iris of its door began to close. Meegan gave him a smile and a friendly wave from within.

"So long, Rico. This time *I'm* the one that got away."

THE END

THE CAPTAIN'S YACHT

About the Author

Your old pal Marcus Alexander Hart is an award-winning novelist, self-proclaimed karaoke star, and default awesome dude. His books include the paranormal thriller *One Must Kill Another* and the subversive teen comedy *Alexis vs. the Afterlife*. Up next is a new sci-fi adventure comedy series entitled *Galaxy Cruise*.

To learn more about Marcus's writing, visit:
OldPalMarcus.com

STAR CADETS

by CW Lamb

THE HOVER BUS came to a jolting stop, bringing Ken to full consciousness and out of the half-sleep he had been enjoying for most of the night. He could still feel his jump bag, pressing against the back of his legs and tucked safely under his seat, as he peered out the window. Squinting through the glare of the morning sun, he dialed up the filtering on the bus window tint, until he could clearly make out the symbol of the Galactic Academy just outside. A silver Rocketship, standing straight and tall, with two diagonal orbital loops intersecting at is center; the emblem was duplicated in miniature on his jacket's left breast.

A smile crossed his lips as he shook off the last of the sleepiness that had accompanied the boredom of the hover bus ride. This was to be his home for the next three years, a childhood dream come true. Reaching between his legs, he found the strap on his bag without looking away from the window, and in one swift move, pivoted from his seat to stand in the center aisle of the bus.

"Hey, watch it," he heard as he bounced off a moving wall with arms and legs.

Landing in his seat once more, Ken looked up in time to see a mass of muscle wearing a uniform identical to his own, only much larger. At nearly six feet tall himself, the other cadet made him feel tiny.

"Sorry, didn't see you," was all he could manage as he worked to keep from sliding off his seat and onto the floor.

"Seriously?" The guy exclaimed as he shook his head in disbelief and then proceeded to the front of the hover bus, to exit behind those ahead of him.

Recovering his balance, Ken waited for an opening in the line of people passing him by, all in the same Cadet Blue uniform as his, before once more attempting to exit the bus. Descending the few steps to the ground, he could see the bus still hovered in place, the gap between the vehicle and the ground no more than a foot at rest. Although it was now low enough to allow the passengers to exit, it was still high enough to lose his duffle underneath if he wasn't there to collect it. Ahead, he could see the open hatch as the attendant tossed bag after bag from the luggage compartment.

"Last one," he heard the man say as a duffle went flying past Ken while he approached the opening.

All around him, cadets were scrambling to identify their nearly identical possessions, packed according to the strict guidelines provided by the Academy. One regulation Jump Bag and Duffle per cadet, no exceptions.

"Hall," he heard someone shout out the name on the duffle in front of them before moving on to the next, continuing the search for their own possessions.

After rushing to claim his bag, Ken adjusted the strap that allowed him to sling it over one shoulder. Then, holding the jump bag by its straps in the other hand, he headed toward the Academy entrance. He lined up behind the other cadets who had arrived there before him, watching as one cadet after another was interrogated by the two security guards before being allowed through the gates. Also dressed in Cadet Blue, he could see the pips on their collars, indicating they were third-year students.

"ID," the one closest to him said as he held out the scanner, his Space Patrol armband denoting his role.

Ken silently presented his wrist, his ID bracelet in place for the device to read.

"Hall, Kenneth. Coeur D'Alene, Idaho," the SP guard read off the display.

"That's me," Ken replied with a nod, his image in the display confirming his identity.

"Head over to Building 3 for room assignment," the other guard directed as he read something off his hand-held display while motioning with his free hand.

Hurrying past, so as to not hold up those behind him, Ken then paused to adjust the shoulder strap on his duffle before he headed in the direction indicated. Doing his best not to gawk as he walked, Ken slowed his pace as he scanned the area around him, thrilled to see all the shimmering glass and steel buildings that made up the Galactic Academy. In every direction, he saw cadets in blue, some with rank pips on their collars denoting their status as second- or third-year cadets like the gate guards.

Mixed in with the sea of blue was the occasional gray of the Galactic Service, all graduates of this academy, and experienced spacers. Ken assumed those in gray were likely instructors, assigned to the school after years of experience in real spaceships, not just the training vessels he was destined for. Returning his attention to the building before him, Ken took the steps two at a time and, in his haste, nearly rear-ended a cadet standing just inside the doorway.

"Star Cadet Kenneth Hall, reporting for duty," he announced to the gray-clad woman sitting at a desk after waiting his turn.

"Hall," she repeated as she scanned the display in front of her.

"Third floor, room 327, take those stairs," she announced after finding the proper entry, then motioning to the stairwell past her desk and on the right.

"Yes, ma'am," Ken replied, not sure if he was supposed to salute or not.

Fresh out of the public university, where he graduated near the overall top of his class with a degree in astrophysics, he had yet to go through the Academy orientation. Galactic Service had many branches, some more in line with civilian pursuits like research or exploration, but all adhered to a military organizational structure.

Climbing the stairs to the third floor, he glanced both ways until he determined the numbering sequence. Heading to his left, he went down two doors before he found his room, 327. Inside, he was surprised to see someone was already unpacking.

"Oh, excuse me," he said, stopping in the doorway.

"Looks like we're roomies," the man said in reply.

It didn't take Ken any time at all to recognize the person before him as the one he had collided with on the bus earlier that morning. Unsure if he should say something about it, he was cut off before he could try.

"I'm Max," the man continued. He paused his unpacking for long enough to extend one hand.

As he shook it, Ken was reminded just how large the man was when his hand was swallowed in his grasp.

"Hope you don't mind, but I took the single; bunks

and I don't get along too well," he said as he resumed settling in.

Ken noted that the room held three beds, one single and two more, set up as bunks.

"No problem for me," a voice replied as a small form brushed past Ken, tossing her bags on the lower bunk.

"Dibs on the lower," she said with a smile as she turned to face the two men towering over her.

"Are you in the right room?" Ken blurted before he realized what he had said, not expecting co-ed rooms.

"Star Cadet Sandra Cytherean at your service. You can call me Sandy," she said with a mock salute.

"Cytherean? You're from the Venus colony?" Ken asked. However, now that he's had a good look at her, he realized the question was unnecessary.

Small in stature, white hair, and pale in complexion, she was a clear product of her environment. Dense clouds and slightly lesser gravity made her exactly as described, Earth's smaller sister planet. Truth be told, he didn't know much about Venus, and she was the first Venusian he had ever met so far as he knew, but she was also stunningly beautiful.

"Max," the man mountain said with a return salute as he finished putting his things away.

"Just Max? You a Martian? You sure look like one," she replied casually as she plopped on her bunk, not even bothering to open her bags.

Max just nodded in affirmation as he continued his work.

"Wait, the man is from Mars and the woman is from Venus? Am I the only one who thinks this is going to be a problem?" Ken half-joked as he looked at his two roommates.

"Maybe for you, but I don't see any issues. Hey, you aren't one of those Earth First bigots, are you?" Sandy said, leaning forward with her eyes narrowing as if she were seeing Ken for the first time.

"No, not at all," Ken stuttered. He waved her off, waiting for Sandy to relax while Max just stood watching the pair.

"To be honest, though, you are the first Martian and Venusian I've ever met. It's kind of exciting," Ken added with a shrug as he tossed his bags on the upper bunk.

"So, where are you from?" Max asked, no apparent offense taken by Ken's earlier question.

"Idaho," Ken replied while he inspected his empty wall locker, sizing it up for space, thinking of what was in his duffle.

"I-da-what?" Sandy asked with a smirk, leading him into a joke Ken had heard his whole life.

—

"First of all, let me welcome you to what will become the greatest and most rewarding challenge you have ever faced," the man in the stark while uniform began as the auditorium quieted.

Ken had hardly begun unpacking when the announcement had been made for all first years to gather in the main auditorium. With Sandy leading the way, the three soon found themselves awash in clusters of cadet blue as the other cadets adhered to the instructions for roommates to stay together.

Several times during their walk to the destination, Ken noted other male cadets pointing out Sandy to their companions. She was, apparently, oblivious of her remarkable good looks, as she ignored their attempts to get her attention. However, more than once, he saw the potential suitor waved off with a whispered exchange, the look of disappointment clear on their faces. Ken made a mental note to carefully approach his new roommate on the subject, once he felt more confident with her.

"My name is Admiral O'Brien, and I am the Dean and commanding officer of this Academy," the man continued from the podium.

Behind him, in a row of chairs, sat other men and women in uniforms of either colors of white or gray. From their seats, Ken couldn't make out their exact rank, but he knew that all those dressed in white were senior officers like the admiral. Those in gray were what Ken called the 'doers'—people who still commanded ships of their own and were only here teaching as part of their service rotation.

Ken listened as each of those on the stage were introduced, one by one, and it was then that he noticed one of the officers in gray was also Venusian. Her last name was the same as Sandy and her appearance strikingly similar, although much older.

"Is that your mom?" Ken whispered to Sandy, only to receive a look of confusion in return.

Before he could ask more, the admiral returned to addressing the cadets directly.

"If you followed the instructions issued, and you had better have, you should be sitting with your assigned roommates," the admiral stated with an edge in his voice.

"I want each and every one of you to look to your left and to your right, because these are your shipmates for the next three years. Every training ship has a three-person complement. Your crews consist of a ship's Pilot and Commander, an Astronavigation Officer, and ship's Engineering Officer. If your role is not obvious to you, talk to your partners; it soon will be."

Ken took a deep breath as he looked to his

roommates beside him. Astronavigation 101 was a required class, one that he had barely passed, and mostly by the sympathy of his instructor and lots of late-night study sessions. His engineering skills were slightly better than that, but his model atomic motor proved to be the slowest thrust producer in the class. He liked to think his understanding was solid; it was the execution that challenged him.

It was then that Ken realized both Sandy and Max were staring at him, as well, both were apparently speechless.

—

"Commander Cytherean, there must be some mistake," Sandy repeated emphatically as she leaped from her seat, with the other two cadets still sitting on either side of her.

All were in the Head of Personnel's office. Unlike other institutions, the Galactic Academy was not just a school. One must have already completed a university-level curriculum before being accepted, and then once you graduated here, you were put to work in one of the various divisions of the Galactic Service. Thus, they did not have an academic enrollment department; it was just personnel management.

After the all-hands meeting for First Year cadets in the Auditorium, the three had returned to their quarters where they compared notes. In short order, they realized that, to varying degrees, none of the three completely agreed with the current assignments.

While Max was quite satisfied with his role as Engineering Officer, he was ambivalent about his shipmates as a whole. Ken interpreted it as, *leave me alone and I'll do my job*. Sandy, on the other hand, was beside herself upset that the Academy had neglected to see her innate leadership abilities and hadn't waved the practice of making the ship's Pilot the Commander. She was positive she could perform the duties required and still navigate, thus deserving of the waiver.

"Sandra-9872, please take your seat!" the officer behind the desk instructed firmly.

The woman before them was the same Ken had seen in the auditorium, the one he speculated was Sandy's mom. This close, though noticeably older than Sandy, Ken could still see similar stunning beauty in the woman—the same features, just more mature.

"Now, as to your personnel assignments," the woman started after Sandy had reseated herself, "I can personally vouch for your placement, as I was the one who put you three together."

"Why?" Sandy blurted once more before being silenced with the wave of a hand.

"I assume none of you are questioning your primary assignments, as you are all the very best at what you do."

A small snort escaped Sandy's lips as she rolled her eyes at Ken. During their conversation before coming here, he had been forced to concede his shortfalls in astronavigation and mechanics. The fact that neither roommate had disclosed their placement in astrophysics, nor any deficiencies for that matter, had just dawned on him. He had been so caught up in his own limitations that he had chosen not to press the issue with either of the two.

"Regardless of what opinions you may have formed about one another in the very short time you have been together, it is my opinion, and therefore the Academy's opinion, that the three of you are properly assigned. So, until such time as you are in agreement with the academy's decision, I suggest you hold yourself to the highest standard of Star Cadet behavior and get along."

Ken could see Sandy was not happy with the decision. However, since the entire monologue had been recited with the two women locked in a stare-down, she could hardly question the intent of the message.

"If there is nothing else, you are all dismissed," the woman finished. She began sorting through the papers on her desk.

With that, the three rose and began filing out of the room, their instructions clear. Lagging slightly behind, Ken waited until the others had left the room before turning in place.

"Ma'am," he began.

"Yes, Hall?" the woman replied without looking up.

"Are you and Sandy related? I mean, you have the same last name and you bear a striking resemblance to one another," he offered cautiously.

Looking up from her desk, she at first appeared irritated at the question, but something in his face must have changed her mind, softening her expression and inspiring her to speak more softly than before.

"In a way, but I believe that is a conversation you need to have with her, Hall. Dismissed." She returned her gaze to the paperwork before her once more.

—

Unlike traditional educational institutions, the Galactic Academy had a more hands-on approach to teaching. They took every opportunity to empower the cadet with their own learning, whenever possible. They were also very straightforward about the intent of certain courses. The case in point was the antigravity sports class they were assigned to attend first thing the following morning. The cadets called it Spaceball.

After leaving Personnel, the three roommates had returned to their quarters in silence, spending the rest of the afternoon quietly unpacking and getting settled in. The only interruption was the delivery of their class equipment. Once more, all First Years were called together, only this time into a smaller assembly hall.

In each seat were two devices: one about the size of a book, only half the thickness, and the other a smaller version of the same. Taking his seat next to his roommates, Ken placed both pieces in his lap, resisting the urge to fiddle with the pair, a battle he could see others around him loosing.

An instructor in gray stood next to a table on the stage with the same two objects nearby. As he spoke, he lifted each item and demonstrated its use.

"The small unit is both a personal communicator and a mobile interface. It is to be worn on the outside forearm opposite your dominant hand, i.e. left arm for righties and right for lefties. In this manner, you can operate the unit, using one or many fingers as it suits you. Once synced, you will be able to find and communicate with your teammates, by text, audio, and video, anytime, anywhere."

"Great," Ken heard Sandy mutter as she shook her head sadly.

"The larger unit is for classroom studies and fits into a dock at your station shipboard. You will find that very convenient if you take good notes. Your assignment tonight is to read the Academy Orientation and start studying the Cadet Handbook preloaded in every one."

For the last part, a 3D projection filled the open air between the speaker and the seating area. There, they could see a cadet in blue seating herself in a rocketship station and then placing the device in a docking port convenient to her workspace. As she went about a checklist on the console before her, she would flip screens on the device display, verifying her actions.

Returning to their quarters, the trio had no sooner settled into study than their larger devices chimed in unison.

"Spaceball, 07:30?" Max read aloud.

"It's intended to teach us antigravity maneuvering skills," Ken added absently.

"It's also intended to teach us how to work together as a crew. We're doomed," Sandy finished.

—

The morning class found all three cadets in one-piece, skin-tight jumpsuits, 327 emblazoned in white across the front and back with magnetic boots on their feet. The boots were more like a synthetic moccasin, with soft, flexible soles intended for use aboard a spaceship. The secret of the footwear was in the material they were made of. Once activated, they offered a magnetic attraction to the metal decking that required some effort to break free, mimicking gravitational attraction. They were common attire in space, once the gravitational effect from any of the planets was gone, should one need a solid grounding. They could be turned on and off by touching the small device on their forearms they received yesterday.

In addition, each held a helmet in their hands. The headwear was both safety equipment and communications gear. The same device on their forearms was also a communicator and was synced to their helmet, allowing the team members to talk to one another without the opposing team listening in. Unfortunately, Ken's crewmembers were barely talking to each other in the open, so the advantage of the communicators was questionable.

The three were standing together in a small square room, three other crews with them, making twelve cadets in all.

"In case you haven't figured it out by now, your room number is also your crew designation and will be your ship number once they are assigned to you. Crew 318 breaks down to a First Year crew, ship 18. Next year, your crew designation will start with a 2, and so on," the instructor in gray explained. He pointed to the window against one wall. "In there is your first chance to work as a crew, to develop teamwork that might someday save your lives."

Beyond, Ken could see a spherical room, as if the inside of a ball.

"From here we can see inside, have a sense of up and down, and can feel the effects of gravity. In there, that all disappears. You may become disoriented, lose your sense of direction. You may even panic. That's all normal, but it's up to you and your crewmates to improvise, adapt, and overcome. Only then will you be ready for a spaceship."

"327, 305, you are the first pairing," the instructor declared as he walked toward the hatch.

As explained in the Cadet Handbook, Ken knew the rules were pretty simple. In the center of the room was a ball, hovering in place. Each crew had to pick a goal to defend, and the goals were located uniformly throughout the sphere. In a traditional sense, there were four goals located ninety degrees along the equator of the sphere, like compass points, and one each at the top and bottom or north and south poles.

Conventional strategies had the players selecting a goal exactly opposite their opponents, however, Ken was aware of circumstances where playing to your team's strength or the opponent's weakness suggested otherwise. Having never actually played the game before, he decided they should use the keep it simple principle. Unfortunately, he didn't get a chance to share that strategy.

"In you go," the instructor prompted as he held the hatch open for the six cadets.

"Max, take that goal, Ken you go there," Sandy shouted as she pointed to the goal directly above everyone and then to the wall to their right as they entered.

The goals were nothing more than openings in the wall where the ball would just fit, glancing throws would deflect away. Ken noticed the other team had taken the time to sync up their communications devices and he noted the silence with which they deployed. He also noted that by following Sandy's directions, he was woefully out of position for where they selected their goal.

Before he could reposition, the instructor started the game.

"Go!" he heard announced over his headset and he watched as both his opponent's player and Sandy launched off the walls toward the ball suspended in the center.

While the other team's player was bigger and heavier than Sandy, he was also much stronger and able to launch himself far faster. Ken pushed off as hard as he could to try and make up for the slower-moving Sandy.

"Ken, move!" he heard Sandy shout, just in time for him to contort his body away from her. He was also able to see one of the opponents snag the ball, and then pass it to his crewmate as Sandy bounced off his form.

It was interesting to note that the action of throwing the ball and hitting Sandy caused both to begin tumbling until they impacted with a wall. Both were then able to stabilize themselves once more at that point. Far too late to intercept, Ken decided to try and predict the next pass, launching himself across the void. Unfortunately, Sandy had estimated the same move, and the two of them collided, while the ball sailed past them and into the opponent's hands once again.

"Watch where you're going and pay attention!" Sandy snapped before pushing off him and sending both of them in opposite directions.

With all this going on, Max was doing his best to protect their goal while avoiding being called for goaltending. The rules specifically prohibited any player from completely blocking their goal, like laying over the pocket. They were only allowed to hover nearby, acting as an obstruction or hoping to get a hand or foot in the way of a throw.

With Max's sheer size, he hardly needed to try to get in the way. Their opponents took advantage of that, however, as one faked a throw, causing Max to turn, and then bounced the ball off his back and right into the goal for a score.

"Guys, we need to sync up!" Ken said emphatically as he motioned to his communicator.

"We don't have time for that," Sandy hissed as she retreated to one wall while motioning Ken to the opposite side of the court.

Once again, the ball returned to center court, the only discernable reference point for Ken, having long since lost track of up, down, or sideways.

"Go!" he heard once more as he launched himself.

Ready this time, he actually reached the ball first, but found no one to pass it too, as Sandy sailed past him, landing behind and to his right. With no other option, he shot the ball at Max, using both hands to keep from spinning and increasing his speed until he impacted the wall, knocking the wind out of himself in the process.

Ken was just aware enough to see his pass intercepted at the last moment and then slammed into the goal by a handoff between 305 crewmates. In short order, a hatch opened on the far wall, giving all a target and both teams exited the court, 5-0 the final score.

"You three need to take a break and get your act together! As far as I could see, you had no leader on the court," the instructor chastised the three.

"You, I understand, but I expected more from a Martian and a Venusian," he finished sadly with a shake of his head as he pointed first to Ken and then to his crewmates.

—

"What did he mean by he expected more from you two than me?" Ken asked as the three sat in the Spaceball breakroom.

To their utter embarrassment, they discovered that their game and several others were all viewable from this location. All around them viewports had various matches in play, in real-time and high definition. It all translated to their abject failure on display for any cadet who wished to see.

"Mars has only one-third the gravity of Earth. We are trained from an early age on how to move in low *g's* without flailing about," Max explained casually as he sipped his drink.

"So, we failed to use the one person best suited to the situation at hand," Ken stated. "And why should I care that you are from Venus, more low gravity?" he directed to Sandy.

"Did you even take Xenology in school?" Sandy asked

as she all but railed at Ken.

"It was an elective, and I chose to take more career-focused classes—you know, like survival in space. Somehow, the study of humans who happened to live on other planets didn't rate high on my need-to-know list."

"It's a little more complicated than that," Sandy replied in frustration, then continued on. "Ok, my full name is Sandra-9872, Commander Cytherean is Sandra-4993. We originate from the same genetic pool, but are generations apart. Everyone on Venus is a genetic clone from one of the original female colonists."

"A planet of all women?" Ken asked in confusion.

"Yes. We are an asexual people, and everyone is cloned from the same genetic source material so there is no degradation or dilution of the line. There were twenty-eight original colonists, both men and women, but only twelve survived the crash landing, all women. The mission was planned in secret and it was at a time in Earth's history when fears of total annihilation were rampant. It was admittedly a misguided effort from the beginning, as each colonist was chosen for their genetic and physical purity, both in form and appearance. Everyone on my planet was selected for excellence on something they did on Earth."

"So that's why you are so beautiful—physical perfection?" Ken blurted out.

Everyone paused, as the disclosure seemed to take both of them by surprise. Ken turning bright red and Sandy looking away in embarrassment.

"You were saying..." Max interjected to break the awkwardness of the moment.

"Yes, so since it would be decades before another ship would make planetfall, the scientists developed a cloning process to continue the colonization effort. Each colonist contributed a genetic sample, and those are the roots of the Barbara's, Sandra's, Elizabeth's, Patricia's, and so on. All twelve colonists are equally represented in today's population. I learned it was ten years before the mission was even disclosed to the public on Earth."

"I know my genetics knowledge is weak, but why are you not all characteristically the same, then? From your line, I mean."

"Each clone is gestated for nine months, just like an Earth baby, and then raised by a non-linear parent. My mother was a Patricia. In this environment, we do develop individual personalities, but our genetic propensities endure."

"Which is why you chose Astronavigation, but the Commander is a Psychologist," Ken observed.

"Yet we are both in Galactic Service, similar but different," Sandy finished, completing the thought.

"And the instructor's comment?" Ken asked referring to the comment after their loss.

"Well, Sandra's are notoriously sneaky, devious at times even," she said with a weak smile.

"Good to know," Ken said softly.

"Um, there is one thing," Ken started awkwardly.

"Spill it. Things can't get any more uncomfortable than they already are," she replied.

"Well, on the first day here, I noticed several guys really checking you out, until someone whispered to them. Then they all seemed to lose interest in you," Ken said, his embarrassment evident.

"I can answer that one," Max replied with a smile.

"Please." Sandy waved for him to continue, apparently happy to be rescued from the situation.

"Vesuvians are asexual and all women, as you now know. That doesn't mean they are not social or intimate. What it does mean is their measure of attractiveness is slanted to a particular, less masculine appearance."

Ken pondered the explanation for a moment before a light dawned on his horizon.

"You don't like men," he stated suddenly.

"They kind of disgust me, sorry," Sandy admitted with a shrug.

"And they know that, so they tend to subconsciously dismiss you," Ken went on, more to himself as he began to see how that could help them. "Anything more I should know about *you*, then, Martian?" Ken asked Max sarcastically, turning toward the behemoth.

"I'm with her. Men disgust me, too!"

—

Their break over, the three cadets returned to the staging room, ready to take on their next opponent.

"Let's sync up," Ken proposed as he presented the communicator attached to his left forearm.

"Agreed," Sandy nodded as she presented hers, as well, motioning for Max to join.

Once all three were synced, Ken pulled them aside in the ready room and walked over several simple plays he had worked out based on what he had learned about each of them. This time, he identified their strengths and focused on that.

"Do you really think these are going to work?" Sandy asked as the opposing team entered the room.

Scanning the three men, Ken let a small smile creep across his lips.

"Absolutely."

"321, 327, get ready," the instructor announced as he had each of the crewmembers lined up at the entryway.

Once the hatch opened, all six cadets entered the court with Ken waiting for his opponents to select their goal, and then positioning Max at the opposite side.

Motioning for Sandy to go high, he took a position to one side.

"GO!" the instructor announced.

Suddenly, Max burst forth, his powerful legs jetting him across the open space in plenty of time to snatch the ball first. Turning in place as he flew, he rocketed the ball back to Ken. Max continued to the opposite goal, knocking opponents clear as he did so until he impacted the far wall.

Rather than shooting the ball at the goal from across the court, Ken fired a shot at Sandy, who had slipped near the intended target, her small stature allowing her to easily slide past the player guarding her. Still anchored in place on the wall, Ken was able to quickly rocket the pass to her, where she slipped behind the hovering Max, slamming the ball in place for the first score.

"Yeah!" Max shouted as he fist pumped in place, causing him to turn in time to high-five Sandy as she came by him.

For Round Two, crew 321 had selected a goal ninety degrees from their own in an attempt to prevent a replay of the last round. Ken whispered instructions to his crewmates, positioning Sandy across the opponent's goal while Max took a spot across from their own, and Ken went high.

Once again Max shot across, snatching the ball ahead of their opponents, but this time Sandy had launched for the same point a mere second behind. The coordination allowed Max to pass Sandy the ball by handing it to her and then continuing on to protect their goal while Sandy flew head on at their opponents.

Not to be fooled this time, two of the defenders tried to converge on her small frame, all three colliding just before their goal. Ken however, had repositioned, to allow Sandy to shuffle the ball to him right before contact. With a smile, he slammed the ball home, giving them a 2-0 advantage.

For the next four rounds, Ken passed instructions to his team, setting them up for a 5-1 victory, their only loss coming from an unexpected pass deflection.

—

Undefeated for the rest of the day, the three Cadets found themselves in the cafeteria, their well-earned appetites challenging all that the cooks had prepared.

"We are now one of the top-ranked Spaceball teams this year. I heard one of the instructors say we might get to play the Second Year teams if we keep it up," Sandy said with pride between bites.

"Once we synced up and Ken took over calling the plays, we started working together," Max observed as he glanced between his two crewmates.

"Okay, I admit, maybe I jumped in a little too aggressively," Sandy said with a nod.

"But what changed with you?" she said, directing the question straight at Ken.

"Well, once I took the time to learn about you two, I started to understand what your strengths are. It made me realize that all we had ever talked about were my weaknesses. Focusing on strengths is far more productive, don't you think?"

Ken could see both Sandy and Max thinking about his statement before Max finally spoke. "What *are* your strengths?" he asked openly.

"Astrophysics, like free-floating bodies in space."

"That makes sense," Sandy said with a smile.

"Oh, and I was the starting quarterback for the university football team, called all my own plays," he added before taking a bite of his own.

The revelation caused both Sandy and Max to pause mid-bite before Sandy managed to squeak out a reply.

"Maybe the Academy knew what they were doing all along."

THE END

STAR CADETS

About the Author

CW Lamb started his writing career in Science Fiction, inspired by the greats from the 1950s and '60s. His initial successes encouraged him to branch out into Fantasy and Paranormal tales of adventure and mystery.

To learn more about CW Lamb's writing, visit:
www.cw-lamb.com

THE DAY THE EARTH WAS GRADED

by P. Andrew Floyd

- Message from ???

IT WAS A Tuesday when the first of the Graders arrived. I woke up to the news alert vibrating my phone. It announced, in all caps, the giant interstellar ship parked in orbit above Samara. The second didn't arrive for another hour, which was plenty of time for the internet to explode with Russian-Alien alliance conspiracies. By the end of the day, the Earth was surrounded by twenty hexagonal crafts that must have made our planet look like a soccer ball.

They stayed for two weeks. The two most exciting, scary, and crazy weeks of my life. Of all our lives. No one knew for sure if they departed their ships. Plenty of people claimed to have seen or spoken to a Grader, but nothing verifiable. The ships just sat there in orbit, unmoving, until the day they left. The day they finally sent a message.

The message appeared everywhere. White alien text on a hunter-green background with a vocal track repeating ostensibly what was written over and over again on televisions, radios, and electronic billboards. They even created social media profiles, uploading it to every popular and out-of-style platform you could think of.

There was only one message. But on select social media sites, they also dumped some translation assistance—just enough to confuse the matter further without being truly helpful. Kids' books, an alphabet with corresponding pictures, a dictionary, poetry, and a few videos of a children's program starring alien puppets. (No one knew if the puppets resembled the aliens or if they were the equivalent to humans watching Cookie Monster and Elmo.)

Because the Dump was totally in the alien language, it took nearly two years to translate the message. And it took almost six months beyond that to release it to the public while linguists argued over the validity of the translation as well as what it meant.

In the end, they had no choice but to publish what they had. The message said:

"We have studied humanity and judged it a C minus. As a society and people, it is deemed: fine*."

Apparently, most of the arguing was over the last word, hence the asterisk. Some thought the word 'fine' had too positive a connotation and should have been translated as 'okay', 'alright', or '*just* alright'.

At first, all anyone could talk about was the message itself. Then, people started asking questions. Mostly, "What?" and "Why?"

People formulated all sorts of theories. They argued

over them, in person and especially online. Some thought the grade was far too low, that the technological and social leaps we made in such a short amount of time should have given us a much higher score. Others thought it wasn't low enough. Despite our advances— our greed, oppressions, and ability to let horrible things slide as long as our personal lives weren't affected— should have failed us immediately. And then there were those who were fine with our grade. They felt average was a perfectly respectable thing to be and to strive for. Needless to say, things remained heated for quite a while.

And they stayed that way until we were given something else to be upset about.

A year and a half after the translation went public, the Coalition was announced. A group of twelve people to represent the different theories about the message, and humanity in general, were chosen to somehow confront the Graders. Twelve people made up of nine white men and three white women.

The internet exploded.

Sure, they represented a majority of the theories on the Message, but how could twelve white people, mostly men, represent all of humanity?

A few months of bad press later, the Coalition was reintroduced. Two of the women and two of the men from the original Coalition remained. A white transwoman was added, as well as an Indian man, a Korean-American woman, a Puerto Rican woman, a Native American man, two black men, and a black woman. (I had my own opinions about that 'diversity', but that's what the so-called 'experts' decided was 'representative'.)

The Coalition met officially for the first time on a Thursday. It was all my husband and I talked about on the way to work. After I dropped him off, it was the only topic on the radio. The local shock-jock leaned conservative, and he spent the rest of my drive blaming the C minus on the liberal agenda while his co-host played inappropriate sound effects to go along with it. (If I ever heard another fart noise, it would be too soon.) I was more than happy to get out of my car when I arrived at the Georgia Poverty Law Center, the non-profit I ran to help low-income Georgians.

Guess how many people were answering their phones when I got inside?

I walked past our reception desk and into the center of the mass of cubicles, all with ringing phones.

"Hey! Non-working individuals!" Everyone spun and glared at me for interrupting their gossip. "Yes, *all of you*. It's me, Rachel. Your boss. I know it's an exciting day. Coalition day! Huzzah!" I pumped my fists sarcastically. "But we still have work to do, so—"

"How do you think they're gonna do it? Talk to the Graders, I mean?" Patsy yelled from a nearby cubicle.

I rubbed my eyes with my palms. This was going to be even worse than the day the Graders arrived. "Jesus Christ, we're not gonna get any work done today, are we?"

"Nope," pretty much everyone replied simultaneously.

Patsy added, "Or tomorrow!"

"Okay, fine. Obviously, they're going to resurrect ICQ to contact the Graders. Now, can we just *try* to answer *some* calls?" A few phones stopped ringing. "Thank you. If you need me, I'm going to be doing some *actual* work in my office." I headed toward the rear of the building, playfully batting Patsy on her shoulder as I passed by.

My first client was already waiting on me. I switched to Spanish as I entered by office. "I'm sorry I'm late, Julia.

I guess the Coalition is going to make pretty much everything run behind. It's a really exciting time, huh?"

Julia gave me a blank stare before replying in Spanish. "I am sorry, Miss Wright, but I do not care about the aliens or what they think of us. I just care about my family's safety."

I pulled out a pad and paper and got ready to write. "I'm sorry, I didn't know the severity of the situation. Why don't you let me know what's going on."

"Well, first, I am not here... *legally*."

I nodded and tried to show caring in my voice. It's not that I didn't care, but after doing this job every day for five years, watching people deal with the worst of humanity, it was increasingly difficult to shove down the jaded and bring out the attentive hope. "A lot of our clients are undocumented. Don't worry about that, just let me know your story."

"I came here with my family. I found a job. And then I met a man." I nodded as she spoke. I had heard this story far too many times. "At first, he was so nice and loving. He gave us a place to live and... well, it's not important. It turns out he is not a nice man, and I don't know what to do."

I finished writing a few more things on my pad. Years ago, I would have made eye contact, but the job had made my eyes heavy. I kept them on my writing. "You can't stay with him, but if you leave, he may report you."

"Yes, exactly. If it were just me... but my daughter and my mothe—"

"They're going to speak!" Patsy exclaimed from down the hall by the cubicles.

I couldn't help it; the excitement exploded out of me. "Come on! Let's go check it out!" The look on Julia's face made me realize the inappropriateness, so I cleared my throat and wiped away my smile. "Sorry."

"But, Miss Wright..."

I got up from my chair and walked around my desk. "This will only take a minute, and then we'll get you all taken care of. We deal with people in your exact situation *all* the time. Come on."

I led her out to the cubicles, where we gazed up at the TV hanging from the ceiling in the corner. "Do you need me to translate for you?"

"No, I understand. But, Miss Wright..."

"Okay, good. Look, there they are!"

The news station showed the twelve people standing behind a podium. At the microphone was one of the men from the original Coalition, General Thaddeus Hayes. "Good Morning."

Everyone in the building became quiet. Even the phones stopped ringing.

"I'm General Thaddeus Hayes, and I'm partially responsible for putting together this... Coalition. With me are three people from the Coalition trial run, Dr. Christian Pass, Dr. Karen Pass, and Dr. Suzanne Baker-Grillo." Pretty much the whole world was familiar with those four. Profiles had been done on them by every news station the moment they announced what they were now apparently calling a 'trial run' of the Coalition. The next few days would be the same treatment for the newbies. "Dr. Baker-Grillo will introduce the rest of the team in just a minute, after I explain what this is all about. The rumors are true. We now have the means by which to contact the Graders."

The room exploded into incomprehensible crosstalk. Everyone yammered on about something—except for Julia, who just appeared impatient. I felt the same way. If we were going to find out what was going on, we'd need quiet. I whistled as loud as I could, and everyone's attention snapped back to the General.

"—amongst the Dump. It appears to be a... And we've double checked this translation?" He looked at Dr. Baker-Grillo, who nodded. "A *customer support line*. It came with instructions to build a device that appears to be used for instantaneous communication."

The building was still silent, but I felt the collective gasp. This was big.

"The machine is called an Interocitor, and it connects via a type of network called an Ansible. We've built the machine and performed some initial tests. It appears safe and to do what it claims. We plan to use it to contact the Graders today after some final deliberation on how to approach them. In a matter of hours, we can finally put this grade business behind us."

The room erupted again as Dr. Baker-Grillo began introducing the rest of the Coalition. I started to shush them when Julia tapped my shoulder.

"I'm sorry, Julia," I told her. "It's a crazy day. You know, I bet it's because of people like your ex that the Grade was so low. I'm actually surprised it wasn't lower."

"Excuse me, Miss Wright, but I do not care about any grade." I blinked at her. "My mother and daughter are waiting in the car."

"You can bring them inside, if you want. They'd be safe in here and they could watch the—"

"No, they do not care, either. We just want some help. Please."

I nodded and waved her on. "Follow me." I felt bad about my misstep. Of course she didn't care. I wasn't this distractible when I'd first opened the center. But these days, I'd let a random meme take my mind off reality in order to keep my sanity. At least, that's what I told myself.

I took Julia past a few cubicles where workers and

clients alike were peering over the faux walls to watch the introduction of the new and improved Coalition. When I found the cubicle I was looking for, I tapped on the inside of it.

"John, I need you to call around and see where there's room for Julia and her family."

John didn't take his eyes off the television. "Listen, boss."

I shook my head. "To what?"

"Exactly. Do you hear any phones ringing? All circuits are currently busy. I just tried to make a call out, and it's fast beeps."

"Okay, then drive around and find something."

John glared at me. He did not look happy. "But, I'll miss the profile on Jodi Kwon!"

"It'll be on the radio. Go. Now. The poor family's been waiting in the car. Take care of this and you can have the rest of the day off. I don't think we're gonna be getting much done around here today, anyway."

I turned to Julia and switched back to Spanish. "John will take good care of you and keep you and your family safe. We'll make any other arrangements needed once the phones come back up."

"Thank you, Miss Wright. Thank you very much." Julia took a deep breath then followed John.

As they left, I turned back to the television. Four faces were on the screen. General Thaddeus Hayes, Dr. Karen Pass, Dr. Christian Pass, and Dr. Suzanne Baker-Grillo. Superimposed on the screen were the words, 'The Conservatives'. The screen cut to the married Doctors, Christian and Karen. Christian began, "We don't consider ourselves 'Conservatives'."

Karen continued, "We're more Independents, really."

Christian nodded. "But I guess we side with the

Conservatives on *this* issue."

"Our score should have been much higher." Karen scoffed. "A C minus is bull—*BLEEP*."

Suzanne Baker-Grillo replaced them on the screen. "No doubt, humanity isn't perfect. We still have a lot to work out. But look at all we've accomplished in recent years, both socially and technologically? Just a century ago, we were virtually in the dark ages. I'm not saying we deserve an A plus, but a C minus? Come on!"

General Hayes appeared in her place. As always, he looked perpetually angry. "Who do these aliens think they are, judging us? We, as a people, have gone through a lot to get to where we are today, and these Graders have no right to assign a value to our progress. We intend to find out exactly where they get off giving us such a score and let them know exactly what we think about it."

A bumper asking the stations' viewers to stay tuned for more information on the Coalition flashed on the screen, which led into a commercial for an antidepressant with a screen full of too-small-to-read side effects.

I tore my eyes from the television and plodded to Patsy's desk. She was sitting with an older couple, who looked as if they hadn't showered or changed clothes in a few days. I slapped the side of her cubicle a few times. "Hey, Pats."

She glanced up from her clients. "Yeah, boss?"

"You think the Cons're gonna screw it up?"

She shook her head. "I dunno... Honestly I think the Mods might do a better job of effing it up. I feel like it's normal to have an opposite argument, even if it is bonkers or evil, but it takes a special kinda stupid to try and find a compromise between the two."

"Yeah, you may be right. I think today's gonna be a

bust. Spread the word. Get what you can done, and then we're taking a half-day. Also, anyone who wants to talk about the Graders can meet at the CNN Center for lunch."

Pats smiled and saluted. "Will do, boss!"

"What's this case?" I asked, already knowing the answer from experience.

"Eviction. They can't afford to pay, but their landlord left a lot of things broken and the lease specifically states that he will fix items 'in a timely manner'."

I nodded. "That's vague, but we've worked with worse. Good luck. Phones aren't working, but do what you can. A lot of these cases may not have any movement until tomorrow, unfortunately."

I scanned around a few more cubicles. People were actually working. Then, I heard the station jingle that would most likely end the few minutes of productivity. I swept my eyes to the television and, sure enough, there were four new faces with the caption, 'The Progs', emblazoned in front of them.

Dr. Carla Combs was up first. "Trans people are still murdered every day just for being who they are. We live in a dark and disturbing world and have a long way yet to go."

The camera switched to Dr. Milind Desai. "Look, I agree there are a lot of wonderful things in this world, but the grade was for *humanity as a whole*. There is still genocide and slavery going on as we speak. I just can't believe with the universe as big as it is that our atrocities are considered average. I just can't."

Dr. John Tyson and Dr. Beverly Carson took over the screen. Beverly's leg tapped in an irritated fashion as John spoke. "Our children are being shot. We turn people away for asking for help."

Beverly glared at the camera. "You wanna know why we deserve a lower grade? Look no further than right here. Why do I have to share the camera with him?" She jabbed a thumb toward John.

"Beverly..."

"No, John. It's a serious question. We aren't related or married. We aren't in the same field. Why are we sharing this space? The only thing we have in common is we're Black."

John buried his face in his hands.

Beverly leaned into the camera. "Dr. Combs and Desai got to do theirs solo, so why didn't we? I wonder."

"I agree, but—"

"No, John. No 'buts'. They gave us a platform to tell people what we think, so let's tell them. Who cares about a grade? We know there are issues. So, instead of demanding to speak to the manager, we should: Fix. Our. Problems. You want to know what I think about the grade? Fu—"

The station cut to a bumper and commercial. I stood staring at the screen; trying to process what happened and what it might mean for the Coalition.

"Boss!"

I jumped. "Christ! John! You scared me!"

John grinned. "I noticed."

I scrunched up my brow. "Where's the family I gave you?"

John nodded his head in the general direction of the door. "In the van. Can I have the card? I need gas money."

I rolled my eyes. "Whoever used the van last was supposed to gas it up. Come on, the card's in my office."

"Cool." John hopped after me. "So, I caught the Progs. Dr. Carson really flipped, huh?"

I didn't disagree. I'm sure she had her reasons, but the Coalition was a big deal for the entire world. You'd think she could have some decorum for a few minutes. To say any of that out loud made me uncomfortable, so I went a different route as we entered my office. "John, I expected better from you. You don't know what she has to put up with as a woman, and a woman of color at that. Especially in her field. I'm sure she has to fight for her space all the time."

John swallowed and shuffled his feet back and forth. "Yeah... I guess you're right."

I grabbed the credit card out of my desk and handed it to him. "Remember, we're here to help people, not judge them. Now, go take care of that family."

He grabbed the card, nodded, and sprinted off.

I only felt a little bad for partially agreeing with him.

"The Mods!" It was Patsy again.

I jogged back into the cubicles. Dr. Jodi Kwon was already on the screen. "—are wrong. Some terrible stuff happens on our planet. But so does some really great stuff."

The screen changed to the face of Dr. Ivette Gonzales. "It makes perfect sense to me. It's basically the Hedonic Treadmill. As you succeed in life, your expectations and desires increase, as well. So, as you gain more, your relative happiness remains the same. I don't see why it wouldn't work in this instance. We will always be able to improve, to do better. So no matter how well we do as a society, we would never be able to pass a C minus because perfection is unattainable."

The camera switched to Dr. Daniel Humetewa looking off-camera, his mouth gaped open. "Oh, wow. I like what Ivette just said a whole lot. But to expand on it. I think a C is perfectly respectable. I made Cs in school, and look at me! I got a PhD!"

The camera switched again. Dr. Charles Perkins' eyes darted around whatever room he was in. "Does no one else think this is crazy?"

Silence.

Charles raised an eyebrow at the camera. "Look, I basically agree with Ivette. But apart from that, I really don't care about the grade. This Interocitor thing can communicate over light-years instantaneously! But instead of studying it and adapting it, we use it to challenge a grade?"

More silence.

"Nobody? Okay, whatever. Let's just get this over with." The station bumper replaced his face.

"Wow." Patsy must have snuck up when I was engrossed by the Mods.

I gave her a slight nod. "'Wow' is an understatement. I knew it would be a circus, but I hoped it wouldn't be. And somehow, it's worse."

Patsy's eyes widened above her grin. "But it's *so good!*"

"I know!" I let a quick smile cross my face, then got back to business. "Hey, how's your eviction?"

Patsy shrugged. "No idea. Phones are still busy, but I sent Enrico to talk the landlord into postponing at least until we can talk to a judge."

"Sending some muscle out for a little intimidation?" I waggled my eyebrows. "I like it. Keep up the good work."

I jogged back to my office and sat down at my computer. There was already a Facebook message from my husband: *"Did you see? That was crazy, huh?"*

I laughed to myself and typed back to him. *"I know, right? What about Dr. Carson? I know she has a lot of good points, but this is the freaking Coalition! Show a little decorum!"*

The little animation that indicated he was typing danced along the bottom of the window. *"Totally! Hey, I think they're back on!"*

"Okay, one sec!"

I ran to the office door and peeked out. Pictures of the Coalition were floating by on the screen like some sort of screensaver, but the voice was just an anchor recapping what just happened and speculating what we might hear next, and even when. I slogged back to my desk and slumped into my chair to type. *"Looks like it's going to be punditry for a while."*

"Yeah, looks like. Guess I'll actually have to get some work done!"

I giggled and typed back. *"Yeah, me too, I guess."*

The rest of the morning ended up being uneventful. Whatever the Coalition did during that time, it happened behind closed doors. As predicted, the news mostly ran profiles on all the newbies. I told everyone that Dr. Carson was my favorite, and I did end up liking her a lot, but I actually liked Dr. Gonzales the best. I just couldn't admit that my favorite was one of the Mods. What would my coworkers think?

Work was just as uneventful as the news. The phones cleared up enough for a few calls to get through, but still remained mostly useless. We got what we could done with minimal phones and distracted workers.

When it was time for lunch, I threw my purse over my shoulder, strode out into the cubicles, stuck two fingers in my mouth, and whistled. "Alright, we did the best we could, all things considered, but I'm calling it until tomorrow. Do whatever you need to do to wrap things up, and then you're free. If you wanna continue gabbing about the Graders, I'm going to the CNN Center for some BurgerFi. Rachel out!" I threw up a peace sign with my right hand and walked toward the front door through ironic clapping.

I was about to exit when I noticed Julia and, presumably, her mother and daughter, sitting on the bench in the makeshift waiting area. I stopped in my tracks. "What are you doing here?"

Julia's mother raised an eyebrow.

Oh, right. How could I forget? I switched to Spanish. "I'm sorry, what I meant to say was... What are you doing here?"

Julia shook her head. "I do not know, Miss Wright. We drove around in the van for hours then ended up back here."

What the hell? John had one job! "I am so sorry, Julia. My colleague was supposed to take you to a safe house—"

"Which I did!" John slid in from somewhere. "Several, in fact. And they were all full or not opening their very locked doors. I came back to regroup and see if I had any better luck with land lines. Maybe call some places in DeKalb."

Crap. This was turning into a helluva day to need a safe house. "Okay, make them comfortable here. Set them up to watch the Coalition, or something, and then do what you can."

John nodded as I headed out the door. I felt terrible for Julia and her family, but what was I supposed to do on today of all days? I couldn't force the world to start back up again. Hell, I don't think I could have done it back when I thought I could do anything. Before I found out how wrong I was. John was competent and could handle it, so I hopped in my car and headed to lunch.

—

The CNN Center was the perfect place for Coalition-starved coworkers to yak about the only thing on their mind. There were plenty of restaurants, and a giant TV was playing the news in the shared eating area.

As I chowed down on my burger, Patsy rambled, not

noticing that she'd dropped mustard on her floral top. "I can't believe how much I like the Passes. I feel terrible about it, but they don't come off as your normal Cons."

Theresa held a taco halfway up from her plate. "I know! They're so sweet together!"

It was only us three girls. Everyone else took the half-day as a reason to head home early. I didn't blame them, but my husband couldn't get off, so it was nice to have people to experience this with. I finished chewing some burger and added, "Am I the only one who thinks Dr. Humetewa looks high?"

Both women guffawed.

Theresa slapped the table. "No! I was thinking the same thing!"

Patsy had opened her mouth to add something when the entire Center erupted in a wave of shushes.

All three of us whipped our eyes to the giant screen.

"It seems that we are ahead of schedule," General Hayes announced. "We will begin contact in five minutes. A feed will be fed on a thirty-second delay to all news outlets. That is all."

I have no idea what came on the screen next, as the room became utter chaos. People stood and tried to use their cell phones. Some ran for the exits. Others stayed put but spoke louder to compete with the noise.

I pulled out my own phone and used the center's free Wi-Fi to message my husband. *"Are you watching this?"*

A second later he responded with, *"!!!!"*

"It sucks we can't watch this together!"

"You're telling me! Don't worry, though. I set the DVR for the whole day. We can watch it together on repeat."

I giggled and glanced up at my coworkers. They were both on their phones, too. A feedback screech pulled my gaze to the TV.

It was starting.

The Coalition all sat together across from a machine. The camera panned to show it off. It had a wide base with colorful buttons and dials and a monitor shaped like an upside-down triangle sitting atop a thin neck rising from the base. A wave-shaped rainbow oscillated on the screen as it made a noise that sounded very similar to a phone ringing. By the third ring, everyone in the center was silent and staring at the television.

The screen split. A camera panned across each face on the Coalition in the left pane. And the right showed a close-up of the upside-down triangle monitor.

The ringing stopped. It was replaced by what sounded like the alien language from the Message and the Dump. On the left pane, all eyes were on the linguist of the group, Dr. Humetewa.

He stared at the ground and listened intently. And then, he cackled.

Theresa leaned in and whispered to me, "Yup, definitely high."

On the screen, the General furrowed his brow and groused at Daniel. "Care to share what you find so funny, Dr. Humetewa?"

The linguist stomped a foot and covered his mouth. "I'm sorry, it's just... the translation... We called the support line, and it's saying that our call is important to them and will be answered in the order in which it was received. We're on hold! Aliens have us on hold!" After almost successfully calming down, Dr Humetewa lost it again and almost fell out of his chair.

Some strange music played on the Interocitor as the rainbow waveform danced around the screen. A quick glance to the Coalition revealed they were feeling very awkward just sitting there waiting.

Eventually, the rainbow disappeared and was replaced by a light-blue background. I almost dropped my phone in excitement. The moment was finally here. We were going to see the Graders!

Something rose from the bottom of the screen. It appeared to be fur. The Graders had fur! Dark-green, matted fur and three eyes. Three googly eyes.

Wait, what?

Patsy covered her mouth. "Oh my god, they *do* look like the puppets."

I shook my head. "No, Patsy. I think those *are* the puppets."

Two baggy creatures danced on screen, their mouths flopping up and down. "Blarg! Blarg! Blarg! Blarg! Blarg! Blarg!"

Theresa gave me a confused glance. "What's going on? Is that the same language from the Message?"

I shook my head. I really couldn't tell. On the left side of the screen, everyone was waiting on Dr. Humetewa to translate. He shrugged. "It's gibberish. They're just repeating, 'Blarg'."

The puppets doubled over, and laughter erupted from the Interocitor. General Hayes stood. "What is the meaning of this? We demand answers!"

And then it happened for real. We got our first look at actual, real-life aliens! They only had two eyes and were not, in fact, covered in fur. They did, however, have tall, squat, yellowish beaks and beautifully deep-colored feathers. There were two of them. The one on the left had plumage covered in a green gradient, and the one on the right had blue and pink feathers. The one on the right also wore a t-shirt with what appeared to be English letters on it, but I couldn't make them out.

Their beaks didn't have much movement apart from up and down, but the way they were raised on their faces, lifted up to their squinted eyes, it looked like they were smiling. The one on the left spoke first. "What's up,

Earth folk?"

The entire Coalition gaped at the perfect English.

"My name's Qwee~'roo and this is my bud, Le'caw."

No one responded. After a moment, Qwee~'roo waved a clawed hand back and forth across the Interocitor. "Hello? Earth to humans? Well, not Earth, I guess. Ha!"

General Hayes balled his hands into fists, not at all hiding his grumpiness. "What is the meaning of this?"

The two aliens glanced at each other then back toward the screen. Qwee~'roo spoke again. "What do you mean?"

The General's face reddened, veins popping out of his neck. "We pass your test and make contact, and you greet us with gibberish-speaking puppets!"

The aliens guffawed. Le'caw actually fell off the side of the screen. Qwee~'roo shrugged as he stopped laughing. "We were just having a bit of fun."

Hayes fumed. "*Fun?*"

Dr. Karen Pass stood and placed a calming hand on the General. "I think what the General is trying to say is, we were hoping you could tell us more about the grade you gave us."

The blue and purple Le'caw climbed back on-screen, still laughing. It looked like his (Her? Its?) shirt said 'BTS' and had a group of Asian men pictured on it. That couldn't be right...

Qwee~'roo spoke again. "Hmmm... nah."

Karen blinked. "Excuse me, did you just say... *nah*?"

"Yah."

The General tightened his fists and opened his mouth to start yelling, but Karen patted his shoulder again. Her eyebrows were pinched in anger herself, but she did a very good job at not letting it sound in her voice. "Why leave us a means to contact you if you won't give us any more information? We worked for over a year to build the Interocitor, and we put together a diverse panel to—"

Both aliens cackled and almost fell over again.

Karen composed herself. "I'm sorry, but I don't see what's so funny."

Qwee~'roo spoke through laughter, "Diverse! You said... you said your group was diverse!"

This time, the General did not hold back. "This is ridiculous! If you knew anything about Earth culture, you'd see our panel for what it is. A diverse sampling of our world."

The green alien finally stopped laughing. "Okay, how many of you are from America?"

No one raised their hands, they just glanced to each other in confusion, as if not sure how to answer. The General pointed at Jodi Kown. "Dr. Kwon is South Korean, if I'm not mistaken."

Jodi glared at Thaddeus. "Um, sir... I was born in Scranton..."

The General choked. The blue and pink alien composed itself and gave the panel one of those weird beak-grins. "Are any of you from outside the United States?"

Milind Desai slowly raised his hand.

"Yes, of course, Dr. Desai isn't from the U.S. He's from..." Hayes shifted his gaze to Milind. "What part of India are you from, again?"

Milind raised an eyebrow. "Toronto, Canada."

The General was at a loss for words again, so Karen tried to regain control of the panel. "You're absolutely right, our panel only represents our continent, but the nation we all come from is quite diverse itself, and—"

Qwee~'roo held up a claw. "And how many of you are Christian?"

After a moment of stunned silence, everyone except Milind Desai and Beverly Carson raised their hands.

The General smiled. "See, we have a Hindu and..." He gestured to Dr. Carson. "Muslim?"

Dr. Carson's eyes widened and she stared daggers at Hayes. "Now, why on Earth would you assume that, I wonder? I happen to be an atheist."

Dr. Desai raised his hand. "Me too..."

Daniel Humetawa stood up and glanced around at his colleagues. "I'm sorry... This is all very interesting in a trivial sort of way, but... am I the only one interested in how and why these aliens speak perfect English?"

I gave the CNN Center a quick glance. Everyone was glued to the screen. I wondered if they were as confused by these creatures as I was.

The green alien gave a shrug. "Well, the hardcore fans learn the native language so they don't have to read subs. Le'caw, here, is heavy into K-Pop."

Le'caw waved at the screen. "By the way, Dr. Kwon, I was very excited when you were announced as part of the Coalition." She bowed. "Anyoung haseyo. Juhneun Le'caw yiehyo."

Dr. Kwon's eyes darted back and forth. "I, um... I don't speak Korean."

Beverly Carson leaned over and covered her mouth. "Holy crap, even the aliens are racist."

General Hayes stomped closer to the Interocitor. "What is going on here? Is this some kind of *joke*?"

The aliens glanced at each other, then swiveled back to the camera and nodded. "Yes. Yes, it is."

The General stumbled backward. "What?"

I glanced down at my phone, there were too many notifications to see if any were important. Whatever they were could wait. My eyes darted back up to the screen.

Le'caw's beak bobbed a few times. "Congrats! You actually figured it out! You guys are all part of our prank show!"

Hayes shook his head. "No, no, no. Do you know how much money we spent?"

Daniel Humetawa cocked his head. "Wait, so you're not actually aliens? That doesn't make any sense."

Qwee~'roo shook his head. "Oh, no. We're from a very far away planet. We just really like pranks."

Dr. Carson actually laughed. "So, you came all this way to prank us? Did the grade actually even mean anything?"

Le'caw grinned. "Nope! We show up to random planets and archive all of your entertainment, then leave a random message and go home. The stuff we pirate, plus the running feed of your reactions, provide years of entertainment! Earth has been one of my favorite shows in a *long* time!"

The green alien nodded. "Oh, definitely. Your guys' reactions have been *choice*."

The General's face reddened, his knees locked, and he got incredibly still. I was afraid he was going to pass out. "So, the grade... meant *nothing*? It wasn't real?"

The aliens responded, but I didn't hear what they said. Hayes saying, 'The grade meant nothing', played in my head over and over. It was all fake. The past four years had been wasted. *Four years*!

I glanced back down at my phone and unlocked it. With a swipe, I scrolled through endless notifications. Like the grade, they meant nothing. I tapped 'close all' and opened up Facebook Messenger. The phone lines would be unusable for some time, but Wi-Fi should still be fine. I tapped out a message to my husband and left the table.

Patsy waved at me. "Hey, Rache! Where you going?"

"I'm opening the office back up. You don't have to come back in if you don't want to, but our work's more important than a dumb prank."

I swiped through my contacts until I found John and initiated a voice call to him. A moment later he picked up.

"Oh my God, Rachel! Are you watching this?"

"Not anymore. Are you still with Julia and her family?"

"Oh, yeah. We're not gonna be able to move forward on them today. Maybe not even tomorrow."

"Oh, we will. They're going to stay with me." It's what the me who started the center would have done years ago, and it's what I should have done that morning.

"What? You serious?"

"Already messaged my husband. Let them know I'm on my way. I'll get them settled in at my place, then we'll get back to work."

"You're opening back up? You do realize that you're not going to be able to get anything done, right?"

"Watch me."

I hung up the phone and walked out of the CNN Center. Doctor Carson was right. It was time to stop worrying about why we got a fake grade and should start acting like we deserved better.

THE END

THE DAY THE EARTH WAS GRADED

About the Author

P. Andrew Floyd fell in love with science fiction the first time he saw a Ferengi try to use an energy whip on Commander Riker. He's been immersed in it ever since and decided it was about frakking time he wrote some of his own. He lives on *Sqee'kra* in Knoxville, Tennessee, with his wife, two children, dog, and demon-possessed cat. When not translating stories from his brain to the page, he loves making costumes and going to cons with his family. Though, to be fair, he loves doing that even when he is writing and can often be spotted in convention lines typing away on his phone.

To learn more about P. Andrew Floyd's writing, visit:
pandrewfloyd.wordpress.com

RESERVATION EARTH

by David Alan Jones

YEAR: **2021**

LOCATION: **Alpha Centauri A/Planet: Belzzrexx**

CLIFTON RAMSEY, ACE pilot, expert laser marksman, and chief exo-planetary diplomat for the Trans-Solar Union of Earth, met the alien's steely gaze without blinking. Ramsey's set his jaw as he poured on the strength, his impressive muscles bunching under his powder-blue skin suit. His six-armed opponent, a native Belzzrexx whom Ramsey called Bob, hissed through one of its twin voice boxes and groaned a low, sorrowful hum through the other.

"Your arm is shaking, Bob." Ramsey forced his opponent's double-jointed wrist another centimeter closer to the table to emphasize his words as the translator unit sewn into his collar faithfully recast the taunt into a lilting clutch of warbles and hoots Bob could understand.

No fewer than thirty of Bob's people had gathered in the station's bar to cheer him on. They alternately hooted and whistled encouragement and displeasure.

Most had money on Bob to win against the puny, two-armed man from Earth.

"Burn in the heart of your yellow star, Ramsey," Bob sang using his first voice, with all the gusto he could muster, while his second continued to moan. Owing to the belzzar's curious physiology—possessing the equivalent of one and a half brains stuffed into their oblong skulls—every individual exhibited what human psychiatrists would consider dual personalities. Though rarely in conflict, the two sometimes differed in their opinions of a situation. Right now, it sounded like Bob's alter ego knew they stood no chance against Ramsey's strong right arm.

Ramsey grinned, ending the match with a decisive shove that sent Bob's middle right hand inexorably downward. The gathered aliens lifted their misshapen heads to the bar's ceiling and wailed in forty different voices.

Bob slapped two hairy forearms on the table and jiggled the bulbous, gray cheek pads encircling his face to produce a sound like sail canvas rippling under a steady breeze—a sign of both surprise and chagrin. "Incredible, Ramsey."

"I do try." Ramsey hid his quivering arm under the table, working his fingers to encourage blood flow. That last push had turned it into a quivering mass of gelatin.

"I suppose the next round is on me?" Bob spread two sets of arms in a human gesture he had picked up from his time aboard Earth-crewed ships. Though humans and belzzar had known one another a mere eight months, mostly owing to Ramsey's ability to smooth their first contact, the aliens seemed taken with human customs and culture.

A dual-voiced shriek brought the bar to a standstill. A belzzar roughly the size of a long-haul space freighter shoved all six of its hands, even the inarticulate lower set meant for disemboweling prey, under Ramsey's table and hurled it across the bar. Patrons, human and belzzar alike, were forced to dive out of the way lest they get bowled over.

Ramsey's collar translator, incapable of keeping up with the enraged alien's ranting, reverted to one of its original language kernels—a basic model Ramsey and his team of diplomats had used during initial contact. It proved more than adequate to the task.

"You rob me! I lose credits. All your fault!" The giant's voices sang in perfect melody.

No disagreement there.

Without warning, the belzzar's middle right hand flashed toward a pistol strapped to its hip, a simple revolver with a bone handle. By mutual agreement, the aliens weren't allowed to bring loaded weapons aboard a Union ship. Apparently, this brute hadn't received that telegram.

Ramsey dove from his chair, careful to angle himself away from Bob and as many bystanders as possible. No sooner had he moved than the belzzar's gun went off with a deafening boom. A hole appeared on the bar's far wall. Thankfully, the fool had shot toward the adjoining corridor instead of the bar's exterior-facing windows with their exquisite view of Belzzrexx Prime.

Humans and belzzars screamed and scuttled out of the way, some running for the exits, others ducking behind tables or even the bar. Taking a stray bullet might cost a life, but getting sucked into the frigid embrace of vacuum meant near instant death for either species.

Cold fury settled over Ramsey as he rolled to his feet. What sort of ill-bred sociopath valued credits more than sentient life?

With reflexes like a jungle cat, Ramsey drew his T-11

laser pistol even before he had fully spun to meet his attacker. He leveled it on the belzzar's abdomen, center mass, and squeezed the trigger. A beam of coherent blue light punched through the alien's chest and buried itself in the space between the bar and the main exit with a familiar hiss. The monster crumpled to the floor in a heap.

A smell of ozone and fried hair filled the room as the moment stretched out in silence. The aliens and humans looked at one another, no one quite sure what to say or do. Ramsey holstered his pistol, though he kept his hand near it in case more violence broke out.

At last, one of the senior belzzar stepped forward, a grizzled specimen with his silver beard woven with many braids to match his waist-length hair. Bob sank to one knee, all six arms spread wide at the elder's approach. Ramsey remained standing, his ample jaw set, ready for whatever argument the old chieftain planned to launch.

"It is unfortunate Felsess attacked you, honored peacemaker. You have our sincerest apologies. Felsess was a fool, and like all fools he hastened his own demise." The elder stuck out his left upper hand, a sign of peace and fidelity.

"I'm sorry I had to do that." Ramsey relaxed and gripped the alien's hairy paw without shaking for the customary six count.

"You are triple fast," Bob said, regaining some of his composure. "I've never seen a faster gun."

"Wish it wasn't necessary." Ramsey shook his head at the compliment.

"Such is the way of the universe," the elder said. "A wise warrior seeks peace but is ever ready for battle."

The bar's door slid open to admit a pair of corpsmen pushing an anti-grav gurney. With the assistance of three belzzar, they muscled Felsess's body onto it and hustled it away.

Lieutenant Commander Mersen, the ship's second in command, sidled past them on his way inside, his eyes wide. He whistled through his teeth as he approached Ramsey.

"Are you leaving us with an intergalactic incident on our hands?" Mersen's tone remained mild though his gaze roved to the aliens clustered about the bar as if he expected trouble.

"No incident," Bob hooted with the confidence of both voices. "One of my brothers thought he could clear his gambling debt with a gun—Ramsey did it with a laser."

"Quite." Mersen wrinkled his nose at the stench.

"Did you say 'leaving', Commander?" Ramsey asked.

"Yes, I did, *Captain*. Orders just arrived from the Union. You've been stop-lossed, and recommissioned at your old Union rank. There's been an incident back at Earth. You're to report there immediately. Hold up your watch."

Stunned, Ramsey slowly drew back his sleeve to reveal his computer communicator watch, or CCW, the standard issue technological wonder carried by all humans on the Union's payroll, military and civilian. Mersen flipped a tiny dial on his own CCW and a new message appeared on Ramsey's screen: several pages of orders printed in bright orange with the Union's emblem, a circle to represent a star with nine points of light stemming from its center, printed at the top.

"What sort of incident rates a re-commission and a trip home?" Ramsey dropped his arm by his side. He would read the orders in earnest later.

Lieutenant Commander Mersen glanced at Bob and the chieftain as if hesitant to speak, but finally nodded and shifted his gaze back to Ramsey. "Aliens dropped out of the Planck Divide two days ago with an armada of more than a dozen battle cruisers. They say Earth belongs to them, they made a deal for it thousands of years ago, and they've come to collect."

—

LOCATION: Europa Territory/Sol System

Ramsey's ship, which he had named *Silver Sparrow*, burst from the Planck Divide, the medium of unreal space that made faster than light travel possible, with a flare of green coronal energy. Although calculating one's exit point from the Planck Divide proved an inexact science on the whole, Ramsey had long ago mastered what he could of the technique. His calculations placed *Silver Sparrow* less than twenty thousand kilometers from the space station, Bujold, in orbit of Jupiter's moon Europa.

A new message alarm sounded the instant Ramsey arrived. He toggled the playback switch and worked the decryption dial on his computer board until a deep voice resonated through the cockpit.

"Captain Clifton Ramsey, this is Admiral Leeds, flag commander of battle group Tiberius, speaking to you via recorded message. Although your previous orders instructed you to report to Bujold station, matters in the Sol System have worsened considerably. Your expertise is needed at Earth posthaste. Rendezvous with the TSU *Unsullied* immediately to receive a critical briefing and meet your assigned diplomatic partner."

The message paused for five seconds before repeating. Ramsey, his brow knitted, switched it off.

Partner? Never in sixteen years of service as an exo-diplomat had the Union saddled him with a sidekick. Of course, the Sol system had never faced this sort of threat before. Perhaps the governing council wanted one of their green diplomatic corps officers to learn from a proven expert. Magnanimous to a fault, Ramsey considered it a fine idea. He would do the same in their place. Considering how seldom he returned to Earth space these days, it might be years before they got this chance again. But the kid had better stay quiet and melt into the background or there would be trouble. This mission could mean devastating losses for the human race if things got hairy.

Earth simply wasn't prepared for a fight.

Though humanity had begun plumbing the stars forty-five years ago after the discovery of the Planck Divide in 1976, infrastructural and resource limitations had precluded building a large standing space navy. With a mere six battleships and perhaps a dozen lightly armed frigates at their disposal, they possessed little by way of defense. The war hawks in the Union's parliament were probably crowing over their past demands for a heavy military buildup, not that it would make a bit of difference at this point.

Now was the time for diplomacy, and that was Ramsey's department. He just hoped whatever effete academician they saddled him with would stay out of his way and let him do his job.

———

LOCATION: Earth Orbit/Sol System

Ramsey toggled three switches in precise order to trigger his ship's automatic docking sequence with the TSU *Unsullied.* He preferred performing these sorts of tasks by hand, but the Navy insisted all ships couple by computer. Foolish. If they weren't careful, humanity would one day find themselves bereft of all the skills that made a man useful.

A thrum quivered through *Silver Sparrow*, indicating a successful mating of the two ships. Ramsey undogged the safety latches on the port side hatch and spun the stopcock to equalize the pressure between his side and the other. Air hissed as the door swung lazily open to reveal a short, paunchy man dressed in an admiral's uniform standing next to one of the most beautiful women Ramsey had ever seen.

He should know, he had seen her before.

"Captain Ramsey." Admiral Leeds extended a hand, which Ramsey shook with all the attention of an automaton. "I believe you already know Colonel Gabrielle McGovern?"

"Colonel, is it?" Ramsey tried to act natural as he shook Gabrielle's hand, though he couldn't suppress the torrent of old memories threatening to overwhelm his senses.

"Some of us work to get promoted, Clifton." Gabrielle's voice sounded as cool and alluring as ever. Even dressed in a service uniform—black coat, starched white shirt, and knee-length skirt—her athletic figure showed through to good effect.

Ramsey grinned, resolutely keeping his eyes on his ex-fiancée's face. It had been three years, two months, and four days since they had broken off their engagement—since she had chosen her career over him—and though he had tried to put her out of his mind by throwing himself into his work, not a week went by when he didn't think of Gabrielle.

"How long has it been?" he asked with what he consider perfect nonchalance.

Her lips curled. "Not so long you can fool me, Clifton."

Ramsey hoped his return smile hid the sudden flush of guilt and agreement coursing through his veins. She did know him—she knew he still had it bad for her—and she was enjoying the hell out of it.

Women, you couldn't live with them, and you couldn't shoot them with your T-11.

Admiral Leeds, his gaze flitting between them, looked like a man becoming suddenly aware of a game he hadn't meant to join. He cleared his throat and placed a hand on Ramsey's back to lead him onto the *Unsullied*.

"I'm afraid time is short," he said, guiding Ramsey along the corridor. "Colonel McGovern is here to brief you. She has clocked more hours with the aliens than any other human."

They entered an austere, windowless meeting room furnished with a small table and five chairs. Ramsey made to pull one of the chairs for Gabrielle, but she pretended not to notice and took a seat across from him and Admiral Leeds. She withdrew a manila folder from a locked satchel she carried and opened it on the desk.

The first document inside, marked TOP SECRET//SPECIAL HANDLING//ORIGINATOR CONTROLLED, showed a high-definition image of an insect-like alien on military-grade film. Wasp-waisted and sporting six limbs, two of which it used to stand upright, the creature looked like a cross between a bumble bee and a hornet. Its exoskeleton was mostly black, but contrasted by symmetrical patterns of bright yellow that ranged over every part of its body. Though it wore clothes, they appeared more utilitarian than designed for modesty. A silver belt covered in pockets hung low over its hips. A second one, strapped diagonally across its thorax, passed under its lower set of arms. Neither accessory obstructed the creature's doubled, irregularly sectioned wings.

"They call themselves the Pluhron." Gabrielle stabbed a manicured nail at the picture. "That one is named High Armored Attack Wing Commander Mezzrel."

"A handsome fellow," Ramsey quipped.

"She is not a fellow. In fact, so far as we can tell from the few interactions our people have had with the Pluhron, they are all female."

Ramsey sat up straight in his seat. "Is that possible? How do they procreate?"

Gabrielle tilted her head to one side. "Not exactly the most pressing question on our agenda at the moment. They have twelve battle ships orbiting Earth. I doubt making babies is a problem."

"Point." Ramsey dipped his chin to acknowledge her logic.

"That is partly why we've asked Colonel McGovern to accompany you on this mission." Admiral Leeds tossed a hand Gabrielle's way. "She knows the enemy."

"You're the sidekick?" Ramsey winced the instant the words left his mouth.

Gabrielle narrowed her eyes. "I am humanity's leading expert on the Pluhron. The only reason they haven't begun sending drop ships to begin clearing the surface is because of my negotiations with them. If either of us is a sidekick, Clifton, it's you."

"At ease." Admiral Leeds waved a hand in the air like a mother admonishing bickering children. "You both bring unique skill sets to this situation. That's why the Union teamed you up. Show a little maturity and remember what's at stake here."

"Yes, sir," Ramsey and Gabrielle said in unison.

Looking no more contrite than before, Gabrielle flipped to the next page in her dossier. This one bore a block of tightly spaced text, the sort Ramsey had seen in a thousand military briefs.

"From what we've gathered, the Pluhron are extremely long-lived beings. Commander Mezzrel claims to be more than three thousand years old, and that she is middle-aged for their species. I've confirmed this with her on three separate occasions, to the point she became testy with me the last time I asked. Information we've gathered from allies likewise attests to the Pluhrons' longevity, and their rather peculiar mating cycle."

Ramsey lifted an eyebrow. "Peculiar how?"

"The exact details are sketchy, but if intelligence reports we've received are correct, the Pluhron mate in species-wide cycles of about two to three hundred years. During mating and child rearing, the adults revert to a far less sentient state to raise their offspring."

"You mean they grow stupid when their children are born?" Ramsey turned his gaze from Gabrielle to the admiral and back again. "What sort of evolutionary adaptation is that?"

"An effective one, it would seem." Gabrielle turned to the next image in the dossier. It showed what looked to Ramsey like a twelve-by-twelve-foot blue honeycomb. "We've received conflicting reports from several of our second-party friends, so this next bit might contain errors, but they claim only Pluhron females possess a true sense of self. The males are perhaps on par with a baboon or wild gorilla."

"They're studs?"

Gabrielle rolled her eyes. "I prefer the term sires. They have far shorter lifespans than the females, just a century or two."

"Enough to help defend the offspring."

Gabrielle nodded. "I imagine their wild period is key

to defending their nests, but as their children age toward adulthood, the parents—at least the females—grow more intelligent with their brood. Once they're all self-aware, they become peers."

"That might make sense on a planet where other creatures are long-lived." Ramsey tapped his ample chin in thought.

"And that lifespan is integral to the Pluhrons' claim on Earth. Mezzrel insists representatives of her race negotiated the fair purchase of Earth from a female shaman named Lowk about twelve thousand years ago. According to her, that was during her grandmother's lifetime."

Ramsey sat back with a huff, his mind whirling. "You're saying these aliens—"

"The Pluhron."

"These Pluhron perpetrated a Louisiana Purchase for the entire planet with some primitives long before humans could even write? Let me guess, they gave them a few beaded necklaces and some blankets in exchange?"

Gabrielle shook her head. "No, they didn't trade for baubles. If we're to believe Mezzrel, her people gave us agriculture."

—

LOCATION: **Earth Orbit/Sol System**

"I'm glad to see you've kept the old girl in top condition." Gabrielle, sitting in *Silver Sparrow*'s copilot's chair, worked a dial to adjust their vector toward the Pluhron flagship. She moved with aplomb, having mastered the console back when they were dating.

Unwilling to show how much her presence pleased him, Ramsey avoided looking into her green eyes. "She's a good ship, always there for me."

Silence fell between them, and Ramsey found himself biting the inside of his cheek. Stupid. He hadn't meant to reference their breakup, not intentionally. He had thought himself healed from that pain, but some deep-seated part of him still felt the sting of it.

For her part, Gabrielle busied herself with the microphone dangling from the computer board. She twisted its dial to adjust the *Sparrow*'s communications antenna. Once she had it oscillating in time with the Pluhrons' main frequency, she held the bulbous end to her red lips.

Ramsey swallowed.

"Calling Pluhron spacecraft, this is Colonel Gabrielle McGovern. My partner and I are here to rendezvous for our arranged meeting with High Armored Attack Wing Commander Mezzrel."

A low, buzzing voice issued from the communications console. It sounded to Ramsey like a cross between a wad of paper stuck in a fan and kazoo. Gabrielle flipped a couple of switches on her control board to convert the speaker's words into English.

"—offer you a pleasant negotiation with all due safety. Follow the light displays to pilot your craft into hanger bay gamma."

"From everything we've observed, all the smaller ships follow this one by rote," Gabrielle said after switching off her microphone. "We believe they're slaved to follow it through a radio signal tether, which acts like a hive mind."

A port slid open on the side of the beetle-shaped Pluhron ship, its entrance outlined in green light. Ramsey piloted *Silver Sparrow* inside and landed amongst a crowd of sleek black ships lined up in perfect order inside a bay that easily contained a hundred thousand square feet of space. Even the Trans-Solar Union's largest space stations couldn't hope to match it for sheer scale.

"Remember what I said in the briefing, the Pluhrons have become increasingly antsy every time we meet." Gabrielle stabilized the ships' pressures as she spoke. "Don't be surprised if they get testy with us. I swear, it's as if they're on a timetable and the end is drawing near."

"I'll keep a level head."

Ramsey got his first glimpse of the Pluhrons as he and Gabrielle waited for the *Sparrow*'s rear exit to open. Six of them, captured by the ship's external cameras, stood as a greeting party, their multi-faceted black eyes staring up expectantly.

"Be ready," Gabrielle said. "It's loud."

That was the understatement of the decade. During their briefing, she had warned Ramsey that the wasp-like aliens used their wings for communication, but nothing could have prepared him for the infernal buzzing that met his ears as the *Sparrow*'s rear exit ramp descended. Pluhrons shot overhead in every direction, some flitting up to the bay's high roof, others clinging to handholds built into the walls. It was like walking into the galaxy's largest beehive. And it wasn't simply buzzing that filled the space; the aliens supplemented that sound with a sort of squeaking tone produced by rubbing portions of their exoskeletons together.

One of the Pluhrons, taller than her companions, stepped forward to flutter her wings while simultaneously gyrating four of her limbs, producing a shrill stridulation.

"Greetings, Colonel McGovern and Captain Ramsey. Welcome aboard the *Dominance*." Ramsey's collar interpreter dutifully translated the alien's speech, though he struggled to hear it over the din.

"Hello again, High Commander Mezzrel." Gabrielle bowed low and Ramsey followed her example. "Could we speak elsewhere? Perhaps in the conference room we shared last time I was aboard? The sound here is distracting"

Mezzrel fluttered her wings for several seconds, a motion Ramsey's translator didn't interpret, but one he interpreted as agitation. At last, she gestured toward a round portal at one end of the bay. "Very well."

Mezzrel ushered them into a narrow, dimly lit corridor. It felt blissfully quiet after the bay, though Ramsey could hear Pluhron squeaks and buzzes echoing from somewhere in the distance. Muted red lights painted the hall in sinister tones. Ramsey chided himself for thinking that way. Alien meant alien. He knew better than to interpret aesthetic choices from a xenophobic perspective, but he couldn't seem to help himself. The shrill noises the Pluhrons made set him on edge.

Mezzrel guided them to a closed door. She brushed one of her wings across a black rectangle set into the wall next to it and it slid open. The room beyond contained no table, but it boasted a dozen large objects Ramsey at first mistook for high desks. He realized his mistake when Mezzrel and three of her companions each squeezed into one of the contraptions. Structured to accommodate the Pluhrons' many legs with padded shelves set at varying positions and open backrests designed for unobstructed wing movement, the aliens' chairs fit them perfectly. A pair of much smaller, human-style chairs stood at the center of the room.

Ramsey eyed the three Pluhrons who had remained standing, warning klaxons going off in his head.

"Stop staring," Gabrielle whispered as she brushed past him to sit.

"Commander?" Ramsey dragged his gaze away from

the Pluhrons by the door to address Mezzrel.

"Yes?"

"Are there many robots like these on your crew?"

Mezzrel's wings buzzed. Was that a sign of surprise or agitation? Either way, Ramsey felt certain he had caught the Pluhron leader off-guard.

"Robots?" Gabrielle leaned forward to stare at the Pluhrons in question.

"The number of our automatons is no concern of yours," Mezzrel said.

"Of course." Ramsey took the seat next to Gabrielle. "It was idle curiosity. I withdraw the question."

"Again you come to speak with us, Colonel McGovern," Mezzrel said. "May we assume your people will soon abandon our property?"

Ramsey bristled at the suggestion, but kept his mouth shut. He had agreed to let Gabrielle start the negotiation.

"I'm afraid our answer is still no, High Commander." Gabrielle pinned Mezzrel with an unflinching gaze. "We will not abandon our ancestral home simply because your people negotiated an unfair treaty with an ancient, unknown human."

One of Mezzrel's companions held up her center right arm. "Our agreement with the human known as Lowk is legally binding under our laws. You have viewed our recorded proof, yes?"

In the first days after the Pluhrons' arrival, they had provided the Union with several magnetic chips loaded with recordings of ancient humans working alongside Pluhrons to plant crops with pointed sticks. Later sections showed the aliens teaching their human students more advanced techniques. Sharp as the images were, Ramsey found it hard to believe Pluhron documentarians had recorded them so long ago, and yet he couldn't deny what they showed. Early humans had learned farming from Mezzrel's people.

"Yes," Ramsey said. "We've seen it."

"Indeed," Mezzrel said. "As I have thoroughly explained to Colonel McGovern, we trained Lowk and her tribe in the art of agriculture for the better part of five Earth years, and remained to supervise training many others over the course of the next century. Our debt, as negotiated, is paid in full."

"And as I have explained to you, ma'am, our people have no knowledge of these events." Gabrielle kept her tone professional, but Ramsey could hear the frustration underneath it. "How can you expect us to uphold an agreement made by someone wholly unrelated to us?"

"Is ignorance of the law a panacea against punishment in your society?" Mezzrel tilted her triangular head to one side. "Might one kill another and claim they didn't know it was an offense to do so, and thereby fly free?"

"You must see how this situation differs from murder?" Ramsey said.

"No. We do not," said another of the seated aliens. "A society that fails to uphold its laws is no society at all."

According to one of the briefings Gabrielle had penned, she found reason to believe the Pluhrons favored strict adherence to law, almost to the point of religion. Ramsey could see what she meant.

"How can you justify removing us from our home when we have nowhere to go?" Gabrielle tossed her hands up in a gesture of disbelief.

"When a tenant has overstayed her contract and refuses to pay her rent, do you allow her to nest in your property for a thousand years while you are refused the use of your rightful possession?" Mezzrel's buzzing and clicking took on a decidedly agitated sound as she spoke.

"No," Ramsay said, "but neither would I toss a child out on a cold night. Humanity lacks the resources to lift our entire race off the planet. And even if we could, where would you have us go? Mars has one city that barely sustains the five thousand people already living there. The few habitable planets we've discovered in our explorations are all occupied. Would you have us go traipsing around the galaxy like vagabonds for generations?"

"We are sympathetic to your plight," Mezzrel said. "That is why we have decided to offer you favorable rental rates on the Australian continent or the Sahara Desert."

"You want us to squeeze five billion humans into North Africa?" Gabrielle looked from one inscrutable insect face to another, her lips parted.

"At reasonable rates."

"Out of the question." Ramsey had had enough. He stood, slowly to avoid alarming their hosts, and stretched to his full six feet, five inches so that he over-topped the three Pluhrons who had elected to stand. He drew in a deep, cleansing breath. "What will you do if we refuse to leave? Kill us all?"

"Not all." Mezzrel retorted without hesitation. "We will, of course, neutralize your rudimentary space fleet and planet-side defenses. Please understand, we would do so only as a last resort. We prefer to assist you in leaving as quickly as possible without bloodshed. We are not a savage race."

Something of the ancient warrior in Ramsey's genetics yearned to take up the Pluhrons' challenge—to spit defiance in the face of their overconfidence. Except, it wasn't overconfidence. From what Gabrielle and the Union had observed, a fight between them would be a walkover in the Pluhron's favor. By even the most generous estimates, such a conflict would last less than a month, and result in catastrophic losses for humankind. Ramsey glanced at Gabrielle who shook her head, her expression as defeated as he had ever seen it.

"Clearly," Mezzrel said, buzzing her wings with less agitation than before, "you are out of arguments. Do not think us a cruel people. We are willing to give you assistance in leaving."

Assistance. The word rang in Ramsey's mind. With it came an idea.

"Your people taught ours agriculture?"

"Indeed, we did."

"And you consider that a boon to us?"

"Every sentient species can trace it's ascendancy back to farming by one means or another."

"But look at the damage your gift caused." Ramsey spread his arms wide as if to encompass the last twelve thousand years of human development. "Farming allowed humans to settle into villages, and later nation states. It fed armies and resulted in strife and plunder and the avarice of ownership. Every war our people ever fought was buoyed by the food that fueled it. How can you call that a gift?"

Ramsey hoped the Pluhrons wouldn't recognize the desperation in his voice or written on his face. That hope crumbled when the three seated aliens convulsed spasmodically to produce a chirping cacophony his translator interpreted as unabashed laughter.

"What should a buyer do when the seller uses her money in a foolish way?" Mezzrel's words arrived interspersed with her squeaking laugh. "How you squander your riches is no business of ours."

Heat rose up Ramsey's neck, and he knew his face was turning red less from anger than embarrassment. That had been a weak argument, but what other sort did his people have at this point?

Mezzrel sidled out of her chair to brush a wing across the door's actuator and gesture the humans into the hall. "It has been a pleasure speaking with you, as always, but I'm afraid our talks are no longer productive. Your people have five days to begin organizing a global evacuation. Otherwise, you may expect our intervention."

Ramsey got the feeling his interpreter was being too politic. It should have translated that last word as invasion.

—

Location: Earth Orbit/Sol System

"Isn't there anything our allies can do to help, Admiral?" Gabrielle sat next to Ramsey surrounded by the Union's top military and civilian leaders aboard the *Unsullied*. Three hours of debriefing and rehearsing Earth's predicament had thus far come to nothing.

Admiral Leeds, sitting as chairman of the emergency assembly, shook his head, his expression grave. "Most other races are pacifists, Colonel, and even those that aren't lack the capacity to make war on the Pluhrons even if we combined our fleets."

The President of the United States, whose role within the Trans Solar Union was first among equals on the governing council, slapped an open palm on the table, making several of his peers jump in surprise. "I say we take the fight to these winged matriarchs! What we lack in forces, we can make up for in surprise and ingenuity."

"I concur with my ally from America," said the Premier of the Soviet Union. "We fought together in the second world war. Let us lock arms again for this first defense of Earth against an alien invader."

Ramsey found himself nodding at the sentiment, despite knowing it would fail miserably.

Admiral Leeds tapped a finger on an electronic pad fashioned into his desk to reproduce the rap of a gavel that echoed through the room. "Gentlemen, the motion to declare war has been put forward and dismissed by a near unanimous vote. What we need now is solutions that won't see millions of our people killed in the coming months."

"Those same millions are likely to die if we attempt to flee Mother Earth." The US President stood, hands planted firmly on the table before him. "We lack every resource necessary to lift humanity into space, especially the ships. We are being bullied out of our homes, and you people are letting it happen."

Ramsey voiced his agreement, which earned him a scathing look from Gabrielle.

"You know we can't fight the Pluhron," she whispered.

"Better to go down fighting than slink off into nothingness."

Admiral Leeds again brought the room under control, this time by pounding the electronic gavel with his fist. He turned to the Minister of Union Intelligence. "Phillip, is there anything new your people have gleaned about the Pluhron or their ships? Something that might give us an advantage should this conflict, God forbid, result in war?"

"As some of you know, we have managed to sneak operatives on and off one of the Pluhrons vessels." The wizened minster, who spoke with a thick German accent, adjusted his glasses as he stood, a waldo in his hand. He clicked one of its many buttons and a screen dropped from the conference room ceiling. Illuminated by a hidden projector, it lit up with images taken inside one of the aliens' craft, but in a room Ramsey hadn't seen.

They showed long bays filled with honeycombed egg chambers. As the perspective panned out, it became clear the eggs filled several floors running the entire length of the ship.

"There must be thousands of them," Gabrielle whispered, her eyes wide.

"Tens of thousands." Ramsey shook his head in wonder.

"We believe," said the Intelligence Minister, "these eggs represent the Pluhrons' invasion force. A generation of Earth-born aliens come to seize our world."

A general chorus of moans and shouts of outrage followed, but died when Ramsey, his jaw firmed, stood and raised one hand.

"Yes, Captain Ramsey?" Admiral Leeds' tone expressed mild displeasure—clearly he thought Ramsey's part in the process had passed.

"Sir, respectfully, I don't think that's an invasion force of Pluhron offspring."

"And why is that, Captain?"

"Sir, those eggs are nearly six feet long. They're far too big for children."

"With all due respect, Captain Ramsey," the Intelligence Minister said, his voice dripping condescension like melted butter. "We do not know how large Pluhrons are when they hatch. They might be fully developed."

"No, sir, but we do know they lose their intelligence whenever they go into their mating season, and that loss continues until they've raised their children."

"You're point, Captain?"

"If the females aboard that ship laid those eggs,

they'd be incapable of holding talks with us about who owns the Earth right now. Not to mention all the robots we saw aboard their ship—caretakers brought along to help out while they go through their long mating cycle."

The soft chuckles and whispered conversations that had broken out about the chamber died at Ramsey's words. The Intelligence Minister looked like someone had slugged him in the gut.

Gabrielle smiled, nodding slowly, her green eyes bright with interest.

"If the eggs aren't offspring, then what are they?" Admiral Leeds leaned forward, likewise curious.

"Simple," Ramsey said. "They're the males."

—

LOCATION: Earth Orbit/Sol System

Infiltrating the *Dominance* was far easier than Ramsey would have guessed. He had expected extreme surveillance measures set in place on the Pluhrons' flagship, which was true, but Admiral Leeds' covert teams had found a loophole in the aliens' security. Though they could easily detect a highly energized object moving at incredible speed, like a missile fired from Earth or the Moon, their automated radar systems tended to ignore slower objects like space debris that wasn't on a collision course with their ship. Using hydrazine gas propellant, usually reserved for minute orbital course corrections, Ramsey and Gabrielle maneuvered the *Silver Sparrow* to within a few hundred meters of the mile-long alien craft by continually tacking across their intended line of bearing. While tedious and time consuming—the trick took nearly four hours versus a few scant minutes required by conventional thrust—they eventually found themselves scrambling through an access port on the ship's underbelly.

They entered a narrow space that appeared far less finished than the corridor's Mezzrel had shown them on Ramsey's first trip to the *Dominance*. Maintenance panels and odd-shaped interface ports stuck out from the walls every few feet.

Gabrielle unfolded a set of blueprints rendered on ultra-thin paper. She held them up while Ramsey illuminated them with a flashlight from his CCW.

"We're one floor below the egg chamber." She pointed to an access hatch a few feet down the corridor. "Thank God Pluhrons use ladders."

"Makes sense, walls are too close for wings."

Ramsey climbed up, careful to make as little noise as possible. The access hatch opened easily enough when he turned its latch, admitting a frigid stream of super cold air to pour down on his face. He popped his head through the opening and spotted a Pluhron pacing away from him next to an impossibly long bank of freezers filled to capacity with eggs. The unit, made of steel painted blue and gold, reminded him of a supermarket cooler meant to keep TV dinners frozen for display.

Moving with all stealth, Ramsey climbed into the ice-cold chamber, his breath steaming. Gabrielle followed, her gaze locked on the retreating alien insect. Soundlessly, Ramsey drew his T-11 and pointed at the Pluhron.

Gabrielle, the ranking officer on this mission, nodded her agreement.

Ramsey's shot burned through the alien's carapace at the base of the neck half an inch below its armored head. Until that moment, he hadn't known if the guard was biological or a robot like those Mezzrel had brought to their meeting. He didn't enjoy killing. It came with the job, of course, but taking a life felt like a sin against his work as an exo-diplomat. A weight lifted off him when sparks flew from the now decapitated Pluhron's throat.

"You were right about the robots," Gabrielle said.

"Let's hope I'm right about these eggs, as well." Ramsey stood to survey the cold storage unit. It seemed to go on forever. No more Pluhrons, robotic or otherwise, stood in sight, though more might show up any moment. He motioned toward a small room overlooking the bay. "That must be the control room Leeds' teams marked on our schematics."

"I'll go to work there." Gabrielle hoisted the portable mainframe computer she had lugged from the *Sparrow*. "See what you can do about these guys, but stick to the plan. No wanton destruction."

"Hey, I came up with the plan."

"I know. That's what worries me."

Ramsey searched for any sort of controls on the storage units, but found only smooth surfaces. He keyed his mic. "Nothing out here."

Gabrielle, who stood silhouetted in the small control room, nodded. "I think I've patched into their computer banks. It's taking the circuits a moment to warm up. Ah, got it! I'm sending a general shut down command to all refrigeration units, but this is going to take a while, probably three to four hours."

"That's too long." Ramsey drew his T-11.

"Clifton, whatever you're doing, I order you to stop."

Ramsey set the laser to its widest diffusion and squeezed the trigger. With the gun's energy spread this far, it couldn't produce a beam of light. Instead, a cone of invisible photons spewed from it to heat the air like the galaxy's most powerful hair dryer. He tracked it back and forth across the eggs and smiled in disgusted satisfaction as the beings inside began to wiggle. The resulting stench smelled of rancid caviar.

In mere seconds, the first male Pluhron sliced through the flesh-like outer membrane of its egg to rise on unsteady legs. It unfurled its slime-covered wings and stretched its body. Unlike the females of its species, the male's exoskeleton was an electric blue matched with black that covered it in jagged, symmetrical patterns. It stood a hair under six feet tall and moved with the sort of torpid slowness a human displays upon waking after a long sleep. But Ramsey got the feeling the newly hatched male wouldn't remain slow for long. He backed away as more than a dozen more hatched. They clambered down to the floor, some on his side, some on Gabrielle's.

"Clifton, if we survive this, I'm having you committed."

"What are you worried about?" Ramsey shuffled back from the growing crowd of increasingly spry males to heat up another section of eggs. "These guys aren't interested in us. They're looking for some gals to chat up."

Gabrielle stepped out of the control room onto a short landing overlooking the nursery. She had drawn her own pistol. "Think for one second. Sure, these fellas want to find girls, but what do you think natural-born breeding machines need if they're supposed to gin up the next generation?"

Ramsey stopped firing his laser and took a longer look at the aliens crowding their birth chamber. The ones who had first emerged stared back at him, their mandibles glistening.

"Food?"

"Yep."

Ramsey cursed.

Wings buzzing like a motorcycle engine, one of the

nearest male Pluhrons launched itself at him, all four arms extended. He just had time to dive out of the way before it swooped through the spot where he had been standing. Ramsey tucked into a roll, adjusting his T-11 back to the kill setting as he moved, and came up firing. He missed the retreating attacker's thorax, but managed to slice off two of its wings as it soared upward. Handicapped beyond its ability to fly, the creature smacked the crowded floor with a sickening thud.

More laser fire erupted behind Ramsey. He spun to find Gabrielle fending off no fewer than six of the insensate beasts. While she dispatched one with a head shot, two more flung themselves at her.

"No!" Ramsey jumped onto the refrigeration unit and ran across it, his boots splashing through pools of slime left after hatching. He didn't notice. His first shot took out the alien nearest Gabrielle, but his second merely nicked the other one's back armor before it managed to swipe at her.

She screamed in pain as the Pluhron's chitin-covered fingers sank into her arm. Blood flew, drawing more of the males to the melee. Gabrielle scrambled back, tried to open the control room door, but fell away when her attacker took another vicious swipe at her ribs.

Running with all haste, Ramsey batted Pluhrons aside like so many bowling pins until he got a clear shot at Gabrielle's assailant. Growling through his teeth, he squeezed the trigger to saw off the thing's head. He took out two more with one beam to gain the stairs and reach Gabrielle's side. He spun about, laser continually sizzling the air, but despaired at the number of hungry breeders pushing and shoving one another to reach the humans. Even with perfect precision, he wouldn't be able to take out all of them fast enough to stop the mob. He and Gabrielle were doomed.

"You don't have to kill them all," Gabrielle said through a jaw clenched in pain. "Calvary's coming."

Ramsey didn't have time to look at her, but he managed to lift an eyebrow. "What cavalry?"

Before Gabrielle could answer, a set of doors at the far end of the bay slid open to admit several dozen yellow females accompanied by a handful of their robotic servants. As quickly as they had entered, the tide of females shuddered, clicked, and buzzed to a stop, Mezzrel at their fore. She held two laser pistols, but appeared too stunned to use them. Her robotic cohorts, however, kept moving, headed toward the humans.

Taking an immense gamble, Ramsey spun to fire at one of the robot Pluhrons. If this idea failed, the males would be on him in seconds. Blue laser light pierced the robot's thorax, sending up a plume of smoke and sparks. The males, distracted by the noise, followed Ramsey's wayward shot and, as a group, froze in place. Though Pluhron multifaceted eyes couldn't widen, Ramsey could have sworn every one of them goggled at the sight they found across the room. Their meal forgotten, first one then the entire group emitted an ear-shattering keening as they took to the air, darting toward the females like comets.

Some of the females ran, Mezzrel included, but most sprang to meet their male counterparts in a dance older than stars.

"Can you walk?" Ramsey holstered his T-11 and knelt to scoop Gabrielle into his arms before she could even answer.

"Maybe a little, but it hurts." She clung to him, the familiar warmth of her embrace giving him strength.

Ignoring the increasingly desperate sounds emanating from the other side of the room, Ramsey hustled Gabrielle to the access door they had used earlier. She cried out several times before Ramsey managed to lower her to the next floor, but cursed him when he tried to beg off. He followed after her, and breathed a sigh of sweet relief the instant he locked the panel behind them.

Once aboard the *Silver Sparrow*, Ramsey made to tend her wounds, but she batted him toward the pilot's chair.

"We need to move. We haven't much time."

"Why not?" Ramsey asked as he strapped her into the co-pilot's chair—she refused to lay in the ship's med couch despite her injuries. "I think the Pluhrons are a little too busy right now to fool with us."

"I planted a command in their computer banks. This ship—their entire fleet—will be underway in..." Gabrielle checked her CCW, "Five minutes. We need to hurry."

Without the need for stealth, Ramsey kicked the *Sparrow* to its highest non-Planck Divide speed, rocketing away from the Pluhron fleet. Sooner than he would have liked, the *Dominance*'s main engines fired, sending a blast of heat and charged particles across the *Sparrow*'s nose, making it exceedingly hard to maintain course.

Green light flared around the *Dominance*'s hull as it charged away from Earth, its subordinate ships in tow. Like a flight of arrows fired into a night-dark sea, the Pluhron ships disappeared into the Planck Divide.

Ramsey, unable to hide his smile, turned to Gabrielle. "Where did you send them?"

Her return smile looked more like a snarl. "Nowhere."

"What do you—" Ramsey felt his eyes go wide. "You mean, they're going to be flying through the Planck Divide forever?"

"Not forever, just until they come out of their mating fugue in a century or two."

Ramsey started to laugh, but was interrupted when Gabrielle slid out of her belts to kiss him. He returned it wholeheartedly, careful of her wounds.

"How about that med couch now?" he asked once she broke contact.

"Yes, please." She wrapped her arms about his neck so he could lift her. "And when I'm healed up, maybe we'll see about a mating fugue of our own."

Ramsey liked that idea.

THE END

RESERVATION EARTH

About the Author

David Alan Jones is a veteran of the United States Air Force, where he served as an Arabic linguist. A 2016 Writers of the Future silver honorable mention recipient, David's writing spans the science fiction, military sci-fi, fantasy, and urban fantasy genres. He is a martial artist, a husband, and a father of three. David's day job involves programming computers for Uncle Sam.

To learn more about David Alan Jones's writing, visit:
www.facebook.com/author.davidalanjones

INTEGRATION
A CADICLE UNIVERSE SHORT STORY

by A.K. DuBoff

SHADOWS AND LIGHT played in Jason Sietinen's mind, illuminating branches of thought, which stretched into fractals of infinite variations. He floated in a sea of possibilities, unaware of any world beyond the darkness and light around him. His reality could be anything he imagined.

Where was I before this?

His sense of peace quavered. Floating like that... he was disconnected from himself. He'd been somewhere else a moment before, but now he was free in the sea of possibilities, waiting to be drawn by the current.

I came here for something...

His purpose eluded him. At the back of his consciousness, he knew he was forgetting something. Something important. There was a reason he'd opened his mind, but drifting without direction certainly wasn't it.

This isn't right!

Jason fought to orient himself. He was lost in the sea

of light, floating without any sense of time or place to ground him. He'd allowed his mind to journey outside his corporeal form on many occasions, but something about this experience was different. It was almost like he was trapped *inside* himself.

Where am—

A high-pitched whine swelled around him, drowning out even his own thoughts. The luminous ribbons radiating through the darkness began to vibrate, growing brighter with each oscillation. He dissolved into the light.

—

"What's on your mind?"

Jason's awareness snapped back to the lounge on the TSS transport ship and his fellow Agent companion. "Sorry, I was thinking about why we're here."

Agent Curtis Jaconis chuckled, relaxing further into the plush seat next to Jason. "Contemplating existence is some pretty heady philosophy for this early in the day, isn't it?"

Jason rolled his eyes. "That's not what I meant."

Curtis turned his attention out the viewport to the ethereal light of subspace outside, still smiling at his own joke. "This mission is a strange one, yes. Why in the stars are two TSS Agents going to negotiate with a bunch of tech heads?"

"Yeah, that's part of it," Jason replied. *Moreover, why do I have a chaperone?* The mission had to be a test. Jason just couldn't decide what insight his father might hope to glean from the exercise—and why. He'd thought he was beyond needing to prove himself. Going to negotiate with the leaders of one of the few Taran worlds to embrace extensive cybernetic enhancements was well outside Jason's usual assignment scope. To be accompanied by another Agent was even stranger.

"This isn't about your capabilities, Jason," Curtis said. Though he hadn't been privy to Jason's private ruminations, it didn't take much guesswork to infer what had been left unsaid. "He trusts you. I mean, stars! He's had you take out the *Conquest* alone. Multiple times."

Jason raised an eyebrow, not sure that temporary command of the TSS' flagship had much bearing on the present situation. "Then why, with all respect, are *you* here?"

"Because you look like you could still be a teenager, and we want the Lynaedans to take us seriously."

The older man's candor caught Jason by surprise; apparently the deference most officers showed him didn't extend to his father's closest friends. "I'm not that much younger than most new Agents."

Curtis chuckled. "Jason, you've been living in a bubble with the TSS and High Dynasties. Out in the border worlds, the Sietinen name doesn't carry the same weight."

Jason swallowed an instinctive retort and allowed the words to sink in. He couldn't deny that he'd led a life privileged by birthright. Though he'd spent his first sixteen years on Earth, unaware of his dynastic lineage, the years since he'd been brought into the fold of the Taran Empire had been comparatively easy. With his father the TSS High Commander and his grandfather the Head of the influential Sietinen Dynasty, Jason had wanted for nothing. He always told himself that he'd earned his place as a TSS Agent—had worked as hard as his fellow trainees—but there'd never been a question of his qualifications. No matter what he did on his own, he was Wil Sietinen's son.

It was a given he'd be powerful. He was expected to be a leader. The career highlights that would typically mark someone as an exceptional Agent were merely Jason's baseline, from incredible telekinetic feats to winning over his peers. Despite his accomplishments, he'd never been properly challenged.

A mission like this, though, was different. On Lynaeda, technology held a higher value than inherited telekinetic and telepathic abilities. The Taran High Dynasties and their governance were a nuisance rather than a position to be revered. Despite his pedigree, Jason would be no higher than a commoner in their eyes. For once, he wouldn't have a home turf advantage.

The realization slowly came into focus. "Oh."

Curtis gave him a sage smile. "Spending time outside your comfort zone is healthy. You may have graduated without having a formal internship, but I don't think your father ever let you off the hook."

"You and the other Primus Elites never had one, either."

"I went toe-to-toe against the Bakzen in the war inside the rift. Don't try to put your part in ousting the Priesthood on the same level." There was a hint of levity to Curtis' tone, but Jason sensed that there was no room for debate.

The brutal war had ended before Jason was born, and it had scarred those involved in ways he couldn't know. While there was no denying Jason's role in the historic events that followed, he hadn't been fundamentally changed by his experiences. He'd never had to confront his inner self. Facing such bare, personal truth was the cornerstone of the TSS internship experience—to address parts of one's character that were denied in all but the most trying of circumstances. No test had ever pushed Jason to those limits, if he was being honest with himself. He doubted any encounter with the Lynaedans could, either, but maybe it was a valid evaluation of if he could keep a level head in the face of direct opposition.

"I'll try to keep an open mind," Jason finally replied to Curtis.

A chime sounded, indicating an intraship communication. "Sirs, we just received updated telemetry from TSS Ops. There's unexpected activity around Lynaeda. You'll want to see this."

Jason was on his feet before the captain had finished. "We're on our way."

"That doesn't bode well for our negotiations," Curtis said, following Jason toward the door.

"No, it does not."

The two men quickly traversed the short corridor leading to the ship's flight deck. The captain and pilot were seated at control stations in the front, facing a broad viewport with an augmented holographic overlay wrapping around the front third of the room. The information overlay presently displayed a planet schematic with surrounding space traffic. More than half of the ship notations were illuminated in red.

"What's the situation?" Curtis asked.

Captain Ambrose swiveled around in her seat. "It looks like we may be dropping out into a trap."

"I take it those ships aren't normally positioned around the navigation beacon?" Jason speculated, examining the schematic.

"No, they are not. And it's a far cry from the diplomatic envoy we anticipated," the captain replied.

This is turning into a test, after all, Jason thought to himself with an inward sigh. Most of the time, he was able to draw on his superior telekinetic abilities to get himself out of a bind. Diffusing the tensions in this matter, however, would require more finesse in order to come to terms with the Lynaedans—assuming an agreement was possible. It couldn't be a coincidence that Curtis, a seasoned liaison, was along for the ride.

"Were you expecting this kind of reception?" Jason asked the other Agent telepathically.

"We'd considered the possibility, though it had seemed unlikely," Curtis replied, the mental communication almost instantaneous. *"Now you're glad I'm here, aren't you?"*

Jason concealed a smile. *"Maybe."*

"Still, I'm second seat on this. You take the lead."

"I'll try not to start another war."

Curtis groaned in his mind. *"Great, thanks for the clarification. Not that it should be needed."*

"You never know." Jason sensed the older Agent's annoyance with his casual approach, but having the lead meant that he could do things his way. For now, that meant employing sarcasm to diffuse the tension. "How long until we reach Lynaeda?" he asked aloud.

"Seventeen minutes," the pilot replied.

"We could drop out early to avoid the fleet," Captain Ambrose offered. Based on her concerned expression, it was clear she was voting for that option.

"I have every intention to attend that meeting, but this development is worthy of a call ahead. Drop out so we can have a chat with the ambassador," Jason instructed. There was too much riding on the mission for him to call it off prematurely; the presence of the Lynaedan ships wasn't cause enough. *"Not that we could necessarily trust whatever excuse they offer,"* he added privately to Curtis.

"But whether or not they take our call will be quite telling," Curtis replied.

"Yes, sir," Captain Ambrose said. "I'll drop us out at

the next beacon."

"Let us know if there's any change in the conditions around the planet."

"Aye," she acknowledged.

The two Agents returned to the lounge room so they could speak privately with the Lynaedan representative who'd been serving as their point of contact. As soon as they entered the room, there was a moment where time appeared to elongate as the ship returned to normal space.

"Just once, it'd be great if one of my missions went to plan." Jason sighed.

"That's asking a lot."

"Is it?" Jason couldn't help but let out an amused chuckle as he thought back on his prior missions. He was still too green to have a long list of ops on his record, but those he did have had had a tendency to go sideways. "I take it back. This was doomed from the start."

"Get ready for a crash course in politics—and I don't mean the corporate maneuverings your family deals with on Tararia."

Politics. The reason I wanted to stay in the TSS in the first place—to avoid that very thing. The Sietinen family had recently diverged along two paths, with his grandfather assuming political leadership on Tararia and Jason's twin sister electing to learn the family business. Jason's father, however, had abdicated his political claim in favor of the TSS, and Jason was inclined to follow that path. Even so, it was wishful thinking for Jason to believe he'd been able to avoid Taran politicking entirely. He hadn't anticipated he'd be all but on his own when the time came, though.

"Before we call Ambassador Greggor, is there anything not in the mission brief that I should know about the Lynaedans or their feelings toward the TSS?"

Jason asked. If the mission was going to shift from a simple technical evaluation to political dealings, it was time to get caught up on the relevant points. He could fake his way through most conversations, but times like this, his childhood on Earth was a major disadvantage—missing out on knowledge of cultural details that most took for granted.

"To be clear, it's not only the TSS they don't see eye-to-eye with," Curtis replied. "Lynaedans consider any un-modded people to be unevolved."

"Seems a little narrow-minded."

"They'd say the same thing about your mindset," Curtis pointed out. "It's these kind of ideological differences that are the most difficult to navigate."

"All right, fair enough."

"People are willing to put up with the Lynaedans' attitude if they want or need anything done with cybernetics. Being the renowned experts has its perks—treat outsiders however you want, and if they don't like it, tough luck."

"It won't be easy to win over people like that."

Curtis shook his head. "No, but I've heard once there's sufficient mutual trust, they're willing to set aside their insular ways to collaborate."

"Question is, how do we establish that trust?"

"That's what we're here to figure out."

"Well, we need them." That aspect of the proposed Lynaedan partnership has been abundantly clear in Jason's research. Aside from being the group with the highest likelihood of successfully adapting the Aesir's bioelectronic tech, the Lynaedans had a monopoly on ateron.

Ateron was the most efficient known substance for bioelectronic conductivity, making it critical to everything from cybernetic systems to telepathic interfaces to computers. Even with the Sietinen Dynasty's extensive reach, the Lynaedans had claim to the richest mining veins that had yet been discovered. If plans to implement the recently rediscovered tech from the Aesir were ever going to move forward, demand for ateron was about to grow exponentially.

"We're sitting on a goldmine of tech the majority of the population can't use because they don't have innate telepathic abilities to interface," Jason continued. "If we can come up with a scalable means to allow the average person to integrate, we'll be able to unite the population in ways that have been impossible for centuries."

"In lieu of a genetic solution to enable abilities, a technological means to allow at least telepathy," Curtis mused.

"Yeah, but it'd be more than just telepathic communication. The Aesir's nanotech is more advanced than anything widely available across the Taran worlds. Once someone masters control, the feats they could accomplish might be all but indistinguishable from our genetically inherited telekinetic abilities. Of course, that opens an ethical can of worms."

"Indeed. Power is dangerous in unknown hands, but restricting access denies personal liberties."

"I guess that's why we need to find out what the Lynaedans can offer and if they're willing to work with us."

Curtis nodded. "They already have a workable neural interface, but they could never guarantee what might become of the tech if it was put out on the open market."

"Which is why we may determine it's better to keep the Aesir's technology under wraps."

"It's a delicate dance of transparency and shielding people from themselves."

"Stars, look no further than the mission brief," Jason

said. "There was nothing about the Lynaedans' attitude toward outsiders in there, and certainly nothing about the Aesir's tech. We want to know everything but don't want to share anything about ourselves."

"And so it's been for generations, across civilizations at all stages of development."

"You'd think we would have learned by now." Jason let out a slow breath. "We're going to be late for our meeting if we delay much longer. Let's get the call out of the way." He gestured to the viewscreen to bring up the communications interface.

"What will you ask them?" Curtis questioned.

"Opening with 'What the eff?' probably isn't the best move, huh?"

The other Agent cracked a smile. "There are ways to get the point across with more grace."

"I think I've got it." Jason initiated the teleconference.

The viewscreen went black, aside from a spinning animation of the TSS logo. After several seconds, the image of a dark-haired, middle-aged woman appeared. Her eyebrows were raised with surprise, though the eyes beneath were strangely expressionless. Upon closer inspection, Jason realized that the silver irises were a tell that her eyes were artificial—and she didn't care to hide it.

"She answered. That's good," Jason commented to Curtis.

"It will come down to what she has to say."

Jason smiled in greeting. "Ambassador Greggor, hello. I don't believe we've corresponded directly before. I'm Jason Sietinen."

"Ah, yes. The familial resemblance can't be missed," she replied. "I hadn't expected to hear from you before your arrival."

"Well, in our final preparations, we noticed some

unexpected activity around Lynaeda. May I ask why there are ships gathered around the jump point?"

"It's a natural place for ships to convene in preparation for a journey," the ambassador replied.

While technically a fair statement, Jason didn't buy the excuse. Sub-light engines were quick and efficient, so it would take no more than a few minutes to traverse the distance between the expansive spacedocks around Lynaeda to the designated jump points for the navigation beacon servicing the planet and its satellites. The only reason for ships to gather so closely together would be to surround a foe and catch them off-guard.

"Have we done something to indicate our intentions aren't honest?" Jason asked.

"Smooth," Curtis commented in his mind.

"Well, if they're going to play it like that, there's no sense pretending there isn't an issue."

"Honesty often does win out in the end."

Ambassador Greggor appeared unfazed by the question. "It has come to our attention that the TSS has access to a repository of advanced technology, which you failed to disclose in our preliminary discussions."

"With all respect, *this* meeting was intended to be the start of our discussions," Jason replied levelly.

The ambassador cocked her head. "Did you intend to share this information?"

Is it better to lie or tell the truth? Jason telepathically reached out to his colleague, but Curtis unexpectedly had closed off his mind. "Well, uh," Jason stumbled, "information is tricky. It means different things to different people."

"Yes. On that much, we can agree." Ambassador Greggor evaluated him. "Your ship is already in transit, and yet you call me now to discuss this matter. What do you hope to learn?"

"Honestly? If we're about to drop into an ambush."

"You already seem to know the nature and position of our ships in the area."

"But not what you intend to do with them." As he spoke, Jason kept a close watch on the ambassador's body language. The entire conversation was for show, simply to give him an opportunity to study her demeanor.

It was unlikely she would have accepted the call if the Lynaedans intended to make an offensive move, which meant the fleet's presence was an intimidation tactic. Ambassador Greggor's movements supported that conclusion, with squared shoulders and a stern expression that seemed much too rigid for her soft features. She was trying too hard. Were they in the same room, Jason would have been able to glean deeper insights, but the superficial observations told him what he needed to know for now.

"I don't think we're in danger," he relayed to Curtis.

The other Agent received the message, but he kept his mind closed to a response.

"Why are you blocking me?" Jason pressed. *"Is this entire thing a setup to test me, or something?"*

Curtis didn't reply, but the ambassador reacted to Jason's previous statement. "Our ships are gathered not as a show of force, but to display for you what we have."

"Laying all of your cards on the table, as it were," Jason said.

She inclined her head.

"While I appreciate the openness, it does send the wrong message."

"Doesn't it say more about you to interpret an innocuous action as aggression rather than saying anything about us?"

The reversal caught Jason by surprise. Next to him,

Curtis raised an eyebrow questioningly. "I suppose it does," Jason replied after a slight pause. *What in the stars am I walking into with these people?*

"Do you expect us to betray you?" the ambassador asked, her tone growing colder.

"No." Jason held up his hands. "I just wanted to make sure you hadn't already made up your mind about us."

"We make no assumptions, yet you continue to expect the worst from us."

"I'm sorry if it's come across that way, but it isn't our intention. We'd like a closer working relationship with the Lynaedans."

The ambassador's eyes narrowed. "Perhaps you're not ready."

"Please, give us the opportunity to prove our good intentions," Jason urged. "We'll be there soon."

"That's your choice." The ambassador ended the commlink.

Jason shook his head. "What just happened? She was all over the place."

"These interactions will define our relationship moving forward," Curtis said at last.

"What happened to you helping the Lynaedans take me seriously?"

"I allowed you to take the lead. Doesn't that deference send a message?"

"I suppose."

Jason sent an order to the flight deck for them to resume the jump.

As the journey neared its completion, Captain Ambrose made an announcement over the ship's comm. "Dropping out of subspace in one minute."

"Time to see if they'll be any warmer in person," Jason said under his breath. He headed to the flight deck, followed by Curtis.

As he stepped through the flight deck's entry doorway, the scene out the front viewport transitioned from the blue-green light of subspace to a starscape. A multitude of ships snapped into focus as the spatial disruption dissipated.

"Where to, sir?" the pilot asked.

"They should have sent us rendezvous coordinates." Jason's confidence from only minutes earlier vanished. Perhaps the ambassador's cryptic words had actually been a warning to stay away.

"You need to tell them what you really think," Curtis stated. He turned to look Jason in the eyes. "Are you ready?"

Jason's brow knitted. "What—"

A sharp buzz swelled in Jason's skull. He brought his hands to the side of his head in a vain attempt to minimize the pressure. As the high-pitched whine intensified, white light crept in from the corners of his vision until nothing of the transport ship remained.

—

"Should we go over it one more time?" Curtis asked.

Jason startled in his seat, suddenly disoriented. "The Lynaedan fleet. Where...?"

He faded out, realizing he was in the lounge room of the TSS transport ship. Out the viewport, the swirling ribbons of blue-green light danced through subspace.

"You'll need to focus in order for us to see this through," Curtis stated.

"Yeah, I know. I—" Jason shook his head. "Sorry, I was somewhere else for a minute there."

"We were just about to go over our strategy for the negotiations with the Lynaedans. What do you hope to get out of this exchange?" the older Agent prompted.

"Haven't we been over this?" Jason's head swam. He could have sworn he was somewhere else a moment before, but he couldn't remember where.

"Daydreaming again?" Curtis raised an eyebrow.

"I dunno. Guess so." Jason tried to shake off the feeling of déjà vu, but he'd been trained to listen to his instincts, and his gut told him that something was off.

The other Agent folded his hands in his lap. "Well, let's get back to the Lynaedans and what to expect."

"Right. How they distrust us unmodded people."

"What you may find interesting is *why*," Curtis continued.

The echo of a conversation flitted through Jason's mind along with a flash of light. He couldn't catch any of the words, but there was something familiar there. "Are you sure we haven't been over this?"

"Information can take on new meaning, depending on your state of mind."

"All right. What's worth hearing again?"

Curtis repositioned in his chair. "When you hear about a group that's distanced itself from the rest of the civilization, what would you expect to be their motives?"

"Could be anything. In a general sense, I'd wager they don't like the other very much—whether it be ideological differences or something else," Jason replied.

"What about this case with the Lynaedans, knowing their stance on technology?"

Jason shrugged. "The people on most Taran worlds prefer to remain in our natural forms, for one societal reason or another. I'd guess that those who seek extensive augmentations probably consider everyone else weak."

"No, that's not it at all."

"What, then?"

"The Lynaedans' distrust of un-modded people

doesn't have anything to do with our physical forms. It's related to the level of connectivity in our minds."

Jason frowned with confusion. "Us Agents can form telepathic links as effectively—or more—than they can."

"But our methods of doing so also make us exceptionally good at concealing our inner thoughts. Their form of interface, coupled with their augmented senses, make deception extremely difficult. They're guarded against outsiders because it's our nature to withhold information and mislead, whereas their culture values being able to take a statement at face value. Anyone outside of that open, shared network can't be implicitly trusted the way their own people can be."

Jason took a moment to process the revelation. "Wait, so they can't lie to each other?"

"Not in the way we can. When minds are constantly linked and cybernetic sensors can reveal nuanced information about a person's physical state, it's much more difficult to be disingenuous—moreover, it's counterproductive. The rest of the Taran worlds, though, rely on providing just enough information to get by in any given interaction. Finding common ground between such different perspectives is a challenge."

"The only way is through honesty," Jason assessed.

"Yes, but when dealing with Agents, whom have such control over their physical state and mental faculties, a Lynaedan's normal measure of honesty becomes unreliable. In their shoes, wouldn't you be cautious of someone like you, too?"

"I suppose I would."

"So, have fun navigating all of that," Curtis said with a slight smile. "Your innate telekinetic gifts and intelligence have gotten you this far, but it takes more than that to be a true leader."

"I'm here willingly. I want to learn."

Curtis smiled. "Good. I've always valued that trait in your family. It's been a relief to know that your grandfather has the respect of the other High Dynasty leaders, given his inside knowledge of the TSS."

"*You* know that, but I worry that not everyone will agree with generation after generation of Sietinens having command of both the TSS and Tararia."

"Your family is in a unique position, no doubt."

Jason stared out the viewport at the swirling blue-green light of subspace. "I guess that's why it's important I prove myself now."

"It's not a matter of proving yourself, Jason," Curtis said in a fatherly tone. "Think about it, instead, as the best way to make your mark. No one doubts the strength of either your abilities or character. The question is how best you can use those skills to the greatest benefit."

"That sounds like something my grandfather would say."

"He's a wise man. Guess that makes me pretty smart, too. You should listen to me."

Jason rolled his eyes. "Like I said, I'll keep an open mind."

The older Agent turned serious. "You should. You never know what you might learn about yourself by looking at things from someone else's perspective."

Something about the sudden change in demeanor caught Jason off-guard. "Finding common ground is what we're here to do."

Curtis' relaxed posture had gone rigid. His gaze was fixed intently on Jason. "You seem so willing to keep technology from the Lynaedans. What happened to equal sharing among the Taran worlds?"

"Whoa, what do you mean? I never said that."

"But you're thinking it. The High Dynasties, the TSS. Really, what use are the Lynaedans to people with such connections?"

Jason hesitated. "Haven't we been over this? The Aesir tech isn't something to take lightly."

"Yes, the Aesir. They've been kept under wraps, too. Even if the tech from their information repository comes to light, I doubt anyone would say where it came from."

"Curtis, what's going on with you? We're on the same side here."

"We are, but not in the way you might think."

None of this is right. Jason took an unsteady breath. "What's going on? You don't seem like... you."

The other man chuckled to himself. "Remember how I said you can learn something new when you look at the same information in different ways?"

Jason nodded.

"Well, you have made quite an interesting specimen to study."

Yeah, definitely *not right.* Jason tried to bolt from his seat, but he was unable to move. He detected none of the telltale electric tingle of a telekinetic vise or any telepathic control, which was even more worrying than the prospect that the other Agent had somehow overpowered him. Though he tried to struggle against the invisible restraints, Jason was trapped.

"Who are you working for?" he demanded. It seemed impossible that Curtis had turned against his TSS family after decades of service, but he wouldn't have been the first to defect.

The other Agent shook his head, laughing. "And here I thought we were getting to know each other! You really think such a loyal family friend would disregard you so easily?"

"I don't want to think that, but you—"

"Think about everything you've been thinking and feeling, Jason." Curtis looked at him levelly. "What explanation makes more sense?"

Jason thought back to the sensation of déjà vu earlier and his sense that he'd been elsewhere before the conversation began. *Why can't I remember where I was?*

There were a number of potential explanations, ranging from straightforward to absurd. It was possible Curtis had been taken over by someone, or maybe even that Jason was being mind-controlled himself. But, as he considered the possibilities, a more plausible scenario came to the forefront.

"I'm in a simulation," Jason stated confidently, though it was only an educated guess.

The other man gave a slight nod. "An over-simplification, but that's close enough for the sake of discussion."

The confirmation did little to relieve Jason's mounting anxiety about the situation. He remained unable to move from his seat, and his companion was clearly not the longtime colleague with whom he'd thought he'd been conversing.

A wave of panic washed through him. *What have I said?*

They'd discussed the upcoming negotiations with Lynaeda. His family. The TSS. And the Aesir tech.

Shit! What have I said about the Aesir? He ran through the conversation in his head, remembering what details he could. To the best of his recollection, he hadn't given away any specifics about *what* technology, only that it required a level of bioelectronic interface that the Lynaedans were best equipped to bring to scale. *Stars, and they might still be trying to read my thoughts!*

He quickly closed off his mind—as best he could, not knowing in what manner he was being observed—and returned his attention to figuring out how to get out of his present predicament.

"Who are you?" Jason asked his apparent captor.

"I am a representation of your colleague formed from your memories," the Curtis-facsimile replied.

Great, so they can *view my memories.* Perhaps the sensitive information related to the Aesir had already been discovered, even without direct discussion. For that matter, there were a number of highly classified details about the TSS' operations that could easily spark a new civil war if the information fell into the wrong hands.

Jason swallowed. "What do you want?"

"Our intent was to get to know you," the other man replied. "The real you—not the one you presented to us. We hoped that exploring your recent memories would offer more insights than we could otherwise glean."

"Yeah, that's not how we go about building a friendship where I'm from."

"You were so guarded. We didn't know how else to quickly determine if there's good potential for us to work together."

Jason scowled. "Whoever you are, you can consider that chance destroyed. We couldn't possibly work with anyone who'd violate someone's mind like this. It goes against our deepest moral codes in the TSS."

The Curtis-facsimile studied him. "Members of your organization have done much worse than this."

"In times of war, when entire planets were at risk, perhaps. But us, right now, we're not enemies. At least, we weren't before you trapped me here."

"You're not trapped."

Jason flexed his arms, still unable to move. "I beg to differ."

"You're still under the influence of the simulation. You haven't come to terms with the information before you."

"Come to terms with *what*?" Jason demanded. "You're speaking in riddles, and I still have no idea who you are."

The Curtis-facsimile made an all-encompassing gesture with his hand. "You were here, before you arrived to speak with us at Lynaeda. You discussed everything we've talked about here with your colleague, but at the time, you didn't hear what needed to be understood. You keep thinking about us as some adversary that needs to be won over. That isn't the case at all."

"Really? Because this interaction hasn't given me an 'old pals' vibe."

"We wanted to explore your thoughts about us, just as you would have a chance to re-examine your opinions. We placed you in this open simulation to allow your mind to construct a stage through which you could act out your thought process. As you developed the scenario, we exerted measured control over the avatar representing your colleague to offer a perspective that would challenge your preconceptions. The first run-through hit a block, but we tried again, and already you are more open than you were before."

Jason wasn't sure whether to be horrified or impressed that the Lynaedans had such abilities. *These aren't people we want as enemies, that's for sure.* Since he was there as an official TSS representative—and the real Curtis was nowhere to been seen—he'd need to find a way forward, despite his personal feelings about the mental violation. For as unethical as the Lynaedans' actions seemed, he didn't sense malicious intent.

"What is it you wanted me to see?" Jason asked.

"We've already told you. But you need to believe it."

Jason revisited the recent conversation once more. "This is about how the Lynaedans don't trust other

Tarans—because our minds aren't networked the way yours are."

The Curtis-facsimile nodded. "We've given you ample opportunities to be honest with us. Why do you keep holding back?"

"I don't know you. Trust is earned."

"Why take that approach? It's so much easier to assume the best of someone."

"Right." Jason scoffed. "When does *anything* play out that way?"

The other man tilted his head. "What about in matters of love?"

"Pardon?"

"When starting a new romantic relationship, at least in those that work, both parties begin with open hearts and minds—even on a first date. They endeavor to share their inner selves. They either connect, or they don't. But in either case, they get to see the other person in their true form, because that's who ultimately needs to be accepted in any lasting relationship. Why should business matters be approached in any other way?"

The argument made complete sense to Jason, though it went against his innately skeptical and guarded nature. Why should intimate relationships be built on assuming the best of people while all others assumed the worst? What had become broken in society so long ago to have created such a divide?

"I can't disagree. We *should* be more open with one another," Jason conceded.

"May we begin our discussions now from that place of open honesty?" the Curtis-facsimile asked.

"After you twisted my memories like this and trapped me in my own mind?"

"To us, your intention to come here and use our technology without sharing your true motivations is a far worse crime."

Jason's own biases forced him to disagree with the sentiment, but that didn't change the fact that the TSS needed to be on good working terms with the Lynaedans for the future benefit of the Taran Empire. Finding common ground started with him.

"Yes, I'd like to start over with you. Properly."

The Curtis-facsimile inclined his head. "Remember what you learned here."

White light, sudden and intense, blocked out Jason's vision. A sharp buzzing filled his mind, deafening at first, but it quickly faded. As the ringing subsided, the light also diminished, and Jason found himself surrounded by a network of illuminated threads—a web he now realized represented his own thoughts and memories. The branches were more tightly knitted than when he'd witnessed the neural map before, evidencing his changes in perception over the course of the exercise. Though part of him had felt like he was simply playing along with the Lynaedans' wishes for the benefit of the TSS, perhaps deep down he did honestly want to have another chance to begin their relationship anew, without omissions or deception.

The illuminated branches faded and fractured into blackness. After a moment, Jason realized his eyes were closed. His breath was once again his own, and he was free to move.

His eyes shot open and he bolted upright from a slightly reclined chair. "That was so real…"

Curtis was standing next to him, watching him expectantly. "I take it the interface was successful?"

Jason scrambled from the chair in the center of a white-walled lab, wanting to distance himself from any tech capable of putting him under. His heart pounded in his chest. "Maybe too much so."

"Jason, what's wrong?" the other Agent asked telepathically.

"It was a simulation of our journey over here. They pulled it from my memory."

"Memory interface wasn't part of our agreement."

"I'm well aware." Jason realized a Lynaedan scientist was standing behind the head of the chair, and he pivoted to confront the man. "Why pretend this was a test of the interface? It was never about that."

"We reasoned it was the only way you would agree to a link," the young scientist replied. He smoothed his white lab coat. "We wanted to get to know you—beyond what you would normally share with others. This technology connects us more deeply than the superficial interactions in which most engage. We needed to be confident that your intentions for using this technology were pure."

"By deceiving us?" Jason shook his head.

"Think how much you kept from us," the scientist stated. "Are the deceptions so different?"

"You dug into my inner, private mind."

"And you kept those inner truths from us while asking us to share ours with you."

Jason could see his point. By the Lynaedans' culture, the violations were on the same level. The only way forward was to accept their perception as a shared truth. "You're right. That was wrong of us," he admitted. "We're not used to looking at autonomy and privacy in the same way as you are."

Across the room, a smooth metal door slid open.

Ambassador Greggor stepped inside, accompanied by two companions. "And I wish we hadn't needed to resort to these tactics to confront those differences," she said, stopping several paces from Jason. "We've wanted to finally reconnect with the other Taran worlds, but little has changed since we began to pull away."

"Was it you, seeding those thoughts in my mind?" Jason asked, fixing her in a piercing gaze.

"Among others," she replied, as composed as she'd been in their simulated discussion. "We needed to be sure you'd be receptive."

Curtis passed his attention around the parties in the room before coming to rest on the Lynaedan ambassador. "Your actions have only served to reinforce our initial caution."

"Just as your deception justifies our measures to seek the truth," Ambassador Greggor replied.

Jason agreed with the Lynaedans' logic, just as he had in the simulation. Both sides had caught each other in deceptive means to achieve their own ends. He couldn't very well condone the TSS' behavior without suggesting an unfair double standard. Other diplomats may have no problem favoring their own side's interests, but that wasn't his style.

"My father suspected they'd employ these kind of tactics, didn't he?" Jason asked Curtis privately.

"It wouldn't surprise me."

With the deeper issues behind the mission coming to light, Jason's pairing with the older Agent now made perfect sense. Jason was, in fact, not there purely as a TSS representative, but rather was a liaison with the High Dynasties based on his family ties. Curtis was the true TSS—a respected officer, whose clout and position had been earned by years of service through wartime and the following peace. He had no claim to a title or riches beyond his own accomplishments, making him a fair representative for the naturally Gifted to contrast against the enhanced individuals the Lynaedans had made through their technological interventions.

For a moment, Jason wondered why his father hadn't

come himself in his place, knowing the importance of the meeting and what it meant for future collaborations. *He already didn't trust them. He needed to send someone who'd have an open mind.*

Jason realized that he'd never suspected treachery or deceit. He'd gone into the mission with the expectation of forging a partnership with the Lynaedans, with their mutual best interests in mind. His father had been through too much to not immediately jump to seeing the worst in people—to close off a collaborative relationship before they had a chance to work through their differences. Jason was a clean slate, less burdened by those biases. It was up to him to find common ground, if it was possible.

Jason took a deep breath. "We got off to a bad start."

The Lynaedans still seemed on edge, but Curtis' stern expression softened.

"We'll need each other one day," Jason continued. "It may be in decades, or it could be tomorrow. But eventually, Lynaeda will need to cooperate with the rest of the Taran worlds. We have the opportunity now to begin building those bridges."

Ambassador Greggor finally relaxed. "Yes, now you see. There are mutually exclusive belief systems, but ours are not. We need only be open and honest with one another."

"That's how agreements *should* be," Jason responded.

"And yet, for generations, we haven't been able to come to terms. The Priesthood liked their secrets."

Jason nodded. "They did."

"We hoped the new Taran leadership would be open to evaluating new policies regarding freedom of information."

"We are. But we also recognize the risks and dangers of sharing information with those who won't give it proper consideration."

Ambassador Greggor inclined her head. "It is one of the reasons we were so interested in interfacing with you—someone walking the line between the TSS and High Dynasties. We have seen the purity of your intentions."

"But others—"

"Yes, others do not show such care. Despite our openness, we have the same concerns about members of our own population. I assure you, there are safeguards."

"So, what do you propose?" Jason asked.

"A dedicated, discreet research team to work with yours in the TSS to determine which tech, if any, is appropriate to bring to scale. If any is identified, we will negotiate further involvement and resources to bring those plans to fruition."

"That's—"

"Everything you asked for, yes," the ambassador said with a cautious smile. "See how much easier this would have been if you'd simply been honest with us from the outset?"

"Lesson learned," Jason acknowledged, returning her smile.

"To be fair, we can't apply these same communication standards to all cultures," Curtis interjected.

"No," Ambassador Greggor replied, "but this is the common ground for our people, and it is how we will find our way forward. You must find that with each of your allies—and enemies, to resolve those conflicts."

Jason nodded. "We'll do our best."

The ambassador smiled. "Now, what do you say we get to work?"

THE END

INTEGRATION

About the Author

Nebula Award finalist and *USA Today* bestselling author A.K. (Amy) DuBoff has always loved science fiction in all forms, including books, movies, shows, and games. If it involves outer space, even better! She is most known for her acclaimed Cadicle Universe, which serves as the backdrop for the "Integration" short story; this broader story universe includes numerous novel series and short stories by Amy and co-authors. As a full-time author, Amy can frequently be found traveling the world while writing timeless space-based science fiction and fantasy. When she's not writing, she enjoys wine tasting, binge-watching TV series, and playing epic strategy board games.

To learn more about A.K. DuBoff's writing, visit:
www.amyduboff.com

Thank you for reading this issue of

THE
GREAT BEYOND
ANTHOLOGY

Until next time, happy reading!

Printed in Great Britain
by Amazon

48438759R10156